It rose above the inane chatter of the late night disc jockey on the radio beside his bed. It pierced his sleep like a psychopath's knife; it peeled it away from him layer by layer, as if it were an onion . . . or layers of flesh. He tried, instinctively, to run further into the safety of his dreams, applying for asylum in that country we visit in sleep.

His application was denied.

It pulled him from the depths of his sleep and upright on the cot, eyes widening, throat constricted and dry, heart pounding.

Something was outside, close outside, and it was howling.

It was a challenge, he knew. An invitation: Come into my parlor . . . The noise tapered off slowly and did not return, but he knew it wasn't leaving. It was waiting. He knew, without a hint of doubt, that if he failed to go to it, it would surely come to him.

He opened the door wide and fast, and just then it stepped out from behind the tree trunks and bushes and revealed itself to him.

He froze. He thought he said, "Oh God. Oh no, oh my God," but he made no sound at all. His lips didn't even move.

The waning moon lit everything with a glow like skim milk, but it was enough. It was too much. . . .

CRY WOLF

CRY WOLF
BY ALAN B. CHRONISTER

ZEBRA BOOKS
KENSINGTON PUBLISHING CORP.

ZEBRA BOOKS

are published by

Kensington Publishing Corp.
475 Park Avenue South
New York, NY 10016

First printing: June 1987

Printed in the United States of America

Conception

His barrel chest swelled and he began.

His voice was deep, mellow, operatic. It filled the small church in which he preached as if it had mass, volume. It boomed in righteous baritone, careening off the walls and vibrating the high beams of the ceiling like tuning fork tones. Looking down he could see the homely face of Eleanor Marcheji turned up toward him in ecstacy. There were tears forming in the corners of her small grey eyes and flowing unheeded down her sallow cheeks and around her thin white lips. Father Gimball graced her with a beatific smile; her expression showed that he had, that simply, redoubled her joy.

He swept his gaze across his congregation, using it like a powerful searchlight upon which the few members of his flock who were straying could focus. Justin Gimball had little trouble with dozing or boredom during his sermons. A natural speaker, he was both eloquent and powerful, his well-modulated baritone commanding attention. He was also a natural dramatist, weaving his parables and commentaries together as if they were a collaboration between the Brothers Grimm and Agatha Christie. People were not forced to hear his conclusions; they thirsted to do so.

A pause. He was not thirsty, yet still reached for the glass of water before him on the podium and drank. His flock was baited, waiting impatiently. Yes, he thought, you're mine. He let his eyes drop imperceptibly and took in Eleanor, who was glutting herself upon him as he towered above her. Such adulation in her eyes, such . . . willingness. Something stirred in his groin, pulsing, rising. Ah, yes, the resurrection. Inwardly, he smiled. That was what called him to her; the willingness expressed as pliancy. And, no doubt, that was what called her to him; he, too, was willing . . . to dominate. His groin spasmed and he managed an undetected glance downward. Behind the podium his cassock was tented far away from his thighs. Immediately he gripped his fantasies and forced them back into a dark corner of his mind where they could not effect him so. It would not do, after all, for the members of the congregation to see their righteous, pure, and chaste shepherd Father Justin Gimball standing before them, preaching God's work, with a hard-on. Managing to contain his cynical laughter, he cast his gaze over them again, spreading the radiance of his smile like fairy dust over them, enchanting them, drawing and binding them to him.

He touched Eleanor Marcheji lightly with his smile; caressed her ever so tenderly with his grey-green eyes. And as she beamed up at him, enraptured, seduced, his groin stirred yet again.

He thought, What the hell? Perhaps one of them

6

will see me like this. And he gave her his most saintly even-toothed grin.

When Tommy Dodds, the altar boy, came and said that to her, she thought she'd die.

All he'd said was, "Miz Eleanor, the Father'd like to see you in his chambers if you please." Then he'd just turned right around and walked away. It was unthinkable to him that anyone would say no to a request from Father Gimball.

Yes, that was all he'd said, and when enough time had passed that Eleanor was able to think again, her first thought was, "Oh, Sweet Lord, what'd I do wrong?" It was just as unthinkable to Eleanor that a man like Father Gimball would want to see her for any reason other than punishment for a transgression.

As she collected her Sunday hat—the new one for spring, with the bumblebees and little blue flowers on it—and pocketbook off the seat of the pew, she shuddered. Perhaps he *knew*. Maybe he knew what she was thinking when she stared at him way up above her, standing there like a giant, or Moses. Or God. It wasn't that she didn't want to listen to the sermon, but sometimes she just got to thinking how good he looked standing there with that gold hair shinin' like a halo and those wide shoulders and . . . Eleanor giggled behind her hand, embarrassed, as if she were speaking aloud or someone could read her thoughts.

"Now girl," she reprimanded herself as her mother used to, even slapping her own hand, "you just stop them sinful thoughts this minute. You a God-fearin' woman an' him bein' a preacher, yet." She looked around the church suddenly, thinking someone there

7

might overhear her; maybe those kids. The kids always teased her cruelly.

No. She was alone.

"And just what do you think he'd do if he *did* find out what you're thinkin'?" What would he do?

She shambled slowly up the aisle toward his chambers, confused, her coat sleeve dragging on the dusty floor. Then she thought perhaps he wanted to compliment her on her attendance record—she hadn't missed a service since he had gotten there eight months ago—and her steps became more hopeful.

Gimball had gotten out the crystal decanter of wine and two glasses and placed them on the low table in front of the couch. Not that he thought he would have to get her drunk first; Eleanor was, besides being of uneducated peasant stock, distressingly feeble-minded. He was positive that those things, combined with his subtlety, sophistication, and angelic good looks, would win the day. And then, of course, there was his trump card; he was a "Man of the Cloth." He chuckled, and the tone was more demonic than angelic. Gullible women were not the singular province of psychiatrists and psychologists. Priests, reverends, rabbis, and others of his ilk had more than ample opportunities to tend to the more physical needs of those they served. Something to do with acting . . . performing, he thought. Just like actors, musicians, and sports stars, he was before the public constantly offering entertainment. Even more, the good Father Gimball offered up answers. Justin Gimball was, by virtue of his vestment, God's man. He was good, he was kind, he was trustworthy. He was, in short, what every woman wants her husband, boyfriend, or lover to be . . . what every woman wanted their father to be—and what most thought he was. Was it any wonder that he was *Father* Gimball? Was it any wonder that, knowing this, he got laid whenever the hell he wanted?

He raised the wine-filled glass before him to the ceiling in tribute. "Here's to the Electra complex," he toasted. "A pity you're not around to see it."

Ah tonight, he thought. And tomorrow night. And whenever else.

He had just refilled his glass when he heard Eleanor's timid knock.

She was shocked to see him in blue jeans and white T-shirt, but she did her best to hide it. Even if she didn't know that priests were allowed to dress like that, it was really none of her business. Besides, why would the Father dress like that if he weren't allowed? He motioned her over to the couch and they both sat down—so close. Her skin grew all warm and tingly.

"Drink?" he asked.

Eleanor nodded, unable to speak, unable to do anything at all but look at him this close—so close she could smell his sweet smell and feel his warmth as it poured from him and washed over her in waves that made her so dizzy she thought she must swoon. And oh, Sweet Jesus, wasn't he just beautiful, all gold and broad and muscular like an angel must be and . . . She watched as his hand reached out in slow motion and gripped her hand tenderly, warmly. Her heart raced so she thought the whole world could probably hear it throwing itself against her ribs. Looking finally at his face, she saw his lips moving.

"Eleanor," he grinned, not removing his hand from hers. "I hope you don't mind if I call you that. I've seen you so much it seems that we're the closest of friends." Putting the wine glass in her free hand, he could feel her trembling.

Talk. She must talk. "Oh . . . no, Father," she stumbled, "You can call me anything you like." What was that to say? Dumb, dumb. Just like those nasty ol' kids were always sayin'. Dummy, dummy, dumbo. A drop of wine sloshed over the edge of her glass and ran down her knuckles to drop off and stain her dress. She started for a moment, thinking she was bleeding.

For just a moment Gimball watched the stain spread through the worn fabric. Yes, he thought, you're mine now. "And you, please, call me Justin." An endearing grin, a squeeze of the hand. I should stop, he thought, before she has a heart attack and dies thanking me right here on the couch. It was all he could do not to laugh at the scene as it played itself out in his mind.

Eleanor coughed nervously, and when Justin looked up his eyes were unfocused and she thought she saw something in them that she'd never seen before. Something mean. Like an electric shock. Oh my, now I've done it, she thought. But just as quickly it was gone—whatever it was—and Justin was as she knew—wanted—him to be. She watched him avert his eyes, almost shyly, and it was so touching and so unexpected that she almost reached out to hold and reassure him.

"Well," he said, sipping his wine delicately as if putting off a task hard for him. "Well, here I am taking up your valuable time when I'm sure there are a million other things you'd rather be doing." Eleanor opened her mouth to protest, but Justin pushed on without seeming to notice. "So . . . I'll tell you right out why I asked you to come." Another sip of wine. A sigh. "A man in my line of work finds a great deal of satisfaction in what he does, as you might imagine . . ." A pause; Eleanor filled the emptiness by nodding. ". . . but he also feels, at times, a great frustration and loneliness. You see, my dear, Satan thwarts our efforts toward goodness at every turn, and many—yes, even in our own little flock—many are so willing to succumb to the Devil's temptations. The Lord knows that, at times, I despair that I do any good at all."

Eleanor gripped his hand more tightly and said, "Oh no, Justin . . ." But then the tears were burning the back of her throat like lye and he was shaking his head and grinning sheepishly.

"Now, Eleanor, let me finish while I have the courage."

He waited for her nod of assent.

"It is the good, the truly beautiful people like yourself who give me the courage and the will to go on." He saw her blush and thought, Yes. "It is through people like yourself that God reveals his face to me, and his everlasting love. It is the joy of my life and yet . . . and yet the root of my greatest longing."

She was stunned. There was a tear, a single, jewelike tear, softly tracking down his dear cheek. His eyes were misty as if they were covered with God's own dew, and Eleanor thought, Oh, God, how can you let this man, this truly good, beautiful man, be so sad? And then she thought with a jolt, He's given it over to me to tend this man. He's given it over to me to relieve this man's suffering.

And she was suddenly, radiantly, glad.

"Oh Justin . . . if you only . . . I mean I . . . all these months and . . ." But there were too many thoughts, too many emotions, and they were all tangled up and she just couldn't, for the life of her, seem to find the right darned words. If I could just stop my insides from shaking, she thought. If I could just stop that place between my legs from feeling so blamed quivery. I'm tryin' but I can't. I'm tryin', Lord, but . . . oh shit. And she blushed a deep, dark red. Justin reached forward and lightly placed his finger on her lips to stop her from saying any more, and suddenly it felt just like she had wet herself like a baby and she couldn't have said any more if it'd meant her life.

"When I see a good, strong, beautiful woman like you, bathed in the light and love of the Lord, I feel the joy of His bounty, true. But I *am* a man and also feel the loneliness of being denied what every other man takes for granted—the love of a good woman. What I want to ask you, Eleanor—if it is not too much to ask you—is for just a little of your time. If we could meet outside of church as friends, perhaps see a movie. Go bowling some evening. I need to see more of you, my dear, lovely Eleanor. I love you, you see, and if I cannot have you as a man was meant by God to have a woman . . . If I can't . . . if . . ." And tears streaming down his cheeks, he pulled his hand from hers and turned away.

Eleanor took no time to think; she couldn't. Her love for this golden man of God had been a dream for

12

so long, a fantasy repressed and unacknowledged. Now it was free, and it coursed wildly through her with the accumulated force of months of denial. It possessed her and spurred her on to boldness. She reached for him and grabbed his face between her hands, pulling him around to face her. "No, Justin, no," she pleaded. "Don't turn away. I love you. I love you, too, and God knows . . . God knows . . ."

Enough talk, he thought, and pressed his lips against hers roughly. He felt her shocked intake of breath but thrust his tongue past her teeth and deep into her mouth, and as she finally relaxed, he pushed her relentlessly back onto the couch and quickly removed her clothing. As he entered her he felt the slight resistance and heard the faint gasp of pain that told of her virginity. This amused more than pleased him, but he did smile as the word "amen" flitted across his mind.

Eleanor knew what was happening, though no one had ever taken the time to tell her anything about it. We're *doing it,* she thought, little dumb Eleanor is *doing it* with Father Gimball. She didn't recall really wanting to do it and it hurt a little, but her own mommy and dad had done it, after all—she knew that much, at least—and there really didn't seem to be that much to it one way or the other. Seems that someone had told her that priests weren't supposed to do it, but maybe that wasn't the truth or maybe it was just certain kinds of priests, like Lutherans or some of them others. With Justin laboring on top of her she doubted that it could be wrong; he certainly wouldn't do anything wrong, and especially not to her. Justin loved her.

13

She looked up at him and he was smiling. Oh God, look. I made him happy. Dear Lord, thank you for letting me make Justin happy and, God, don't let this be a bad thing.

Please don't let this be a bad thing . . . .

The next April, with the flowers sending tentative blossoms to peek through the brown soil and the sap rising to the delicate new buds on the trees, Eleanor discovered she was with child. This neither shocked or dismayed her; rather it seemed to her in the natural, and therefore expected, order of things. Justin had not made love to her for over a month. In fact, he seemed to be spending less and less time with her and more and more with that little Lettie Snipes, but everyone knew she was a trollop and Justin said he was just trying to bring her around to Righteousness. And if anyone could bring such as Lettie around to a different path it certainly was Justin Gimball, she reflected proudly. Yessir. Father Justin Gimball could charm the spots off a snake, and no doubt about it.

And Eleanor went to Justin Gimball and proudly announced the miracle of God's newest blessing upon them. Whereupon, after many shouts and disclaimers, Justin threw Eleanor out of his church on her proverbial ear and returned to his diligent pursuit of saving poor Lettie Snipe's soul—poor Lettie having almost frozen to death while hiding in the confessional naked as the old jaybird.

For the next two months Justin would not talk to her, barely acknowledging her existence at all, even with a glance. Finally, in the beginning of June, Eleanor went to her parents in a daze and attempted to explain her predicament.

Her parents, being upstanding, God-fearing folk, declared her to be no longer their daughter and ordered both her and her few possessions out of their house by the full moon.

Before she left home her parents, wallowing in guilt, took her late one night to Father Gimball and made her confess to two sins: the sin of the flesh and the sin of bearing false witness against, of all people, the good Father.

That night she was forgiven both her lust and her delusions.

Even later that night, while Mr. and Mrs. Marcheji slept secure in their righteousness and Eleanor slept upright in grueling discomfort upon the seat of the outbound train, her face smashed grotesquely against a smeared, bug-splattered window, the Father Justin Gimball strove mightily and in many novel ways to save the soul of poor, wayward Lettie Snipes.

And so it came to pass that Eleanor Marcheji, ex-member in good standing of the House of Divine Guidance, Father Justin R. Gimball presiding, came to the house of one Danny Loong Gar both pregnant and alone. Here, in the city of Chicago, Illinois, she came to rest, getting a job as a presser in the Loong Gar Laundry, where she worked by day, and living in a small, crusty, vermin-infested flat above it where she spent her nights.

It was in that flat, lying on a stinking and stained mattress and attended by two women whose speech she could not understand, that she gave slow, painful birth to a son she would later call Joshua David. A son whose first cry, whose first expression of life, was so full of rage and hate and anger that even the Chinese midwives took a few steps toward the door, mumbling between themselves. A son whose first cry was not a cry at all but a howl, seeping through the cracked and soot-encrusted window into the bone-chilling cold winter air; floating over the trash and blackened snow and freezing winos that littered the streets; rising toward the bloated full moon that lorded over the dissipation that was that part of Chicago at night.

It took with it the last dregs of sanity that Eleanor Marcheji possessed. . .

. . . and it was not human. . . .

Birth

The library had closed hours ago and he supposed that he should be going home. His mother could be such a pain in the ass with her curfews and dos and don'ts, and that damned religious bullshit she spouted every time you gave her the chance. He took another drag of his cigarette and stared, grinning, at the glowing end. What the hell would she do if he ever smoked in front of her? She'd probably have a fucking heart attack. Give him another lecture on the tools that Satan uses to tempt the flesh. He chuckled, inhaled more of the burning tobacco smoke, and tossed the butt into the darkness. If poor, crazy Mom ever found out damned near anything he enjoyed . . . The last time he'd sworn in front of her she'd rinsed his mouth out with soap and given him an hour-long lecture on profanity and blasphemy and the Devil's language. And he'd been fifteen at the time, for Christsakes! A grin reappeared on his face as a warmth spread across his groin. If she could see what he and Kathy did. . .

The sensation in his groin was becoming uncomfortable, and he unthinkingly stuck his hand into his pocket.

"Joshua Marcheji," he commented wryly to himself, "you are getting weirder every day." He shook his head. "Very fucking weird." Shrugging his shoulders he walked toward the apartment that was his home. Joshua looked at the things around him with bitterness. He hated this city with its cold and wind in winter, its oppressive heat and humidity in summer, and all year long its poverty and filth and empty despair. He longed to be out of here, to be gone, to be any-fucking-place else but living in Chicago with his goddamned crazy mother and her asshole religion.

"Soon," he whispered to the streets. "You can't hold me. I'm getting out. I'm different."

And he was getting out—soon. At the end of the school year he would be going to college on a scholarship, his only problem being which to accept. Wide of shoulder and slim of hip, he was thin but exceptionally well-muscled, and his coordination and overall athletic ability were considered by many a minor miracle. Having lettered in any sport he chose to play, the athletic scholarships were not slow in coming, nor did his straight-A average do much to staunch the torrent of offers from various colleges across the United States. The future higher education of Joshua Marcheji was definitely not in doubt.

In fact, this last school year in Chicago was dedicated to something other than the certainty of good grades and graduation with honors. These last months he would begin a single-minded search for his roots. His past. His father.

18

His father. It was a forbidden topic in his home; Mother would never discuss it. And on those few occasions—when he won the letter for debating; when he told her he wanted to major in philosophy and religion, minor in psych; sometimes when he caught her staring at him at night in his T-shirt and Levi's and came over to run her fingers through his silver-blond hair or lock his grey-green eyes with hers—on those occasions, at these times, sometimes she would say, "Josh, you put me in mind so much of your father," and there was deep sadness and regret in her voice, and just maybe anger.

His father was still a mystery to him, but he would be patient and learn, in time, what there was to know. Just as he had with The Nightmares.

But they weren't nightmares and they weren't dreams and they weren't hallucinations. He wasn't crazy like his mother, although for many shattering, horrifying weeks he had thought he was, and then he had thought he was evil for being what he was . . . for doing what he did.

Damn you for that, Mother. Damn you to hell, if there is such a place.

Now he didn't think any of those things. Joshua just thought—no, he knew now. He *knew* . . . that he was different.

And he *was* different. So very, very different.

Kicking a can down the block with a sobering clatter and murmuring, "Damn right," Joshua turned into a darkened alley and smoothly picked up his pace. It was getting really late, and if he didn't take this shortcut and hurry home, his already-due lecture on timeliness and filial responsibility would be increased tenfold. He grimaced and began seeing his mother . . .

. . . in her chair. Shabby cardigan with the pockets bulging with used tissues. Hair dishevelled. Sallow face puckering, tears forming in her eyes, jaw working as she readies herself to speak. Such an effort. The Bible in her hands, held so tight her knuckles are corpse-white. She's been praying again, always . . . always. Awshit, here it comes: " . . . and don't you know better than to stay out so late I'm your mother I worry and haven't I told you that the Devil does his work in the darkness his minions roam the world in darkness it isn't safe to . . ."

With a start his senses became alert to something and snapped him back rudely to reality. His mother forgotten, he peered into the murky bowels of the alley before him and waited, watched, tensed. Had it been a sound? A shadow? Just a feeling? He didn't know; had been too distracted.

But as he slowly and silently took his first step, he saw.

They stepped out of the shadows on cue, appearing all at once backlit against the streetlight a block away. They hadn't broken that one just so they could produce this effect; it was their best trick. The leader's name was Angelo but he made people call him Angel. He was short, swarthy, with powerful arms and chest and a white scar that ran diagonally across his face from his forehead to his chin like a hash mark. Although he had a switchblade crammed into his boot, he carried a torn-off car antenna in his hands, not lethal but painful, and capable of drawing a lot of blood if used correctly. In his experience, most of the straight community feared pain and blood and disfigurement much more than they feared an end to their boring little lives. He watched the Angelo, his victim, back up a few steps, and called out, "Hey, brother, don' run away now. Me an' my frens, we jus' wanna chat a little, huh?" Then he motioned, and the others followed him toward Joshua.

Miguel: very Latino and very macho, wiry and quick. Although his knuckles were deeply scarred, he felt the cold weight and hardness of the new brass covering them was well worth the price he had paid. He ached to break them in.

Rubin: tall and gangly black, with the carriage and deceptive strength of a professional basketball player. The three-foot chain looked very small in his hands. Light. Harmless. It wasn't.

And Paulie: looking just like everyone's little brother except for the four-inch studded bracelets he wore on his forearms and the pair of nunchaku he carried so casually in his hand.

Joshua sized up the opposition and saw he was in trouble. If there had only been two or even three . . . but four was too much, even for a person of his abilities. And then he smiled. His abilities. He had never tried it voluntarily before and never . . . never *done* anything to anybody before but . . .

"Hey, asshole, you hear wha' I'm sayin'?" Angel hissed.

. . . but these punks were going to kick his ass no matter what he did and . . .

Paulie jabbed his leader in the ribs with his elbow as they walked up to where Joshua stood, deep in thought. "Mebbe the fucker's deaf er somethin', man," he sneered.

. . . you could never reason with these fuckers. No, they'd just take what they wanted off of him and then fuck him up real bad and leave him laying here in this stinking alley in stinking Chicago and go wherever bastards like this went and laugh at him. Laugh . . .

"I dunno," Angel answered. "What you say, brother? Cat got your tongue?"

"Shee-it," Rubin spat. "I think the muthafucka's deaf and dumb boff. Dat, or his fuckin' ass is too fuckin' good to talk to lowlife trash like us." He spat again and rattled the chain threateningly against his leg.

. . . laugh at him laying here bleeding and all broken up, dead, in the hospital, paralyzed for the rest of his life . . . the rest of his life in a wheelchair in his mother's apartment in Chicago and never, ever getting out. Ohno, ohfuckingno, you bastards. I'm getting out, you fucking animals . . .

"That's shonuff what I think, Angel. It shonuff is."

"Well, we oughtta do somethin' 'bout that, then. Don't you think, Paulie my man?"

A grin of anticipation hit Paulie's child-face. "Yeah, Angel, I think . . . Yeah . . ."

. . . animals, Joshua thought, and seeing the irony there he smiled just as his eyes focused and he saw a dark face with a scar across it nod to a little boy with some kind of toy in his hand, and he realized (oh shit!) they were on top of him now. Before he could move at all he saw the flash of something shiny like snakeskin as it went toward his stomach (oh shit!) and felt it take him low, near the belt. Felt the pain spread like fire through his torso and burn the air out of his lungs . . .

Paulie sunk his right into the Anglo's guts, reaching for the spine the way the Chink had taught him. The Chink had called it penetration or something, he didn't quite remember what, but whatever it was it was a good thing to know 'cause it sure helped you put a fuckin' hurtin' on people. He stepped back and watched the white boy slump to his knees. Shit, the fucker was almost pretty's a chick. Maybe he's a fuckin' queer. Probably. But man, there was somethin' scary about this dude . . . weird like . . . like . . .

Paulie didn't know, so he stepped back and played with his nunchaku, considering, while he watched Angel kick Joshua in the ribs to put him on his back. Rubin and Miguel stepped forward for some of the action but Angel waved them off, kneeling over his victim's body and grabbing it up one-handed by the collar to peer into his face. Paulie watched while Angel spat into the white dude's face and then asked, "Do we have your attention now, mother fucker?"

Joshua saw the face inches from his, felt the slimy trail left behind as the ball of phlegm, like a greenish-white snail, crawled down over his cheek. His stomach was cramping severely and his rib cage felt afire, but he knew he had to do something now, before he was injured further. Before they could stop him from escaping . . . from them, from this city, from his mother. And he felt something else; it was a burning, a pain, a rage that went beyond his body, even beyond

23

his mind and flamed out of control in a part of him he didn't know. It was a desire, like lust. No. More than lust, more than desire, it was . . .

A hunger. Growing. Consuming.

He welcomed it.

Angel said, "Do we have your attention now, mother fucker?"

And Joshua replied, "Oh, yes, you fucking bastard. Oh, yes, you certainly do." This he did with his lips and tongue, with language. When Angel, shocked by the words and even more so by the menace in the tone, faltered, Joshua replied with violence.

Grabbing the hand in which Angel held his antenna, Joshua brought his knee up hard between his assailant's legs and twisted, throwing him off and gaining possession of his weapon in one motion. He got to his feet quickly and met Miguel's rush with a slash across the Latino's face that blinded him and brought dark blood welling to the surface and spattering on the asphalt. Rubin came on, chain hissing in the night air, and Joshua tucked and rolled behind a group of trash cans, the hard steel links flattening the side of one just behind him. As he righted himself he saw an old wine bottle wrapped in brown paper and, picking it up like a fumbled football, whirled and pitched it into the oncoming giant's face. A gout of fluid erupted as it struck his nose dead on. Rubin screamed in pain and rage and, dropping his chain, covered his face with both of his enormous hands and stumbled backward to the alley wall.

Joshua spun to face Paulie, but the fourth member of the gang just stood there shaking his head and mumbling, so he turned and ran down the alley into the darkness.

Paulie, looking after him, shook his head again and turned to Angel, who was hobbling toward him. "I knew he was trouble, man," Paulie said with resignation in his voice. "I jus' knew."

Angel grabbed him and shook him angrily. "What da fuck you doin', asshole? You don' fight with us no more? He damn near fuckin' killed us, man, an' you jus' stan' here and tell me you *knew*? You knew shit, man . . . shit! You hear me? Paulie, you hear?"

"I knew, bro. I mean, you can feel . . . somethin'."

"Shit, man. Feel his knee in my balls, Paulie. I can feel that. An' I'm damn sure gonna get that cocksucker for it, too."

When Paulie sighed, it was the sigh of a parent trying to correct a willful child. "Let 'im go, Angel. He's gone, man. How you gonna find 'im now anyway? He's fucking gone an' I'm damn glad, man."

Rubin walked over to the two of them. Miguel staggered behind. Blood caked the tall black's face and neck and gloved his hands. His broken nose was starting to swell badly, but his eyes gleamed with pain and hate, and he carried his chain. Rubin towered over Paulie and Angel, and he spat into the trash along the curb. "I been lis'nin' to what you two bin sayin' an' ain't nuffin' bu' jive. Shee-it. That alley the white boy gone down, ain't no way outta there an' you know it. Where your haids at, man? That mutha fucka done fuck'd me up, an' now I gone down there an' do him up right." He spat some blood. "Shee-it." Turning, he walked down the alley alone.

It had all been said; even Paulie conceded wordlessly. It was no longer a matter of profit. It was now a matter of honor. Angel pulled the knife out of his boot and fell in behind Rubin; Paulie gripped his "sticks" tightly and followed, too. Miguel, still dazed and partially blinded, lagged farther behind. Each knew without telling, without being told, that it was no longer a violent game. It had changed somehow, somewhere. Now someone had to die.

As the four of them stalked down the alley the night changed. Suddenly it became threatening, overpowering. The new moon cast a surreal light into every corner. It was too bright, the night too quiet. Even the air seemed to grow heavy, muffling the sound of their steps and lying heavily around their shoulders like a shroud. It lay like smoke in their lungs, making normal breathing into labor. They stole down the alley on edge, making their way to where their quarry had to be. Against the wall at the end there was a large green trash bin. There was no place to hide besides that. He was either behind it . . . or in it. So they drew near to it, and as they did they heard the white dude.

He was talking to himself.

Rubin heard it first and stopped short, cocking his head and piling Angel up behind him. Paulie walked abreast of Rubin, heard it too, and stopped to listen.

"What that mo'fuckin' honkey doin' in there, Paulie?" Rubin's chain rattled against his leg. He broke out in gooseflesh.

"Sounds like he's talkin' to himself," Paulie answered, but it didn't sound right.

26

Angel wiped his knife on his sleeve. "Mebbe the man's prayin'."

Closer, Paulie mused. That's closer but . . .

Then, clearly, they heard a growl. A snarl. It was low and infinitely threatening, evil and fatally menacing. Paulie thought it had stopped his heart.

"He's got a dog back there?" Angel looked very pale.

Rubin said, "Umm . . . umm . . . Aw, man, what the fuck do I know 'bout a dog? Where'd he get a dog from, huh? Man ain't got no damned dog an' I'm goin' in an' gettin' the muthafucker right muthafuckin' now!" He walked forward resolutely, and Paulie realized that Rubin had to go now, and Angel, too. They were so damned scared that if they didn't go now, they'd turn and run out of there, out of Chicago, out of Illinois maybe. Like Paulie wanted to, only he couldn't, either. So he walked behind his friends until the black waved them over to one side of the bin and signed that he'd take the other. As they got in position Paulie looked at Rubin and thought that he looked like a big fuckin' tree and hoped that dog back there didn't piss on him. His brain kept whispering, Not prayer, not prayer, and he giggled at the thought of a dog pissing on Rubin's leg. Suddenly the dog back there howled and Paulie started to cry. Then he saw Rubin hold his chain out in front of him with both hands and disappear from view. Before he heard the black man screaming, Angel had rushed behind the trash bin too, and Paulie followed like air rushing in to fill a vacuum. Then he heard Angel talking in a high voice, just like a woman, saying, "Oh God. Oh God no. No. Stay away from me. Please stay away from me, please, nonononoNONONONO. . . ." Then a thud like maybe he hit somebody or got hit, and then a growl that sounded like . . .

. . . a chant. A chant, not a prayer. He knew and . . .

. . . he didn't know why he couldn't see until he realized his eyes were closed, and he opened them and saw and then he knew, knew for fucking sure, and there was screaming and roaring and blood, blood everywhere. All hell was breaking loose back here. And he saw and he knew that he was going to die.

Miguel could see very little as he stumbled up the dark length of the alley in search of his amigos. Joshua's whiplike blow with the car aerial had struck him almost horizontally across the face, damaging his right eye severely even though it had angled downward and spared his left. The good eye was tearing heavily in sympathy for its neighbor. The makeshift weapon's track across his face was swollen, still oozing blood and fluids, and hurt as if he'd been branded with a red-hot iron. His agony was so great, in fact, that he had heard the riotous commotion behind the distant trash bin in only the most disconnected manner. The implications of the beast-sounds and screaming made no impression on his anguished consciousness. Miguel walked drunkenly onward, rubbing his face with both hands as if he could physically tear away the cowl of pain that had settled upon him. Alone, now. In shock. Oblivious.

He saw the trash bin slowly materialize at the end of long, dark tunnel that was the alley. His eyes made the image grainy, the outline waver, the whole thing look smeared. The hackles on the back of his neck rose suddenly and his body shivered as if it were the middle of winter. The bin had a shadow, even in this darkness. It had a darker-than-dark shadow, and that shadow was getting bigger or changing shape or . . . something. For a minute it looked as if the sun were moving real fast around the back of the dumpster, making its shadow spread quickly toward the curb, and Miguel looked up, startled and confused. But there wasn't any sun, not even a moon. He looked back and saw that the shadow was running down the curb now and into the gutter, moving slowly down the street.

"Water," he breathed.

No, not water, 'cause it's moving too slow. It looks thick like chocolate syrup, thick like Aunt Jemima's or Mrs. Butterworth's or . . .

"Blood."

The impact of the word knocked him back like a jab to the chin. Then he shook his head—shaking off the blow, denying its power—and lurched forward toward the only place where anyone could be in this damned dark place.

A shadow detached itself from the hulking murk that was the bin and moved to the alley wall, where it stood, silent and still, staring at the young Latino. Miguel first sensed, then saw it. He stopped, craning his neck like a gangling bird to try to bring the low-slung dark blot into focus, to make sense of what looked nonsensical to his injured eyes.

Slowly, tediously, his vision cleared and he saw— saw what Paulie had seen, and Rubin, and Angel. He saw, too, what had become of those that had seen first

29

. . . what was left of them. Miguel saw and didn't believe at first because he didn't want to. Then he quit looking and gave himself totally to the scream that reflected the horror that rooted his feet where he stood. It erupted into the air around him from his deepest self, gargling when the contents of his stomach rose with it and cascaded down his shirt front. It was much more than a scream; it was a statement. When it ended, there was not much left to say, nor any better way to say it. Except for what Miguel did say after that. He said, "Mother of God!"

"Mother of God!" Miguel said. And then he whined, "Oh Jesus."

The huge, enormous beast in front of him cringed for a second as if it had received a physical blow. Then it dropped the dismembered forearm it held in its mouth, the studded armband on it clacking as it hit the concrete, and began to advance, its body lowered. Stalking. Fixing Miguel with its oddly luminous grey-green eyes. A sound like a chain saw filled the boy's ears and he realized the beast was growling low in its chest.

"Oh, Jesus," Miguel choked out. "Oh, Jesus Christ . . ."

The beast stopped whining and then came toward him again, more quickly this time and somehow, it seemed, less gracefully. Then Miguel saw what was happening and understood, and with the understanding came acceptance. Even the fear lessened slightly, although he saw that he would die, for he knew now what it was. His mother had told him the stories of brujos who could do this, could changed their very

30

shapes and become . . .

It barked sharply, drawing his attention. It was standing as erect as its hind legs would let it, much more hairless. The hands extended toward him were clearly human but sharply clawed, and the teeth were long, jutting sabers . . . canine. It walked toward him, now doing its best to smile, and went to grab him by the shoulders.

"Jesus," Miguel said, more awed than afraid now.

The thing drew back again and winced. Then, becoming less canine with every passing second, its claws locked into the heavy cloth of his jacket and it was pulling him toward itself. The teeth were still long and razor sharp, but before it lowered its head and used them to rip out his throat, it spoke. The voice emerged from a throat not quite made for speech, sounding rusty, as if the words flowed over sandpaper or ground glass before being thrust rudely into the air. The words were a violation to Miguel's ears and made him sick to his stomach to hear their sound, but he understood them. The thing said, against his throat, "Such blasphemy is very rude, boy."

Then the deed was done.

The new moon passed from behind the clouds as he finished his walk home. Very late now, very late. It didn't really bother him much now, though. He kept repeating under his breath, "It works! Goddammit, it works!" He looked at the glowing, fingernail-paring moon and grinned broadly. He was very happy, indeed.

Eleanor was waiting impatiently in her chair when

he strolled, whistling, into the apartment. As she started to complain he held up his hand and shook his head, not saying a word, and there was just something about him that stopped Eleanor cold. He walked past her toward the cramped kitchen and she thought that he even looked different. Hairier . . . or something. She dismissed the thought, saying "Joshua, have you eaten? Can I make you something?"

And the voice from the kitchen said, almost laughing aloud, "No thanks, Mother. I ate a huge meal on the way home."

Maturity

Moonshadow.

name to the name of his father after Eleanor had
ball, nee Marcheji. He had legally changed that hated
name to the name of his father after Eleanor hads
died of cancer two years ago. It was a graduation
present of sorts, coming just in time to spice up his
graduate degree in philosophy. Of course, that wasn't
his only field of interest or expertise. He dabbled in
theology for his amusement, and his aptitude for the
more mystic/occult psychological theories, as well as
his vaunted proficiency at hypnotic techniques and
hypnotherapy, was already achieving him a well-
rounded reputation in academic circles. Yet, though
all of this provided for both his comfortable position
as a full professor at the Larksboro Area Community
College and financial security, his most treasured
advances were in reference to his peculiar abilities,
and Moonshadow.

Standing on his wooden front porch he looked over
his domain—twenty acres of mountain land, most
heavily wooded, ten miles from Larksboro proper.
One single-lane dirt road led from his front door to

town and back, and that was damned-near impassable in all but the most hospitable weather unless a four-wheel drive vehicle was used. Joshua had a fine four-wheel drive pickup for general use and two dirt bikes in the barn beside the eight-room house. He had his own generator for power, fresh well water, and indoor plumbing. There were fireplaces in the living room, kitchen, and master bedroom, and a wood stove for daily use. There was a large garden in back, although he ate very few vegetables and no fruit. All this made up the body of Mooshadow, while the spirit was comprised of solitude, self-containment, independence, wildness . . . ferity. Joshua Gimball himself was the brain. There were also eyes, ears, and other organs for sensing and doing. Not here, for they'd do no good here. They were . . . other places. The eye is no good that sees only itself, Joshua mused; the ear no good that hears only its own silence. To survive one must see others, hear others, but be neither seen nor heard in return. An organism must look out on its environment and know it, use it, to survive. One that doesn't is insane. And so, it perishes.

That would not happen to Moonshadow, because this place was the beginning of his greatest dreams, his greatest triumphs. Here it would start and from here it would spread, feeding off the body of society. Not unlike a cancer in that aspect, he had to admit. But unlike a cancer this would not ultimately be self-destructive. No, this would be carefully monitored growth, controlled to achieve the optimum possible benefit. This did not have the lack of restraint that characterizes the self-destructive. This plan possessed the watchful self-control of true genius.

There was a sudden noise—the snapping of a twig—and he turned toward it. It was not a tense or hurried movement, for his keen senses told him that there was no threat, no imminent danger. He had a passing feeling of pleasure at his reaction; how far he had come since that long-past night in Chicago. How familiar he was with his being, how at one with his nature. His eyes fell upon Alec as the other man approached him. Joshua watched his lithe movement and upright posture, the firm control he had over his hard musculature. Alec Wall had the distinctive self-possession of the dancer, which he had been. Before. Joshua smiled at Alec, his closest friend and disciple. He smiled but still shook his head, the disappointed teacher admonishing his favorite pupil, and said, "Alec, I thought you had transcended such untoward clumsiness."

Alec looked sheepish. "Yes, Joshua. I'm sorry."

Six years ago an aspiring, talented young dancer named Alec Robinson Wall met an equally talented young academician named Joshua Marcheji, and the attraction had been spontaneous and mutual. It was not the pull of opposites, art versus science, which is the parent of so many short-lived college relationships. This was the immediate acknowledgement of like natures and kindred spirits, more the attraction of one for himself. In Alec, Joshua found a man of will, of control; a man in touch, and in tune, with his manifold being. In Joshua, Alec found the same, but more intensely than he had ever felt possible. A veritable Renaisance man, an ideal made flesh. Joshua's physical abilities made him feel clumsy as a newborn, and the intellect that sparkled in his eyes

35

and poured forth in his actions and speech made Alec feel like a Neanderthal. Joshua was a man both awesome and fearsome, a soaring thing that could, at any moment, plunge into the darkness that seems always to underlie true genius.

Before that happens, Alec remembered thinking then, I must learn all I can from this man. And Alec Wall remembered one other thing as he stood in the warm sun that blanketed Moonshadow this fine afternoon, looking at his friend standing bemused on the porch like a noble surveying his fiefdom. A thing that had been said long ago, and a thing no longer true. Having never seen Joshua in rapport with anyone other than himself, Alec had boldly asked the young scholar if he had any other friends. Joshua had fixed him with those curious grey-green eyes of his, replying that he had never made many friends nor did he feel the need for them. Then, smiling slightly, he had closed the topic by finishing, "I seem to be, Alec, what you might call a 'lone wolf.'"

It had been almost a year before Alec had learned of the black humor in that statement. And five since, rendering it false. After all of that and with much work ahead, Wall was still grateful. True, he wasn't the dancer he'd wanted to be, but when he perfected his new talents, that could be remedied. More importantly, Joshua had led him away from all those seductive promises and bleak threats, equally empty, that constituted organized religion. Heaven and Hell and Hogwash, as Joshua often said. What Moonshadow was . . . was a way of life. A simple and true way of living whose sole tenants were: find out what you are, acknowledge and accept that being, live it;

Never regret or look back.

It was line, chapter, and verse of a thousand songs and scores of works on pop psychology; what made Moonshadow different was simply that here the words were lived.

That, plus the fact that the members of the Moonshadow community themselves were rather : . . . different.

In the final examination, Alec mused, it could well be the extremity of that difference that held the group together so tightly. Indeed, they were less a group than a hive, a mound, a pack. The reward for social compliance was survival; asocial behavior would mean almost certain discovery and more certainly death.

Once you were admitted into the Society of the Moonshadow, *it* became *you*.

Alec Wall shook himself back from his reverie, and the movement was not quite human. "Daydreaming again," he chided himself, chagrined. "How positively *human* of you, to slip into waking dreams and let the moment slip by unlived." Sticking his nose in the air, he sniffed a few times. Then smiling, and much more conscious of his step, he walked past his mentor into the house.

Gimball turned to follow him, waiting until the other's back was turned before he allowed himself to smile. After all, it wouldn't be seemly for even his best student and friend to witness his amusement.

The transition was hard, even for those gifted few like Alec. It demanded constant awareness to give up the last vestiges of this habit of humanity. There must only be now: the moon, the night, the forest, the hunt

37

. . . the moment.

No distractions.

No parts.

And how long, Gimball thought, had it taken even him, born to this life, to accept what he was?

To welcome it.

Those thoughts, and this scene:

Joshua Gimball. Tall, silver-blond, athletic of build. Penetrating grey-green eyes. Moving in his graceful, loping walk across the sunlit porch of his home toward the front door, smiling. Scratching the day-old stubble of hair that itches the palms of either hand. Reaching up to feel a similar situation over the bridge of his nose, making his two eyebrows into one.

Joshua Gimball thinking, as Sunday's sun starts its descent toward the western hills, that he must rise early enough tomorrow to shave; thinking in great, good humor, "I yam what I yam . . ."

Feeling the desire to bay the rising moon.

BOOK I

"Beware of false prophets, which come to you in sheep's clothing but inwardly they are ravening wolves."

—Matthew's Gospel
vii, 15

might overhear her, maybe those kids. The kids
always wanted her to walk

Chapter 1

Larksboro might have been called a typical mid-sized Pennsylvania town. It was far too small for towering buildings or urban sprawl or any of the other symptoms that things had gotten a little out of hand with civilization around here. It was that small, yet large enough to support the Larksboro Area Community College, a Western Auto run by Fred and Mattie Zimmer, two local banks (both insured by the FDIC), a smattering of dentists and M.D.s (two apiece), an eight-man police force with two squad cars (nine-man if you counted Myron Aimsley, but he was only part-time on Saturdays), a florist and pottery shop combination, a few clothing stores, and a drug store. There was also what used to be called a "dry goods" store, which sold most of what couldn't be found in any of the other local establishments and much of what could. This was called the Larksboro Emporium and was run by Agatha Cooper almost as a hobby. Her husband Martin, mayor of Larksboro, had learned long ago that some concessions must be evaluated more in terms of mental health than material wealth. The Emporium was such an investment. Without something to occupy her time and energy, Aggie could have a man talking to himself—like she did—in a week and answering himself—as she also did—in two.

A town reflects its people, and the people of Larksboro were generally fair in their dealings and friendly to, if slightly exclusive of, outsiders. All in all, Larksboro was the type of place that prompted remarks like, "Wouldn't this be a nice place to live, John?" or "God, Helen, this would be the perfect place to move to when I retire next May!" or even "This is how it used to be when I was *your* age, Harry . . ." Five miles outside the town limits, most forgot Larksboro even existed.

This isn't to say no one came there. Spring and summer brought the backpackers, hikers, campers, and trout fishermen who, in turn, brought litter, noise, an occasional fire, and outside dollars into the area. Autumn and winter brought the hunters with their need for ammunition, beer, food, beer and beer. Few of these visitors even stayed in town. They ate at the Four Starr diner (Walter Starr, Prop.) or the Mountain House if they could afford that. They shopped the Emporium and the Western Auto. Some found their way to church on Sunday morning or the jail Friday or Saturday nights. More importantly, they all, eventually, found their way back home. They came wanting to use Mother Nature and looking for someone they could pay for the privilege. The outsiders bought, the locals pimped, and both sides parted smiling. The cycle was as regular as the seasons, a normal procession in the normal life of a normal little town. An unremarkable town, perhaps even boring. The rhythm of Larksboro was a lullaby, and when things started to change no one was awake enough to notice.

Things had been changing for quite some time.

"My God, will you look at this? I mean, just look at this place! I still can't believe it," Evelyn crooned, tucking her long blond hair behind her ears. "I mean, I feel like I wrote this place or something, you know?"

Rudy took his eyes off the winding road for a second to look at her. She was the love of his life, no doubt about that, and his partner in more ways than one, but even after living together and working together for the past three and a half years, he was still amazed at her capacity for childish exuberance. Considering her profession, perhaps it should have come as no surprise to him at all. Reluctantly he returned his attention to his driving; the road was a winding two-lane downgrade, not conducive to daydreaming. They rode smoothly past the sign warning of falling rocks and then the high chain-link fence that the Pennsylvania Department of Transportation had put around the base of Stuckey's Peak to catch them if, and when, they did fall. He passed the steep road that led up to the top of the three-hundred-foot-high formation, remembering Fred Zimmer at the hardware store telling him it was the local lover's lane. Ahead, a yellow diamond warned of an impending S turn. The shape reminded him of Evelyn's petite form; she had been a gymnast in college and still worked out with almost religious devotion and zeal to keep herself fit and firm. To touch her was to feel steel sheathed in velvet. Groaning inwardly at his hyperactive libido, evidenced by an increasing tightness in his jeans, he forced his attention toward less arousing topics.

Larksboro sat in a hollow surrounded by forested slopes, and Rudy had to admit that the view, as they approached down the winding road with the sun setting in front of them, was breathtaking. He put his hand on Evelyn's thigh and squeezed affectionately. "You're right, Eve, it could be a town in a children's book. Or a Chamber of Commerce pamphlet," he added, not being able to resist the jibe.

Eve gave him the evil eye. "C'mon, Scrooge. I mean, have you ever seen any place like it? Ever?" She looked wistfully out her window at the deepening twilight.

"Once," Rudy answered straight-faced.

"Oh yeah, smartass? Where?"

"When I was in Appalachia with the Peace Corps."

"Fuck off," she growled, trying not to laugh, raising the middle finger of her left hand and waving it in front of his nose.

"Or maybe it was Tijuana . . . " he mumbled.

Rudy received a solid punch on the shoulder (black and blue again, he mused) for his attempt at wry humor. Then they smiled warmly at each other and settled back in their seats to enjoy the drive and the cool evening air flowing in the windows. Godzilla a Great Dane/Newfoundland mix that took up the entire back seat of their late model Camaro, whuffed contentedly and went back to sleep. The rest of their trip to Larksboro was spent in intimate, companionable silence.

Even though they arrived at their new home in full darkness, it looked just as good to them as it had the first time they had seen it. Prior to moving here they

44

had lived in New York City, and for people trying to peddle their artistic skills to a limited demand market, it had been a wise place to be. The Apple was still widely considered the cultural Mecca of the east coast: The theaters, the playhouses, the operas, the galleries, and the publishing houses were there. They had met in a sidestreet bar called Down and Out and, from the first, the combination seemed both fortuitous and predestined. Evelyn Sangellis was a young author trying to sell her manuscripts for the children's books she loved to write. Rudy Vardon had recently given up his pretensions for a career in "serious art," realizing he had neither the talent nor the dedication it takes to become great but thinking that he had sufficient technical skill and imagination to be a passable illustrator. After an evening of drinks, mutual self-pity and self-praise, and long overdue honest self-appraisal, Eve had "hired him" to illustrate her books—should she ever succeed in getting any published.

It had taken time, but eventually they discovered the key to unlock the doors to success. Soon after that they realized that they were in love and began living together.

The books were modest but steady sellers and their relationship seemed to have few peaks or troughs, just a steady, dependable line that led to tomorrow. For those needing more excitement, such a relationship would have proven terminally boring, but both Eve and Rudy seemed to find their excitement in the creativity of their work. Creating together, as they did to form a cohesive whole, seemed to lend an almost mystic intimacy to what they felt for each other.

Though the city had changed little during all this time, they had changed—their needs, wants, and demands from life. With success blooming both within their relationship and without it, Eve and Rudy had looked around themselves with a different eye and asked if New York City was home. They answered no.

No to the expensive rental fees, which were considered suitable amounts only for mortgage payments—and sizeable ones at that—in other less urbane cities and towns in the East.

No to the almost compulsive pace of the city, the smog, and the noise. The greed, the strikes. The whole hyperkinetic gestalt that was distracting them from doing their best work.

No to the paranoia that seemed to swell deep inside you like a fetus, growing a little stronger every day until you thought you would die in the throes of some grotesquerie of birth. But you wouldn't, and finally you realized with horror that you'd never come to that; there was no "full term", and what was in you would just keep growing . . . growing . . .

So you didn't look your fellow man in the eye when you passed him on the street; you quickened your pace when you heard him behind you. You gripped your purse for dear life until your knuckles were white. If you walked you were not a pedestrian, you were a daredevil crossing streets, a broken-field runner on the sidewalks. To drive was to become a kamikaze pilot who depended far more on bluff and other's brakes than good motoring habits and courtesy of the road.

46

And, in time you began to treat everyone you came in contact with as one of two groups—adversaries or strangers. Even your kids, your girl, your wife.

No.

Six months after making their decision, Rudy and Evelyn were following their belongings to Larksboro.

The morning was beautiful—cool for the season, bright, and clear. The sun washed through the kitchen windows and flooded the whole room with a brilliance that gave the swirling dust motes the appearance of small jewels and soon had Rudy, sitting at the breakfast bar with a cup of strong coffee in front of him, anxious to get out and explore his new domain.

"I guess there's a lot of unevolved animal in me." He grinned at Evelyn after his labors—she was *not* a morning person—having finally gotten her into a sitting position, back propped against the headboard of their bed, squinting comically at him. "I feel like I have to go out and mark some trees or something."

Eve placed her feet on the as yet uncovered wood floor and gasped at the chill. Finally she rose and headed toward the hall bathroom, shuffling her feet and scratching various parts of her anatomy, as needed. "Mark some trees," she mumbled. "God, it's times like these that I know why I haven't married you."

Rudy chuckled and headed for the stairs. "I'll make you some coffee."

The town was just beginning to stir, most people leaving for their jobs in larger cities. Rudy and

Evelyn decided to try the cuisine at the Four Starr Diner when the mountain air finally started Eve's stomach growling like a German shepherd. They found the food to be remarkably well-prepared and, even more enjoyably, learned that the Four Starr Diner was one of the town's nerve centers . . . the place to come if you wanted a passable breakfast spiced heartily with the latest in town gossip, news of local events, and a smattering of historical reminiscences. Walter Starr seemed to divide his time between captaining the grill, refilling cups with rich black coffee, and simply standing with his immense stomach resting upon the counter, rubbing his pink and sparkling head. His smile was wide and truly infectious, and he presided over both the news and culinary functions of the diner benevolently, settling disputes, listening, and offering what his own ears had culled during the course of his twelve-plus hour day. When he learned that both of them were new residents of his community he put the full resources of his establishment at their disposal, graciously giving them the "Welcome Wagon" special. "It's on the house, folks. Real nice to have a young couple like you aboard."

"Why thanks, Mr. Starr," Rudy stammered, slightly embarrassed. "That's—"

"Walt, please. You want to call somebody 'Mister,' you'd better go up to the Mountain House. I hear you have to call the waiters 'Mister' up there."

"And don't thank him," a loud voice came from the back. "If he starts thinkin' the food's good, he'll raise the damn prices again."

Starr waved his huge sausage-fingered hand dismissingly in the air. "Yeah, nice to have new blood in town," he remarked in a stage voice. "Mebbe we'll put some manners back into these old farts around here." The clientele laughed appreciatively at the banter, and Rudy could see a grizzled man in a filthy red baseball cap being battered about by his cronies at the back of the diner. "That's Claude Reiner," Walt said, back in a normal conversational tone. "He owns the filling station over on Mulberry. Reiner's Amoco. Good place to go if your car goes out; that man knows more about cars than a flea knows about dogs. Jus' don't tell him I said so, now," the big man finished with a wink.

"Right," Rudy agreed conspiratorially. He looked at Eve and saw that she was done eating. Pushing himself away from the counter with an exaggerated groan, he reached out and shook the owner's hand. "Real nice to meet you, Walt. And thanks for the free meal."

"Hey, no problem. Like I said, real nice to have you folks movin' in. Real nice, Rudy. An' . . . Evelyn."

"Eve," she said, taking the proffered hand but using it to balance herself as she stood on tiptoe to kiss Starr's pudgy cheek. "I can tell I'm going to love it in Larksboro."

"Oh Gawd," Reiner moaned from the back. "Food won't be worth a shit all day, now."

Starr flushed a deep crimson. "Well, I sure hope you do, Eve. I sure do." He glanced at Rudy, questioning with his eyes, looking for any signs of jealousy or anger.

Vardon smiled. "I'm sure we will. Well . . . see you

later." He grabbed Evelyn's arm gently and they walked toward the door.

"Oh, Walt?" Eve said, turning, and Starr became all ears. "Can you tell me where I could buy some typing paper and carbons?"

"And some art supplies," Rudy added.

"Sure. Over to the Emporium would prob'ly be the best place. Mayor's wife runs it. It's right on the square; you can't miss it."

"Less you can't find the square," Reiner said.

The couple chuckled at the retort and walked out into the bright sunlight, smiling cheerfully as each thought his private thoughts about their new home. Slowly strolling languidly, the idyllic drone of small town life accompanying a chorus of shouted greetings and a choreography of waves and smiles from the people they passed, the lovers made their way to the square and the Larksboro Emporium.

It was a large building, deep and high, with two huge bow windows filled with houseplants flanking an intricately carved wooden door. The hanging sign was a modern multi-colored rendition of "old-time" script, the entire place seemingly done in a manner meant to convey a message of history. Unfortunately the message was garbled and, besides, to Rudy and Evelyn the fifties were B.C.

Eve, shaking her head sadly, said, "My God."

"It's a common enough style, Evelyn, my love. I think Howard Johnson's adopting it in a few years."

"Rudy!" she scolded. She cocked her head and gave the place an appraising gaze. "Well, it is kind of quaint, I guess."

"Oh, quaint. Yes. Very," mocked Rudy as he moved toward the door. When Eve started to follow, he opened the door gallantly, bowed, then said quickly, "Oops, watch out for that dog shit."

Just as quickly Evelyn came to a halt, trying to keep her balance, keep her feet still, and keep her eye out for unwanted objects on the sidewalk at the same time. When at last she realized what was happening, she strode up to her lover, who was quaking with repressed laughter, cuffed him sharply on the shoulder, and spat as haughtily as she could, "Won't you ever grow up!" Without a backward look she strode firmly through the door . . . and into the thin, waiting arms of Agatha Cooper, who had hurried from her place by the entrance to the back room to greet her first customers of the day. Eve heard her host's starting gambit of incessant chatter even before she felt her hand being pressed by something that felt vaguely like a bird's foot . . . cool, dry, boney with the tips of incredibly long nails pressed lightly against the back of her hand. Even as her eyes became used to the rather dingy interior of the store, she had trouble making sense of the pale mass that bobbed like some haunting ghost at the level of her nose, until a strong scent of hair spray made her realize that this was the top of a woman's head.

Rudy moved into the darkness behind his lady wondering why the woman was chattering so rapidly and in such an odd voice. Totally intrigued, he moved slightly to the side to see what Eve's petite frame might be hiding. What he saw was so bizarre that he had to feign coughing to hide his sudden fit of giggling.

The woman in front of Evelyn was tiny in every possible sense of the word. She couldn't have been over five feet tall, and was so thin and flat-chested that she looked almost two-dimensional in the darkness. The largest thing about her was her hairdo—a bouffant-type thing that piled up on top of her narrow head, stiff and glowing platinum, for what seemed like yards.

She looks like a fucking Q-tip, Rudy thought suddenly, and launched into another coughing fit.

This diminutive creature was positively attacking Eve's arm, shaking her hand convulsively while talking so quickly that he couldn't make sense of anything she was saying.

Evelyn stood, baring the Q-tip lady's onslaught with total disbelief and consternation written all over her face. Her eyes were wide and staring down into the bird's nest that jiggled under her nose. Her mouth worked as she tried to fit a word in somewhere. Finally, blessedly, the cloying odor of hair spray became too much for Eve's overstimulated system, and she sneezed loudly.

Agatha Cooper dropped her customer's hand as if it were leprous, stepped back, and quietly stared.

Rudy moved beside his wife, coughing lightly into his fist. "Hi," he beamed. "I'm Rudy Vardon, and this is Evelyn Sangellis." The Q-tip lady just stared to him bluntly, so he decided she might need prompting now. Maybe her batteries are dead, he thought, and coughed again. He extended his hand, "You're—"

Mrs. Cooper stared at them, totally confused. She started to say, "You two must be new in town," and then, even though she didn't understand why this seemed so hilarious, she began to laugh, whooping like some kind of crane. The young couple in front of her joined in wholeheartedly.

After all had dried their eyes and groaned about their cramped stomachs and facial muscles, Agatha told them to call her Aggie and wouldn't rest until she had escorted them into her back room, sat them at a small table, and made them each a cup of hot tea on a hot plate.

"It's green tea," she explained, sitting down across from them and sipping hers as a wine taster would savor wine. "Martin, that's my husband, he gets it special for me from an importer in New York. A few years ago we vacationed in Japan, and I just fell in love with it."

"Do you travel a lot?" Eve asked.

"No, not really. Martin is so busy here in Larksboro. It's not a big town, you know, but he takes his job as mayor so seriously. He wants to preserve the raw spirit of America here, he says. I guess that's alright, but I think New York City's so-o-o-o exciting. I go there as often as I can. Didn't you say you lived there? In New York?"

"For years," Rudy nodded. "Maybe Larksboro isn't more exciting to you, Aggie, but you can believe me when I tell you that you have much more of life's"—he searched for the word he wanted—"fullness here." Good choice, Rudy old man. Maybe you should try your hand at this writing business.

As if she could read his thoughts, Aggie agreed with them. "Why, Rudy, here I thought you said your wife was the writer. Hmmm, 'life's fullness' . . . I like that. It's so poetic. You sound so much like

Professor Gimball—he teaches at the Community College—but then you're a college man too, aren't you?" Rudy nodded again. "Lord, but it must be nice to have been blessed with brains and talent. And beauty," she added, tilting her head at Eve. "Like your wife here. As you can see, I—"

"Aggie," Evelyn interrupted gently, "I'm not Rudy's wife, yet."

"Oh. Oh my," Aggie fumbled. "Well, I didn't mean . . . you young people today just do things so differently that . . ."

". . . that you tend to confuse people of Agatha's age and limited experience."

The voice reached out in the small room, reverberating, commanding. At the first sound of it, the small hairs on the back of Rudy's neck and arms stood up, and ice formed somewhere deep in his stomach. Challenged, he reflected, I feel challenged. His heart pounded, his skin grew cold and clammy, his senses alert.

Jesus Christ, what the fuck is going on here?

He saw Aggie look up, startled, at a point directly above his head, eyes widening. And then she seemed to recognize whoever it was who had managed to enter so silently, and her look became . . . fawning. It occurred to Rudy that if Aggie Cooper had a tail, she'd be wagging it.

Then he saw his mate's look—strange way to think of her—change from momentary fright to fear, to awe, and finally, gaining composure, to polite inquisitiveness.

And he realized he would have to turn completely

around to face this person, and get off his chair and stand. He tried to pull himself together as he did these things, but his movements were hurried nonetheless—tensed, ready to repel an attack, to defend against some violent aggression. Finally, clumsily, he gained his feet and looked up from his own six-foot height into a face that seemed to contain nothing except two riveting grey-green orbs . . . penetrating, somehow menacing.

I'm going to die. Oh God, he's going to . . .

He wanted to protect his throat.

A few seconds later the feelings had passed. The world speeded up almost audibly, and as his frozen blood thawed, Rudy could feel rivulets of sweat snaking down his spine and ribs. The Greek god that stood only inches from him smiled warmly and totally engulfed Rudy's hand in his, grasping it in an almost viselike grip that seemed to be no effort at all.

"Sorry to have startled you so," he purred. "My name is Josh Gimball. And you must be the famous Rudolph Vardon."

There would have been silence, but Agatha Cooper jumped deftly into it and exorcised it with her tongue.

"That's right, Professor. That's Rudy Vardon and this is Eve—"

"Sangellis," Eve finished for her.

"Sangellis, yes. They just moved here from New York City, can you imagine? Rudy paints, and Evelyn writes children's books. They're *very* talented, Joshua."

"From New York City," Joshua mused.

"That's right," Agatha blurted. "Rudy says we have 'fullness of life' here. Isn't that right, Rudy?"

"Fullness of life," Gimball cocked his head toward the other man and fixed him with his eyes. "Really?"

Vardon nodded once, dumbly. Struggling against his torpor, he thought, My God, the man is overwhelming!

"And you, Evelyn . . . Ms. Sangellis, what do you think of our little town?"

The baritone voice seemed to wash over her like a wave, but it was cold, Evelyn thought, so cold . . . "So far, Professor Gimball, I haven't found anything about it I don't like." I don't think.

Gimball held out his massive, long-fingered hands in a gesture of supplicaton. "Please, call me Josh. Or, at least, Joshua. Professor Gimball sounds so formal, as if I had something to teach you, when I'm sure just the opposite is true."

"Okay," Eve conceded, "I'll call you Josh, but I don't really think—" But Gimball turned toward Rudy.

"And may I call you Rudy?" he asked pleasantly.

"Certainly."

"Fantastic. I paint also, Rudy. I'd feel privileged to talk to you about painting sometime. Perhaps we could show each other our work. I'd love to have your suggestions on improving my style."

"Actually," Rudy admitted, feeling more himself but still ill at ease, "I'm an illustrator, not a painter."

"Damn you, Rudy!" Evelyn scolded, grabbing his hand and squeezing. "You graduated with a degree in fine arts and you can too paint. When you let yourself." She turned to Joshua. "We have quite a few of his paintings at home, and he'd love to show them to you." She yanked his arm, "Wouldn't you?"

"Well—"

She turned back to Gimball as if the matter had been decisively decided. "There," she huffed victoriously, "that settles it."

Joshua Gimball laughed deep in his chest, and Rudy was uncomfortably reminded of a growl. "Excellent. I commend you on your choice of women, Rudy. True spirit is an infinitely precious commodity. Well, I'll call you soon. Perhaps we can get together at my place for dinner and a few drinks some evening, yes? It's going to be such a pleasure talking to people of maturity and talent. I can't begin to tell you how enjoyable such evenings are to me." He put his long, thick arm around Rudy's shoulders in a comradely gesture and squeezed. Vardon thought he could almost feel the power—enormous, awesome, untapped—coursing through that arm, barely restrained. He realized that, should he decide to, Gimball could crush him into pulp in an instant, and there would be no hope of salvation.

It was not a good feeling.

"You'd better marry this girl," Joshua advised him, "before someone else takes a liking to her." Rudy had a feeling Gimball spoke more in warning than in jest.

Evelyn snaked her arm around her lover's waist and glared at Josh in mock insult. "I think I have something to say about that!" she asserted.

Gimball smiled, but somehow it wasn't reflected in his eyes. He reached out and stroked Aggie's cheek— she leaned her head into the caress and Rudy had the

57

impression that she could've been purring . . . or else
. . . what? —and said, "Why of course, Eve, of
course." Then he flashed stunning white teeth and
walked out.

He seemed to leave a vacuum behind him, or a
time warp or something. It took quite a while for any
of the three of them to get the energy to break the
glassine silence, and when it happened it was Aggie's
doing. Suddenly she shook violently from cotton-
head to pigeon-toe, bursting into voice and motion at
the selfsame instant.

Evelyn thought, This woman has got to be doing
speeders.

Rudy thought, Walt's a bloodhound. Agatha's a
rat terrier. And Joshua Gimball's a . . . What the
hell *is* Joshua Gimball, anyway?

They walked home arm in arm, discussing what
they'd seen of their new home, carrying the things
they'd finally purchased at the Emporium, bumping
together occasionally in that planned/unplanned way
lovers have of touching. They could see the red ball of
the sun impaling itself on Stuckey's Peak as they
walked.

They had decided to paint the kitchen yellow, to
eat breakfast every morning at the Four Starr, that
they liked Walt and Aggie, to build Godzilla a
doghouse but mostly to let him inside, to accept
Joshua's invitation if and when he called, to make
love tonight—and to go to bed early—and that they
liked Larksboro.

They walked on. The sun breathed its last red
breath into the sky, and night fell softly but quickly.

The stars winked down at them flirtatiously; the moon was half a phosphorous pie. Eve leaned her head on her man's shoulder and sighed.

"It was time we did this, Rudy," she breathed. "It was good."

Rudy pulled her closer to him, relishing her feel, her warmth. Everything had been good and could only get better. "Yeah. The Apple was starting to go to the dogs."

The howl broke into the cacophony of nightsong, stilling it instantly. It was a hellish, ululating sound that dropped the temperature of the night air below freezing. It rose above the mountains, rose until Rudy thought he would scream and Eve felt her bowels trying to loosen. It rose, and suddenly . . .

It stopped.

Alone on the street, between the mountains, in the night, the man and woman looked at each other and forced nervous grins.

Evelyn said, "You rang?"

Deep in the forest, embracing the blackness, feeling the old desire—not the Hunger, the Other— Joshua Gimball pointed his face toward the glowing moon and sang out his desire, thinking, Evelyn. Eve. How apropos . . .

Chapter 2

It moved through the high woodland, downhill, steadily through the trees, swift and silent. It breathed evenly and rhythmically, the warm air clouding in the still chill night air, streaming out of its mouth and nose as if it were exhaling smoke. Padding swiftly on enormous paws, it advanced to the very edge of the forest, to the narrow buffer of overgrown fields of weeds and grasses and the occasional brown scabs of newly turned farmland and gardens, which acted as a buffer between the town and the surrounding mountains. It stood with its canine senses alert for even the smallest hint of threat or danger but found nothing. Field mice and raccoons scuttled through the verge. An owl questioned his presence from the wise security of a high pine branch. From somewhere close came the cautious step of an invisible whitetail, not alerted yet to the presence of this predator but stealthy just the same. It could smell these things with its preternaturally keen nose, hear them with its radarlike ears. Its eyes collected the available light as fully as the most advanced man-made night optics, turning the near darkness into a panorama of shapes and forms illumined by ghost-light.

It growled deep in its muscle-banded chest, alternately flexing and relaxing its corded haunches. Hunger was upon it, and had it been less of a creature like some of the others, it would have forgotten its mission and gone off in search of fresh meat to curb its desire, fresh blood to slake its thirst. But this creature was older and wiser, and did not take such animal urges as an imperative. This creature was no simple beast. There was a well-developed brain protected by this canine skull, a mind the equal of any man. And now there was a new purpose to its nocturnal wanderings—this night, at least. It was time to find a mate, to settle into a new life. To spawn a new generation of beings that would become, in due course, the covert rulers of the planet. The next evolutionary step for intelligent life on Earth. A hybrid that not even the most visionary biologist could have envisioned as a possibility, much less a reality, although the ancients did, as well as the superstitious and ignorant peasants, no better than cattle, which littered the world and defaced the history of this globe. But now it could exist and thrive and prosper. Now it could exist in its rightful place in nature, a niche that had been vacant for so long.

The ultimate predator.

A dark canine form moved out of the trees and disappeared into the edge growth that bordered Larksboro. It was large, much larger than any dog had ever been, but exceptionally well-proportioned. The physical configuration would have reminded an onlooker of that of a monstrous German shepherd, had there been such an onlooker. And if there had been such a one and he had been close enough, he might have seen the rubbery black gums drawn back over dazzlingly white six-inch canine teeth, the lolling dark tongue, and thought, Sweet Jesus, that thing's smiling.

Or he might have seen the piercing grey-green of its eyes.

In their new house on Cooper's Point Road (there had been Coopers in Larksboro for generations), Rudy and Eve had never quite made it to bed as they had planned. After putting away the supplies they had bought at the Emporium, they had started a roaring fire in the living room fireplace, both to ward off the chill of the night and the scare of that single, lunatic howl. Then Eve had gotten some wine and cheese and crackers, laid the sheepskin in front of the fire grate, and turned off the lights. They sat now in the flickering light, gazing into the yellowish clarity of their drinks and into each other's eyes. It was a moment of total peace and contentment, and they prolonged it as best they could.

Eve leaned over and nibbled Rudy's earlobe playfully, whispering, "I'm hungry."

Rudy pushed the plate of cheese and crackers toward her, momentarily distracted by unwanted thoughts of canine aspects of personality, of Agatha Cooper's fawning attitude, of her almost doglike shake after Professor Gimball had left, of Joshua's unsettling magnetism . . .

Of that ungodly howl.

Evelyn pushed the plate away, peeved, and aggressively shoved the man onto his back. "I'm not hungry for *that*, Casanova," she reproved, and then settled into his arms, cutting off his reply with her lips and tongue.

As things progressed, becoming more and more heated as clothes were shed and things were kissed, stroked, and suckled, Godzilla haltingly raised his bulk and moved toward the writhing shapes on the floor. He sensed vaguely, by smell, what was going on between these two humans, but he didn't really care. The dog knew only that, at times like these, his masters were not so observant as they normally were and less inclined to discipline. And there on the floor, pushed toward him as if in offering, was a round thing piled with food. He lowered his broad head, daintily picked piece after piece off the plate, and quietly gulped them down, taking little time to chew.

There was another canine form just outside the house on Cooper's Point Road, its seventy-six-inch length propped against one of the undraped front windows. With its forepaws resting effortlessly on the window ledge, it had no trouble seeing all that went on in the exposed living room, senses that even Godzilla would have envied perceiving more. It watched, statue-still, rapt, as Eve ran her small pink tongue the length of Rudy's body and took him deep into her mouth. Never moving, it silently watched as she straddled Rudy's lying form and lowered herself to engulf him, and they writhed and moaned and sweated in ever-increasing intensity and quickening tempo. It could hear every moan, every muttered curse, every liquid slurp that testified to the coupling going on before its eyes. And more, it could smell the musk, overpowering, as it wafted from even the minutest cracks in the structure. The creature's penis extended slowly, incredibly long and thin—snake-like—and glistening red. Its long, bushy tail started to quiver and writhe with a life of its own, and as the keenness of its perceptions worked against it, increasing the impact of all it saw, heard, and smelled beyond tolerance, it emitted the briefest of tortured snarls.

It was a mistake.

Godzilla's head came up instantly, took in the eyes glittering in the window like twin jewels in a black cloth, rumbled like a passing train, and then leapt, barking furiously, toward this intruder that threatened his domain and his masters. If it hadn't been for his mid-air collision with the female, he would have flown through the window, without pause, at the interloper—to his death.

Evelyn heard the snarl, too, but only vaguely. What launched her into panicked motion was Godzilla's barking. She rose off of Rudy like the well-conditioned athlete that she was, standing suddenly, perfectly bisecting the arc of her dog's final leap.

Rudy felt his woman's peaking excitement and his own imminent orgasm, and gave himself over to it completely. Then there was a noise (thunder?) and Eve was rocketing to her feet as his seed spurted out of him across his stomach and abdomen. He could hear Godzilla barking frantically, then heard the dog's startled yelp and Evelyn's gasp as he saw her plummet, headlong, into the couch they had placed in front of the living room window. As he turned and got to his knees, he saw his dog's massive black shape as it got to its feet and scrambled to Eve's side, whining and nuzzling her face in concern and apology. He saw Eve fall onto the floor with a thud, onto her rump, and look at him, dazed and confused.

And as he looked over her head at the window, he could have sworn he just caught a view of some enormous dog or wolf with laser-beam eyes as it spun and dropped out of sight.

About that same time, he thought he heard somebody yell.

Ellison Hartmen had not had a sober moment of his own choosing for years, but this isn't to say that he didn't have them at all. For the past ten years he had gone to the Safari Lounge with his government disability check tucked firmly in his pocket, claiming poverty and misery and sponging drinks from those he could persuade to contribute. He was a tradition now, and things were better than he could ever remember, not that he could or cared to remember that much. Doris was dead and probably making the Devil Himself miserable, so he didn't have to go on the wagon two or three times a year so's she'd give her gums a rest. And now that the town was getting used to him—accepting him, kinda'—the drinks were flowing freer and he had that government check for the little brown bags that he carried home every night, although the best nights he couldn't find home an' just sacked out in the woods.

This had not been one of his best nights. Not even a good night, actually. The Safari had been damn near empty, and those that were there weren't in a buyin' mood. Then the goddam federal government had fucked up on mailin' his check somehow (probably some asshole in a suit and tie knocked it inta the trash can while he was gettin' blowed by his secretary!) and he didn't even have his own money, for Chrissakes, to get drunk on. So here he was, only half high, not even drunk enough to forget the cold, back on the way to his house to finish whatever he could find, even outta' smokes, and now this!

Down to the end of Cooper's Point, where it came closest to the mountain, there was one fuckin' big bastard of a dog lookin' in the front window of a house, for Chrissakes! It was the damnedest-lookin' thing he'd ever seen in his sixty-one years. Big pointy ears. Teeth what looked bigger'n those bayonets we used to shiv them Krauts with in France. Fuckin' feet looked big as dinner plates. Just one evil-lookin' motherfucker of an animal. And he had to walk right by it to get home. Damn!

Ellison (you can call me El; sorta' rhymes with my ultimate destinashun) hefted his walking stick and waved it in front of him sabrelike. He felt like Fairbanks in one of those swashbuckler movies, and it braced his courage. His leg had shrapnel, impregnated while walking a country road in France during the Second World War (he had been coming back with two chickens "liberated" from a French farm) and, with the onslaught of arthritis fifteen years ago, he had been forced to rely on something other than his game limb to support him. He gave the stick a final flourish, remembering a few years ago when he had beat the tar out of those kids who used to follow him home, heckling him and throwing him down.

Showed them damned brats a thing or two, too, he recalled, and began to creep down Cooper's Point Road.

The closer he got to the dog, the more he didn't want to go any farther. He saw its tail start to twitch and almost turned to retreat, but thought that if the dog saw him leaving now it'd be on him in a second. If it did come for him, he sure as hell wanted to be facing it. He thought. So he moved forward again, painfully slowly, watching in drunken fascination as the animal's genitalia became engorged and slid from the foreskin, a pink glistening worm.

Christ Almighty, he realized with some amusement, the damned thing's gettin' a hard-on. And his brain was just filling with speculation about canine peeping Toms and wondering about just what, exactly, that animal was looking at, when he heard its rumbling snarl and saw it turn toward him.

Ellison Hartmen never remembered screaming (although his throat was raw for two days after) and certainly didn't know what he had screamed, but he knew that he turned and ran back up the street the way he came, forgetting the cane he still carried, forgetting the arthritis, forgetting even the scarred tissue that hindered his step. He knew only that he was running, that his bowels had let loose and soiled his clothing and himself, and that he was never going to quit running until he reached the Safari, 'cause he'd rather die of a heart attack than be . . . killed by whatever that THING was.

When Ellison reached the Safari Lounge, he knew also that he could never tell what he'd just seen. No one would believe him, for one thing—hell, he almost didn't, for Chrissakes, believe it himself—and, secondly, he doubted that he would be able to talk until quite a few shots had numbed his terror. So he just walked, limping severely now, up to the bar and sat, shaking and staring at the reflection of the door in the mirror over the bar.

He looked so bad that the drinks came effortlessly; came so that no one there would have to hear why he looked that way. Came because no one even wanted to know.

The beast dropped to all fours on the grass, aware instantly of his mistake and cursing himself for his lack of control. It saw the older human running as quickly as he could up the street, smelling of alcohol and ill health and fear. There was no threat there, it knew, either now or later, for it knew the man and what position he occupied in the pecking order of the town. Even if he told, no one would ever think to believe him, and so it let him live.

The remarkable ears of the creature detected the commotion inside the house, analyzed it, and realized there would be no confrontation this night unless it so desired. Turning in a blur of coordinated motion, it sprinted the few blocks from the town proper to the fields in a loping, seemingly effortless stride. In flowing motion it merged with the shadows, blended with them, ran deeper and deeper into their wavering embrace until it knew it was safe. Here it stopped and scratched its ear with its hind paw in the way of canines, castigating itself, seething with anger and unfulfilled desire. It paced back and forth nervously, feeling the hunger and the rage and the desire course through it like hot blood. Then, unable to calm itself by movement or by reason, it threw its sleek head back and emitted one last sonorous howl before it launched itself demonically into the trees.

It had been quite a few years since they'd done anything like this, and even more since they'd last come to Larksboro, but what with Eileen at summer camp for six weeks and Russell away at Fort Lauderdale with friends, this seemed like just the ticket for getting reacquainted. The tent had finally gone up correctly just before sunset, and the supper of dehydrated beef Stroganoff and dried fruit had been just the thing to quiet their complaining stomachs. Neither of them was used to going without, and it struck him, as he smoked and watched the setting sun, that it had been a long time since he had even been really hungry, eating mainly out of habit instead of need. Patting the respectably large roll of fat that obscured his belt buckle, he resolved to remedy that situation when they returned home. Looking at his wife's overample posterior as she labored over her sleeping bag, he rather hoped that she felt the same way.

When it got too dark to really see and the two of them found that they were talked out, they walked hand in hand to their new Sears tent, crawled in, zipped up the flaps, and lay down to sleep. Just before exhaustion overtook him, he thought that it was a shame he couldn't see the stars. Then his romantic musings were disturbed by his unwillingness to share his blood with gnats and mosquitos, and much more appreciative of his removal from the pests of the night, he rolled over with a sigh and closed his eyes.

"Hon," his wife whispered timorously. When she got no answer she repeated more loudly, "Hon?"

Wondering how women could manage to always time things so badly, he said tiredly, "Yes dear?"

"Do you think there are . . . bears or anything . . . out here?"

"No, dear," he sighed deeply, thinking, Oh shit. Next it'll be alligators. "The most vicious creatures out here can be killed by your bug spray, sweetheart. Believe me."

It hurried through the night-dark forest until it smelled the smoke, faint and far away, but there. Immediately the beast changed its course and started up the mountain, panting with the exertion but hurrying now, needing. A quarter hour later it reached the campsite, snuffling softly from the effects of the smoke of the dying campfire, a single red eye that winked out of the darkness. The creature padded silently forward, ears pricked up and hackles raised, all senses alert to the hunt. When it reached the tent it sniffed softly at the colored nylon, checking for an opening as well as gathering data about the occupants. There were two, it realized, a male and a female, and the scene played out before it tonight came back in full torturing force. Him, making love to her, mating with *her* . . . The creature's jaws ground and popped as his muscles corded and tightened with his hate. It sank its teeth into the flimsy nylon side and ripped wide an opening for its entrance, then stood backlit by the light of the heavens and snarled out its challenge to the two humans it confronted.

His eyes opened in time to see his wife's feet exit a gaping hole in the side of the tent. They kicked up and down furiously, like she was trying to run in place, on her back, and he called out "Maggie?" as they disappeared outside and he heard a motorcycle, a big one, revving up somewhere. (Dirt bikes?)

The next instant IT materialized, filling the gaping hole ripped in the tent, filling his vision, filling his mind. He wouldn't let himself think about what it was, but he understood that it had gotten Maggie, dragged her outside, and now it was back for him. He reached for his camp hatchet and raised it over his head as the creature stood there watching, growling ceaselessly, not moving until he moved to strike it with all his strength. Then it darted forward in a blur, seizing his forearm in its huge jaws and crushing the bone instantly. The pain brought tears to his eyes and, whimpering, he tried to crawl to the far wall of the tent. But he couldn't. The beast held fast to his crippled arm, feet braced against his efforts, snarling as if they were playing with some gory new pull-toy. Then the thing shook its head once, sharply, and pulled the forearm off at the elbow joint.

It made the same sound as pulling the drumstick off a Thanksgiving turkey.

Bill was beyond caring. Freed, he crawled rapidly back against the tent wall as the beast passively watched, impacting with such force that the tent tilted crazily and fell around his struggling form like a net.

71

With his quarry so trapped, the beast began his dismemberment at leisure but in earnest. First he dug his muzzle into the warm juncture between the man's legs. . . .

Hours later, when he had taken out his rage upon the mutilated carcass of the man and quenched his hunger and thirst on the flesh and blood of the woman, Maggie, Joshua Gimball, in his wolf-form, returned to Moonshadow. Hanging from his monstrous jaws were some choice parts he would take to the younger ones, those he called the "pups," to nourish them until they learned to hunt on their own.

Then he would have some of his followers come to this place and remove all traces of Bill and Maggie and their fate while he got some much needed sleep.

Tomorrow was, after all, a school day.

Walter Starr clucked his tongue sympathetically.

"It was the damnedest thing I ever saw, Walt." Rudy started to go over it all again. "Luckily neither of us got hurt or anything, but our dog just flew to that window and when I looked up . . ."

"Honey," Eve interrupted, "you've already told Walt everything twice. Why don't you relax?" It wasn't that she really cared how many times he told the story—she was still shaken up about it too—but the tale had obviously been altered before it was revealed to the public, and she was worried that Rudy might slip up and start to tell what the circumstances really were.

"Yeah, you're right. It's just that I've gone over it a jillion times myself, and what I saw . . . what I think I saw . . . just doesn't make any sense." He looked at her pleadingly. "Does it to you?" And when she shook her head, he turned to Walt. "How about you?"

"Nope," Walter mumbled thoughtfully, rubbing his hand over his bald scalp in a motion that looked as if he were waxing it. Then he raised his eyes and looked out the plate glass window, saying, "But I'll tell ya' who—" and then he nodded toward the door and waved at the man who entered. "Speak of the devil," he chuckled.

The man who had come in so conveniently on cue was clearly a game warden. He wore the Smokey Bear hat and distinctive uniform that announced his authority symbolically, and had a carriage and seamed outdoorsman's face that bespoke an authority all its own. He came at Walt's beckoning and, after informal introductions all around, perched his tall, rangy frame on a red vinyl counter stool two down from Rudy and asked what he could do for them this early in the morning. As it was explained to him, a frown settled across his features and he rested his forearms dejectedly on the counter. John Scott had been a game warden for eighteen years, but he had never been able to accept the circumstances— and the mentality—that led to problems like he was beginning to have in the Larksboro area.

"It's the dogs, Mr. Vardon," he stated flatly. "We started to have problems with them in our woods over a year ago. Now it looks like the bolder ones are coming into town to forage."

Confusion showed in Rudy's face. "Well, it certainly looked like a dog . . . sort of . . . I mean, a damned *big* dog, but it could've been a dog, I guess."

73

He fell silent for a moment, deep in thought. There had been something familiar about that dog. Like he'd seen it somewhere before, but that was impossible. Still, there was . . . something. Deeply irritated at his inability to solve that riddle, he focused on another enigma that the game warden had just brought up. "What do you mean you've been having trouble with dogs in the woods? What kind of problems can a dog cause in the woods, John?"

Scott looked at the younger man and thought how naive city people were about their cute little pets. "You're not a hunter, are you?" he asked.

Vardon shook his head emphatically. "Don't believe in it."

"Well, that's a whole 'nother can of worms, as they say. I'll leave that set until another time. But dogs, Rudy, are the most ruthless predators in the woods these days. Some say they took the place of the wolves and bobcats and what-all that civilization chased out decades ago. If you ever saw a wild dog kill, you'd know why most knowledgeable people disagree with that. Wolves and cats and other wild things, they kill for food or self-defense. Dogs gone wild kill just to kill. They're almost evil in their violence sometimes. Besides all that, they have very little fear of man." Scott paused to sip the coffee Walt had served him. "These animals kill deer and other wildlife and throw the whole balance out of whack. That's why we shoot wild dogs on sight."

Eve thought of Godzilla being shot to bits like the villain of some Clint Eastwood movie and she shuddered. "But how do these dogs go wild, John? I mean, how do they get up on the mountain in the

74

first place?"

The tall warden smiled kindly with his eyes. "Well, miss, that's about the most disgusting part. People come up here to camp or fish or hunt. Sometimes they rent the cabins up the slope for a week or two. They bring their wife and kids and they bring the dog. Or else they just bring the dog, their loyal friend, and all that sh—pardon—stuff. Thing is, the dog wanders off because he isn't a good enough friend for them to keep track of, they can't find him and leave the animal behind when they go, and it has no choice but to go wild—feral, they call it. Sometimes these folks can't have dogs where they live, so they pick one up free or cheap when they go on vacation to give to the kids, and then they give the pup the boot when it's time to go back home."

"God," Evelyn was almost crying. "That's so damn cruel."

"Most of 'em wouldn't agree. They figure the dog will find his way back to town, somebody nice'll adopt the poor orphan, and it'll end up peachy. Too bad that's not usually the way it works. The ones that don't starve to death—and there's a lot of *them*—go feral real quick. Eventually their group instinct brings them together to form packs, and those packs are *the* most efficient killing machine in the woods."

Walt, who had been silently listening, put his hand lightly on Eve's arm to get her attention. "An' that's not all," he added. "Because not all of them dogs are from out-of-towners. Nope. There's a lot of people right here in Larksboro that just let their dogs run, and where d'you think they go? Right up the

75

damned mountain, huh, Scotty?"

"Yeah, Walt, that's the truth. Fido and Spot spend a fun day up on the mountain crippling and killing whitetails and what-not, and then come back home around supper time wagging their tails and begging table scraps. Most of the time they don't eat much, or any, of what they kill."

"Sounds like a lot of the 'sportsmen' I know," Rudy quipped acidly, and Scott nodded at him sagely.

"But you got to understand we're not all like that, Rudy. I know that folks like that can put you off all of us, but I wouldn't be a game warden, old buddy, if I didn't love the animals out in those woods. And there are a lot of hunters just like me. God knows I'm not in this for the money."

"Okay," the younger man said. "I think I have a better perspective on it now. But it's still a matter of personal choice, John. You haven't made a hunter out of me today."

"Haven't really tried . . . yet," John chided.

Eve grabbed Rudy's arm firmly as he started to answer and held up her hand. "Look, fellows," she said in her best condescending tone, "I hate to interrupt your conversation, but do you think we could stick with the dogs, huh? You know, Rudy? Dogs like the one that was sizing us up for his entrée last night. Do you think we have anything to worry about, John? I mean, should we stay indoors or what? I can't help but be a little concerned about this."

Scott spoke with an assurance he didn't quite feel. "I don't think you really have to get upset, miss.

That dog last night was probably drawn by the firelight; mostly just curious. As for the ones in the woods, well, I doubt that you'd be able to find them if you were looking for them. They're not all that afraid of us, like I said, but they don't want anything to do with us, either. Just be a little careful when you go in the woods, and I'd keep that dog of yours around home the next few days. I think I'll see what I can turn up, and I wouldn't want to shoot this pony of yours. Other than that, I wouldn't give it another thought."

After that the three of them, joined occasionally by Walter, talked about other things that were not so immediate. By the time John Scott turned down a third cup of coffee, paid his bill, and ambled out the door, the young couple felt as if they had known and liked him for quite a while. They finished their own coffee and headed toward home, Evelyn to a long overdue session at her typewriter, and Rudy to his sketchpad and charcoals.

John Scott headed for his cherished mountain, but his thoughts were heavy and sombre. Things were getting strange around Larksboro. Things were getting positively . . . spooky. There had to be a pack of wild dogs running his mountains, but they weren't behaving like feral dogs. He had found their kills many times in the past year and a half, but he had never found their spoor. Never as much as one damned footprint. . .

Holy shit, now I'm making them human! Make that *paw*print, he thought.

So. Never as much as one damned *paw*print. What

77

did these animals do, clean up after themselves? They had to leave prints. Unless there were ghost-dogs killing deer—and anything else they could find, he guessed—in this forest.

And the kills weren't wild-dog kills. The deer had been quite literally torn apart, the bones not simply gnawed but crushed and sucked dry of marrow, the skulls emptied of brain. These animals had been killed viciously, efficiently, by animals that seemed to enjoy the act of killing. Yet they had also been consumed: The organs were eaten, as well as the intestines and the genitalia. The muscle meat also, but an experienced eye could tell that it was taken last, probably by the pack members lowest in the social structure.

There was one final thing, a thing that made even less sense than anything else: Larksboro had become a high-risk area for dogs in the last year. Fido and Spot and Rover were simply disappearing—out of yards, out of doghouses, off of chains. No place was safe for pet dogs in Larksboro anymore. They couldn't *all* be in these mountains. Some, perhaps, but certainly not all. So they had to be either dognapped or dead, and dognapping wasn't a major law enforcement problem in town. That left dead, and the question was, Who or what would need or want to kill over a dozen dogs in twelve months? That was the question, but what was the answer?

John Scott lit a cigarette as he drove along one of the rutted dirt roads that crisscrossed the lower slopes, thinking, What the hell *is* going on out here, anyway?

Rudy sat cross-legged for hours, trying to capture the essence of an old gnarled oak, which stood paternally halfway across a field of light green grass and small blue flowers, and transfer it to paper with his charcoal. Either the oak looked right but didn't feel right, or else it came out just the opposite. Finally he gave up and thrust his legs out straight in an effort to ease the aches in his knees and ankles. When he looked down at his day's best efforts, he wondered if he had learned anything at all in college—or since, for that matter. The dignified and stately tree out there had been turned into a tree from a Hammer Films set; the reassuring atmosphere of paternalistic benevolence had become, in translation, one of the most malevolent menace. Shit!

Well, he'd do it this way: Just relax the body and mind and doodle right out here in the glowing afternoon sunshine. Mind blank, that's right, no trying, no peeking, just doodling. Fine.

The living room window . . . big, no . . . BIG dark shadow with . . . the ears seem out of proportion . . . Too big, the ears are too big to fit with the head . . . The head is enormous and much broader than it is high . . . high . . . The sill was four feet off the ground at least, and the shoulders were well into the middle of the window . . . Broad shoulders, too. Looks like a Volkswagon with a head, with . . . Eyes. The eyes—oh shit, the EYES—look so familiar, but you sure as Hell would remember an animal with eyes that glowed almost in the dark such a strange shade of green. Dammit! I *know* I've seen those spooky damned eyes before. Where? Where? . . . .

And he shook so violently that his charcoal broke

off with a snap that summoned him forward in time to today, a second too soon. Just one second before his floating subconscious could organize his subliminal perceptions from last night and present him with a clear answer to his question. But even though fate had snatched away this chance for enlightenment, it had allowed one message to come through: When he looked at the sketchpad in his lap, he saw what he had drawn. It wasn't a dog at all, that was obvious. It was a . . . monster of some kind, and it had a squat, blocky head flanked by outsized ears, demonic in scope and configuration. The shoulders, from this front view, were three or four times the width of the head, almost reaching the ends of the paper on either side. Where the eyes should have been there were two large circles, but he had given them no detail. They were blank.

"My God," Rudy stammered. "Even my unconscious is afraid of the eyes," and another violent tremor ran the length of his spine.

He glanced at it as time flowed around him, and when he was finally able to make himself look up he was convinced that his imagination was getting a little out of hand. No animal had ever looked like this unless it was, perhaps, malformed at birth or deformed by some type of radiation. Even these possibilities seemed out of the question. No one sane would own a dog that looked so . . . so *evil*. As for the other alternative, well, he doubted that even the haunting specter of Three Mile Island would cast its shadow this far north and east, even if the utilities and the NRC were lying through their teeth. Rudy concluded that he couldn't have seen a dog like this, because a dog like this simply didn't exist. Packing up his things to reach home before dark, he laughed to himself, thinking, The damned thing doesn't even look like a dog. But his throat tightened and his laughter stopped when another part of him whispered sibilantly, No, it doesn't look like a dog at all. It looks much more like a wolf.

"Look, maybe if you talk this out, you'll feel better. I'll get my jacket and we'll go for a walk, okay?"

Rudy nodded and watched Evelyn walk to the hall closet for some protection from the late evening chill. "I know it sounds like I'm chewing peyote or something, hon, but you saw the drawing. What's it look like to you?"

"It looks like you've OD'd on Lovecraft," she said, grabbing his arm and hustling him out of the house. "Or it would if I didn't know what it takes to get you to read anything. But just because you draw something that looks a little, I'll grant you, like a wolf, that's no reason to assume there's one out here." She swept her free arm around in an arc, indicating the dark humps of the mountains. "Right?"

"Will you quit being so goddammed logical? You're a writer, for Pete's sake; you're supposed to have imagination. You saw something at the window last night too, Evelyn."

"Yes, I did. I was lying flat on the floor, just like you were, and looking up at the window. The fire was in back of us and flickering like mad. My dog had just knocked me ass-over-tin-cup, and I was suffering from the effects of coitus interruptus. None of these things, sir, aid or heighten my powers of objective observation. Do you really think, when you consider all those things, that we can really depend on what our eyes told us we saw out there—especially when we saw it for only the briefest instant. Well?"

Rudy looked up at the diamond-bedecked velvet of the sky in exasperation. "Christ, you just had to minor in psych, didn't you?" he moaned. Then he pulled her closer to him and nuzzled the hair on top of her head. "Alright, Sherlock, I give up. All I can be sure of is that there was *something* outside our window. A learned authority on the area's wildlife suspects it was a dog, ergo it was probably a dog. But"—and he turned her around and peered into her eyes—"I don't have to feel good about it coming to call, and I wish you'd promise to be careful if you decide to go walking around at night, or in the woods, without me. Take Godzilla. Take a gun. . . ."

"We don't own a gun," Eve interrupted gently.

"Well, then take a goddam cross or some garlic or something. I don't care if you take a bath in holy water before you go out. I just want you to be careful, please?"

Evelyn was touched, and she put her arms around his neck, pulling his head down. Their lips met softly, briefly, before she broke the contact just long enough to say, "Okay, Mr. Van Helsing, I promise. And if I should happen upon any men with rather odd dentation or excessive facial hair, I'll run right back home and let you save me like a good little damsel in distress. But since the moon isn't full tonight, I think it might be safe to go home and . . . take care of certain unfinished business. . . ."

"The moon wasn't full last night," Rudy got out, then Eve's warm breath caressed his cheeks, and the sweetness of her smell, the nearness of her body, made him think far different thoughts.

As their lips met for the second time, the howling started.

Chapter 3

The rest of the summer slipped deceptively quickly into the arms of the past, as summers tend to do. It was hot as the blazes the last two weeks of July, and August was drawing to a close before the skies gave up three days of good, steady rains to drop the temperature and humidity and give general relief to an increasingly irritable community. The fine hot weather brought the campers and fishermen and backpackers in droves, and this did nothing to raise the spirits of Larksboro, either. Tourists were both boon and curse to the town and its people, and were tolerated or bemoaned depending on the prevailing mood.

Walter Starr complained daily that the cost of air-conditioning the diner was going to drive him to the brink of bankruptcy, and when Reiner asked him just why the hell he didn't turn it down then—it was cold enough in there anyway to freeze the balls off a penguin—Starr asked him if he'd prefer *wearing* his coffee this morning.

Evelyn took to sitting in front of her typewriter in her panties with the fan blowing across her, but when it became obvious that this was more conducive to procreative than simply creative activities, she insisted they buy three air conditioners so that she could write them back into solvency without worrying about the uncontrolled lusts of her libidinous illustrator. Rudy conceded, then began complaining about the cold. "Maybe if we just hold each other for a few minutes—"

Mattie Zimmer seemed to thrive at the Emporium, greeting all her customers cheerfully, flitting about like a caged canary with claustrophobia. Her husband owned a mint-condition 1968 Lincoln Continental Mark V, which he drove only on special occasions such as the Fourth of July and Labor Day parades. He paid for the fireworks display on both these days out of his own pocket, even though he did purchase them from the Emporium, Aggie having bought them from a New York firm and adding ten percent to the price.

Fred and Mattie Zimmer's Western Auto prospered handily thanks to the heavy tourist traffic; even their son Arthur's live bait concession made enough money for him to afford that neat ATV they had down at the Honda dealers.

Charlie McQuire, who was Larksboro's Chief of Police, and his deputies, Mack Horner and Astin Chubb, were kept busy by a rash of disappearances in the mountains surrounding town. There were a couple of deaths, too, but Charlie said that wasn't anything to worry about. Every year some tourist thinks he for sure *knows* which mushroom ain't poisonous, and another one thinks, hell, that little cliff ain't nothin' to climb, and such as that. Charlie said that you had to expect some accidents, some missing persons, even some deaths when folks who don't know a sycamore from a stoplight set out into the sticks like they were goddamned Jeremiah Johnson. So good old Charlie and Mack and Astin took care of the serious business of cleaning up the mess, doing their level best to not let it spoil the day for any of the taxpayers. It was generally agreed in town that they were three real good men. Martin Cooper himself backed McQuire every election, and that was good enough for most people. And while the rest of the police force seemed to change regularly, Chubb and Horner had been deputies a long time, almost as long as McQuire had been chief. Nobody really knew why that was, but if it was good enough for Charlie McQuire, then it was good enough for them, too.

It had been the worst, the most puzzling summer, in John Scott's life. The deer were still being slaughtered, a henhouse had been decimated, two more dogs were missing, and he still had seen neither hide nor hair of the culprits. At the end of July he had found a collie, scrawny and bedraggled, up near the very top of Stuckey's Peak. He had crept to within ten yards of it before it became aware of his presence, and as it turned toward him he had pumped three shells from his .38 Special into it before he could think. Now, looking back, he knew that he had done the wrong thing. He shouldn't have shot the damned mangy thing; he should have tried to follow it, track it to the den or whatever so he could've gotten the whole damn pack. No, he shouldn't have shot it, and he should have seen that it wouldn't have led him anywhere even if he hadn't, because when the dog had sensed him, even before he started to turn. . .

. . . he was waggin' his tail so hard he'd like to shake his ass apart, and I was so scared and jumpy I just pulled the trigger. Fuck. Oh, shit, I wish I knew what the hell is going on around here. I wish I knew why I'm so goddammed scared.

Joshua and his friends had eaten well this summer, and as things progressed, they would eat better. The taste of human flesh had been so . . . extravagant, at first. Now it was compelling. But it was a dangerous food to obtain, even now, as the pack enlarged steadily. Not that man was so strong or smart—he was quite weak, really, and rather dim-witted—but he was a majority, overwhelmingly. So it was best to wait and grow stronger and more capable. Just for a short time yet. For now, they would subsist mainly on the deer they pulled down, the opossums, raccoons, and rabbits. An occasional chicken or calf, lamb or goat, pig or dog. And, when it could be allowed, a human. For humans were the ultimate predator's natural food.

Things other than food were considered at Moonshadow that summer, however. As the first weeks of September passed, both Alec Wall and Joshua Gimball grew restless with another desire—the need for a mate. Such a need was common enough to both their natures but intricately complicated—and dangerous. Both men were handsome, virile, articulate, witty, intelligent. Neither had a shortage of female admirers. But both had to do more than merely find a mate; they had to *create* one. Equally, both were restrained from even mild promiscuity by what they believed. More, by what they were. Alec and Joshua were very special beings who needed the companionship of other beings equally special, beings who believed exactly as they did and who were as they were. And they had to find and choose their candidates with exceeding care for, once done, it could never be undone. A werewolf, like any wolf, mates for life.

The summer ended toward the end of September, its death heralded by dropping temperatures and falling leaves. In its wake came the chilling autumn rains in the same way that death is rightly followed by tears.

Rudy and Eve walked into the diner out of the rain, hung their damp coats on the coatrack by the cash register, and seated themselves at the counter. Although they would probably have been more comfortable at one of the booths lining the walls, this had become so much a habit that the same two seats were usually left vacant for them every morning. It was the easiest way to have an audience with the large, gentle man who sweated each day over the grill, and so they did it without thought. Both of them had come to love Walter Starr dearly.

The two of them were no sooner seated than Eve whispered that she had to go to the "loo" and scurried to the rear of the diner. Rudy shook his head in mock scorn as Walt served his coffee. "How can they say they're our equals when they can't even hold their water, Walter?"

"Say that three times fast," Reiner bellowed from his usual seat.

Starr laughed, and Rudy looked startled, mumbling, "My God, the man must have bugged my seat."

"Only thing works better'n that man's ears is his mouth," Starr chuckled. "Where did Eve say she was goin' again?"

"The loo," Rudy explained. "That's what they call the bathroom in England."

The big man muttered, "The loo, huh?" and turned back to his grill full of frying eggs.

"So, what's new this morning?" Rudy asked when Eve was back and seated and there was a plate full of eggs, home fries, and bacon in front of each of them.

Starr deftly scooped up two easy-overs with his spatula and slid/shook them onto a plate. Then he wiped his hands on the starched white apron that girdled him and turned to face his young friends. "Well," he said, obviously relishing the moment, "I guess you haven't heard yet."

"Heard what?" Eve managed around a piece of wheat bread dripping with yolk.

"Coupla' hunters came into the diner here this morning, early, shoutin' about these incredible big dogs they saw out to Greystone Creek after the rain started lettin' up this morning. Said they were the biggest dogs they'd ever seen, and they were goin' to go somewhere where there was more sensible-sized dogs. The one guy said there was no way he was goin' to spend another night out there knowin' those dogs were around, and he said—now mind, I don't know what he was smokin' up there—he said what they saw looked more like wolves."

Eve turned to her boyfriend, saw that he was pale and wide-eyed, and thought, Oh, shit. Knowing she had to do something fast to prevent Rudy from using this to substantiate his theories, she turned to Walt and rushed, "There aren't any wolves around here, though, are there, Walt?"

"Nope. Been here all my life, and I never saw one. My Daddy lived here all his life, too, and hunted all over these hills same as me, and he never mentioned seein' one either. Fact is, I don't know of anybody who ever saw a wolf around these parts—that's how long there haven't been any around here. Nope. Just dogs, sweetheart. You don't have to worry about any wolves."

Eve kicked Rudy sharply in the shins and gave him a look that said, Now don't start that whole thing up again. You heard the man, there are NO WOLVES around here.

Rudy gave her his most innocent "Who, me?" look and began wiping up his plate with a corner of toast. He was very quiet as they sat and drank their second cup of coffee.

As Rudy walked between the dripping trees, he doubted both his quest and his sanity. No one had seen a wolf in this area for years, but he, on the basis of hearsay evidence heard at the Four Starr Diner, was certainly out here looking for one. He wasn't a hunter or a woodsman. In fact, aside from an artistic appreciation for its beauty and an intellectual under-standing of its importance, he had never even been comfortable in the forest, for God's sake.

Plus, if the wolves he felt were out here *were* out here, he was going to be in trouble anyway. He was only armed with a tree branch he had picked up along the way.

"So here I am," he quipped amusedly as he walked. "Twentieth-century man, sallying forth to confront nature on Her own ground. Walking, as it were, in the very jaws of—"

No, that definitely was not a good way to put it.

The rain had stopped completely an hour ago, but he couldn't tell that walking here. Every few steps a stately oak or maple would shake its balding head and send huge drops of freezing water down the back of his neck. His jogging shoes were soaked and so were his jeans up to the knees, and he was fast becoming miserable. The one reason he didn't turn right around and go home was Eve's last, tightly controlled words, "You and I are going to have a little family discussion about this obsession of yours when you get back, pal."

Greystone Creek gurgled and cooed alongside him as he followed its twisting course uphill. How could she act like he was being so irrational when she had seen that damned thing at the window just as well as he did? When something like that almost jumps in your window, it's only natural to want to find out what's going on, isn't it? He still had dreams about it, and . . .

Mind on his self-dialogue, Rudy failed to see the fallen limb that stretched out full length across his path, dipping its end into the creek like a boa constrictor entering the water. His foot wedged firmly under it, and he pitched forward headfirst onto the soggy creek bank.

"Oh my God," he screamed before the fall knocked all the air from his lungs with a whoosh. He felt that his foot was trapped and pulled crazily until it came loose, not once looking back, struggling to free himself from the wolf that he was *sure* was attacking him. Finally he was released and, half crawling and half slithering, Rudy moved upstream in hasty retreat, plucked his tree branch from the muck, and turned with his back to a large rock. He thought he had known his last day on Earth. Braced to give a good account of himself during this, his last battle, he finally sighted his enemy where it lay cunningly camouflaged. The rough tree branch sparkled like scales with moisture, but that is as close as it came to resembling anything living. It didn't press its advantage.

I will NEVER, Rudy swore, tell ANYONE about this if I live to be a thousand years old. Not Mom and Dad, not Eve, not a priest or a psychiatraist. Nobody, nowhere, no time. No way! He tried to laugh at himself, but his heart was still lodged in his throat, so he gave the attempt up as feeble and started to pick himself up off the ground. That was when he saw it.

There beside the rock, deep in the soft sandlike soil of the creek bank, was a pawprint. It could have been a dog's or it could have been a wolf's, he didn't know. But what he did know was that it was here, and he knew also from the size of it that it was important. He estimated it to be about 9½ inches across. Whatever made this print, Rudy realized, was either the size of a rhinoceros or badly deformed.

Vardon squatted beside the rock, holding his limb like a club and trying to decide what to do. If this dog-wolf had been here once it could come here again, so staying here was definitely not in the cards.

There was movement in the brambles to his right and he almost knocked himself out as he ducked behind the rock, putting it between himself and the sound. When the fox squirrel finally darted out, grabbed a snack, and dashed back under cover, he breathed again, thinking, My God, that's what I'm acting like. I really don't think I'm cut out for a life of high adventure.

Tell someone, of course, was what he had to do, and he could only think of one person with the expertise to unravel this mystery: John Scott. We'll get to the bottom of this yet, he announced to himself, and it even sounded corny to him.

"Unbelievable!" he muttered as he headed quickly back toward town. "I really think I'm starting to like this detective shit!"

John Scott lived in a small white clapboard house close to the Four Starr, at the corner of Third and Orchard. His Bronco was parked alongside the curb, and when Rudy went to the door and knocked, he found the man home.

The warden looked him over questioningly but said only, "Come on in, Mr. Vardon. You're just in time for a late lunch," and ushered him into his home.

Rudy looked around and saw the neat, homey place he would have expected. Aside from a few nature photographs, the walls were bare; the furniture was simple, inexpensive, and functional. What would be called the "woman's touch" was conspicuously absent, and Rudy realized the whole thing put him more in mind of a rather luxuriously furnished hunting camp than a permanent residence. Copies of the *Pennsylvania Game News* littered the coffee table, and beside a worn-but-comfortable-looking recliner a stack of *Outdoor Life*s and *Sports Afield*s spilled onto the threadbare green carpet. It was the house of a man rarely at home but one who wanted to simply be comfortable when he was there, and Rudy thought he must have been lucky to find him in at all.

"Not married, John?"

Scott chuckled. "Naw. Wardens work pretty odd hours, you know. I don't get much chance to meet anybody by way of a social life." He looked at the young man appraisingly. "How'd you tell that? Hear it from Walt?"

"No," Rudy shrugged. "The place just looks like a man's idea of home. It's pretty hard to explain."

"Yeah. It's not as hard to figure as you might think." He brought two large BLTs from the kitchen, on plates with potato chips and dill pickles, and motioned Vardon to sit on the couch. After he had placed his guest's meal in front of him and his own on a table by the recliner, he got two large mugs of coffee, gave Rudy one, and sat down across from him. "So, what can I do for you? You decide to buy a huntin' license this year, after all?"

Vardon realized Scott was looking at his soiled, damp clothing and felt a qualm of guilt for sitting on his couch in this condition. "No, but I have been hunting, sort of."

The warden settled back in his chair and took a dainty bite of his sandwich, waiting.

"I heard about what those two hunters told Walt this morning, about there maybe being wolves around

Greystone Creek. Well, John, I know there haven't been any wolves around here for years and all that, but I've thought a lot about that thing that was outside my window a couple of months back, and the more I think about it, the more it *didn't* look like a dog. And Eve and I have both heard something howling at night on several occasions. Well, whatever, I decided to go out and see if I could find anything around the creek and . . . well . . . I did."

Scott felt like jumping out of his chair. After all these months of looking for a clue, for anything . . . and now, if Rudy Vardon really had found something . . . "Just what was it you found, Rudy?" Scott asked, trying to keep the impatience and excitement out of his voice.

"I found a paw print. Just one, though, because after I saw it I got the hell out of there and came right down here to tell you."

"Did it look like a dog print?"

"Not like any dog print I ever saw, John. I mean, I'm not Marlin Perkins or anything, but I don't think dog prints can look like this."

Scott scratched his face. "About how big is this thing?"

Rudy held his hands up, adjusted them minutely, and got what he thought to be the proper width.

The game warden exhaled so hard he sounded like a balloon exploding. "Come on, Rudy, that's the size of a dinner plate. Do you know how big an animal would have to be to make a print like that, for Christ's sake? It would take one hell of a respectable-sized bear to make a print that big, son. Can you imagine the size dog it would take? You sure you

95

wouldn't like to guess again?"

"Look, John, this is how big the damned thing looked to me. I think it belonged to that . . . whatever that looked in my window. It was big, too, remember? Plenty big enough to make tracks like this, I'd say. And not only that, that animal looked deformed. Couldn't it be possible that this print was made by a deformed . . . creature? That could mean that it might not be as big as this print would indicate because its proportions would be out of whack. Well? Isn't that a possibility, at least?"

"Possible, son, but just possible. Look, we're not going to settle this sitting here, so if you're done eating, why don't we go on up there and take a closer look at this thing?"

Rudy jumped up eagerly. "Sounds good to me, John. There's something about this whole thing that seems to be taking my appetite anyway."

When they got to the spot and John Scott saw the enormity of the print, he could think of nothing to say for quite some time. While Vardon looked on he simply knelt beside the rock, running a finger along the edges of the track wonderingly. Part of it was his relief at finding, at long last, something to go on. But most of his awe was inspired by the sheer physical presence of the thing itself. Never had he seen anything like it. At first he had thought that Rudy's report of its massive dimensions would be due to the sandy soil in which he had found it. Sand tended to cave in when it was wet, and the effect often made marks left in it seem to grow, a distortion that snow also produced when it melted. But even if that were somewhat the case, this pawprint was far and away the biggest canine track that he had ever encountered. And, as the young artist had hinted, it didn't look so much like the track of a dog as it did that of a wolf.

It was hard to tell because of the deformations that were evident, even in the soft earth. First there was the sheer size and the fact that the configuration seemed to indicate a supported weight that no wolf or dog would ever reach. Secondly, the toes were disproportionately elongated and seemed to be strangely jointed, giving the effect of a structure more like a pudgy, foreshortened hand than a paw. There even seemed to be evidence of a thumb, but Scott rubbed his eyes and steadfastly refused to believe that, closing off his mind to all further supposition.

"Look, Rudy, why don't you just go on back into town? I'm sure your wife is worried sick about you by now. I've got a little cabin just up the hill a ways, so I think I'll go on up there and pick up a few things, come back, and try to make a cast of this thing to send off to Harrisburg. The print didn't hold well enough in this to give me much to identify it by."

"Well—"

"Go on now, you get on home to your wife. I'll take care of everything up here, and I can't thank you enough for finding this for me. Really. I'll be just fine."

"Okay, John. You're probably right," Rudy admitted. "I'd probably just be in your road up here anyway. And Eve's probably worried, too. But if you need any help, I want you to come right down this mountain and get me, you hear? And tell me as soon as you can what made that damned thing, right?"

"Believe me, Rudy, you'll be the first person I tell. Now, will you scat so I can get to work here?" He made a shooing motion with his hand, grinning widely. Then he watched the young man walk reluctantly away through the trees. When he was out of sight, Scott pulled out his .38 and checked to see that it was loaded. He didn't know what made this track, but he did know he didn't want that boy around if it showed up here again. Something this size, which killed in the way he had seen, could make a widow out of that pretty wife of his real quick. In fact, he thought somberly, I don't want to be here either if that beast comes back. Giving his weapon a reassuring pat, he moved up the slope toward his cabin.

Damn! the creature thought as it watched the rangy human climb out of sight among the trees. Joshua will skin me alive for this. It sniffed the air tentatively, trying to determine the man's exact position. Trying to figure out exactly what action to take. When it was certain it would be unobserved, it moved to the creek bank and obliterated the evidential pawprint with its own forepaws, being extremely careful not to leave tracks of its own. Then it decided to defer all decisions to a higher authority and swiftly padded in the direction of Moonshadow, the imminence of possible discovery lending speed to its already preternatural step.

The cabin welcomed him like the old friend that it was, inviting him in and bidding him to relax. It was an offer that John Scott would have like to take up, but there was too much to do and the light was already being leached out of the sky by the closing night. He packed the few things he would need to make a serviceable cast of his new exhibit and exited swiftly, hurrying back down the slopes to the soggy banks of Greystone Creek. Tensed with excitement, he mused as to whether the creature was a dog or if it could possibly be just what his eyes told him was the more likely choice—that it was, indeed, a wolf. With any luck, Rudy Vardon would never know just how right his instincts had been about that beast outside his window last summer. If this was the same animal, and it certainly was deformed enough to be if you judged from the print, all hell could have broken loose in the boy's new home that night, that was for sure. If just for that reason alone, Scott planned that no one in town know about this—not now, not when it was long over and finished. Wolves were one of those animals that had a bad reputation in human circles, even though they didn't deserve most of their infamy. Mention wolves and the human imagination went into high gear, never mind that they were really quite man-shy and certainly not the vicious brutes the tall tale-tellers made them out to be. No, if folks thought there was—or even had been—a wolf running loose around Larksboro, there'd be a panic like this little town had never seen before. And, if word got out to the bigger papers around the state, they'd feel the economic pinch from a flagging tourist industry for years to come. It was, the warden concluded, time to use a little discretion and deal with this problem himself before it got out of hand. Just how a wolf got into these woods . . . well, he couldn't rightly say. He'd seen ads in his outdoor magazines for wolf/dog mixes up to three-quarters wolf, and he supposed somebody could have set one of them loose up here just the same as they did to mutts and beagles and poodles. Hell, that might even go a ways toward explaining why the damned tracks were so oddball in the first place. Maybe when you mixed the two canines it affected the conformation of the paws or something? He didn't really know, but it made some sense. More than anything else had so far, anyway.

So thinking, he bulled his way through the last barrier of briars between himself and his prize, and was confounded by a fresh mystery: The cleanup crew had struck again. The track was gone.

Scott's jaw dropped and he hissed, "Damn. I'll be damned!" Shaking his head in disbelief, he dropped to his knees and thoroughly examined the area where the imprint had been, but to no avail. The pawprint had been wiped from the ground irrevocably, nothing of it remained. Where it had been, the ground was freshly turned, furrowed as if for some mysterious planting. Scott sat back on his haunches, perplexed. Could a squirrel have done this? Digging for seeds or roots, maybe looking to stash away an acorn or two? But no, it wasn't a hole, and the area of it was much larger than a squirrel would have made—even those damned big fox squirrels that thrived up this way. Unless he were trying to bury a pumpkin, the warden mused wryly. With a sigh, he resigned himself to accepting the illogical, the irrational, but the inevitable. Something had been here after he had gone to the cabin and had wiped the track clean out of the bank. Someone or something had known that the track was here, waited, and come back just to make sure that no one would see it. And, although that line of thinking made no sense, it was very coherent when you remembered that there hadn't been any tracks or spoor at any of the kills he'd found . . . none. Never. And now there weren't any tracks here either, John. So what does that prove?

It proves that something doesn't want to be found out. It proves that something is killing in these mountains that doesn't want its existence revealed . . . yet. Someone or something.

He stood and tried to shake the thoughts from his head. They were getting too strange now . . . too scary. . . .

It proves that it thinks, John. And you haven't caught it, John, and that proves it thinks better than you; it's smarter than you. And what if it knows that you know about it now? What if it knows? Will it come after you, then, and leave you in pieces of ripped flesh and sucked-dry bones on the forest floor? Will it wipe out all its tracks then, John and leave people saying, "Don't know how them dogs could'a took ol' John Scott. Thought he was too canny for somethin' like that."

He noticed he was sweating, and his hands shook. Thinking, I'm out of my league here, just plain out of my league, he turned and walked hurriedly back up the mountain. He forgot the casting paraphernalia he had brought, leaving it where it had rolled when he stood up so suddenly, under a corner of the rock where his evidence had been. He thought no more about what was roaming these mountains, which he would have called *his* mountains. Really, he

101

didn't even think about his destination. He just walked noisily up the incline toward the closest shelter, toward the nearest place of light and warmth and walls and safety. It was getting very dark now, so very dark, and for the first time he could remember he shivered at the thought of being caught in the woods at full dark . . . at night. Thinking only of the half-full bottle of Jim Beam in the kitchen cabinet and forcing all else from his mind, a terribly frightened John Scott made his way, as directly as he could, to his cabin.

It had taken the remainder of the Jim Beam to calm his nerves and act as balm to his fears. Even now he wasn't close to being drunk, but he felt tired and groggy enough to finally get some sleep, and that was good enough. Outside it was a clear, crisp night. He could hear the night creatures—the raccoons and opossums and deer—rustling around in the dried leaves and undergrowth. It made him think of what else might be out there also, and he pulled the drapes shut to seal off the world from his eyes. Then he walked to the nightstand and turned on his transistor radio until its tiny squeals were all he heard. Better. There might be something out there tonight, but he wasn't going to see it or hear it. He drew the double-barreled twelve-gauge down from over the fireplace and broke it open. Then he slid two shells filled with double-aught buckshot into their respective chambers and snapped it shut decisively. "And I'm not going to feed it, either," he announced into the empty room. He made one more check on the locks and latches, which made five checks since he'd gotten in (better to be safe), and carried his shotgun to the cot by the fire.

Sleep. I need some sleep.

Setting his weapon beside him tenderly—almost like a lover—he lay down fully clothed on the thin mattress and closed his eyes. As he drifted into sleep, he thought that tomorrow he would take some sort of action. Tomorrow . . . in the light.

It rose above the inane chatter of the late night disc jockey on the radio beside his bed. It pierced his sleep like a psychopath's knife; it peeled it away from him layer by layer, as if it were an onion . . . or layers of flesh. He tried, instinctively, to run further into the safety of his dreams, applying for asylum in that country we visit in sleep.

His application was denied.

And it chased him through the corridors of his own mind until it caught him, seized him by the throat, and pulled him from the depths of his sleep and upright on the cot, eyes widening, throat constricted and dry, heart pounding. The shotgun seemed to leap into his lap like an obedient pet. The recognition washed over him and nearly made him cry. Something was outside, close outside, and it was howling.

It was a challenge, he knew. An invitation: Come into my parlor . . . The noise tapered off slowly and did not return, but he knew it wasn't leaving. It was waiting. John Scott knew, without a hint of doubt, that if he failed to go to it, it would surely come to him.

He eased the safety to off and stood.

Walking to the door was surprisingly easy. He wasn't shaking or dizzy or anything like that, and the

103

fact amazed him. Even the fact that his eyes were slowly seeping tears didn't bother him much as he threw the bolts on the door and flung it open.

He opened the door wide and fast, and just then it stepped out from behind the tree trunks and bushes and revealed itself to him.

Scott froze. He thought he said, "Oh God. Oh no, oh my God," but he made no sound at all. His lips didn't even move.

The waning moon lit everything with a glow like skim milk, but it was enough. It was too much.

It wasn't as tall as he was, maybe only five feet nine or five feet ten, but it was the most horrible thing that Scott had ever seen. The face was canine, with thin mottled lips stretched tightly over protruding beastlike teeth. Drool oozed like syrup from the corners of its wide mouth and ran thickly off its short chin. The face was spottily haired, like a mange-ridden dog, and flanked by two pointed ears that were hairless and pink save for a tasseling of brown at the very tips. The torso was powerfully muscled, especially the shoulders and chest, the legs and groin covered with thick fur. It was totally naked and grotesquely, lasciviously male.

Crazily, Scott thought, It looks like a . . . Centaur. Half man, half goat. No, not goat . . . half man half . . .

Then it sprang.

Scott fired at the same time, the twelve-gauge sounding like an exploding case of dynamite in his ears, and began backing through the open door. As if by magic, and the beast twisted in mid-leap and avoided the brunt of the blast, catching only a few of the pellets. But it was enough to make the effort fall short by a good six feet, and when it landed, crouched and bleeding, that distance from the warden, he loosed the death in his other barrel, point blank. The effect was instantaneous: The creature flew backward, as if pulled by some invisible spring, blood and bits of flesh showering from its chest, finally rolling to a halt five yards back, a crumpled, bleeding mass.

John Scott waited until it stopped moving, whirled inside, and slammed the door. He threw the bolts reflexively, then pulled the drapes away from the window and stared. It still wasn't moving. It was dead. He breathed for what seemed like the first time in hours. It was dead. He had killed it. Yes, it was dead. Letting the drape fall back into place, he turned and walked to his cot and sat down. Now all he had to figure out was what the hell it was in the first place, because he sure as hell had never seen anything like it before. The thought came to him that it might have been a man dressed up like that, some nut or crazy or whatever, but no, it hadn't moved like a man. That jump . . . no man could jump like that. Well, one thing was damned certain: Dead or not, he wasn't going outside until morning with that bastard out there. Still shaking, he fumbled his shells from the night table, shook two from the box, and opened the gun in his lap.

"Holy shit!" he remembered as he worked to reload. "That damned thing's eyes were *blue*!"

The door cracked with a noise like a sonic boom as it shattered inward, accompanied by the sound of breaking glass. The shells jumped from Scott's hand with a life of their own as his head snapped up in time to see the hirsuite thing he had killed just moments ago fill the new emptiness of the doorway. "How—?" he started to ask, remembered hearing glass fall, and turned toward the window. Now there were two of them, and this new one looked even more like a man. It looked like . . .

The thing in the doorway moved suddenly. Scott raised his weapon like a club to strike it down, but the beast was too fast. It raised its rippling arm and brushed the improvised bat out of his grip with such speed and power that the stock splintered and the barrel bent upon impact. Then it picked him up like a bag of popcorn and hurled him into the center of the room. Scott hit on his knees, feeling one of them fracture painfully, and slid facedown across the floor to the other creature's feet. He hear his attacker padding softly across the floor toward him and knew that he was finished. Leg broken, weaponless, outnumbered, there was only one thing remaining to a dead man: He would see his killers. In agony, he rolled onto his back.

This . . . thing. The ears are pointed, and there are inhuman claws and teeth, but it's pretty much hairless and it looks like . . .

The first beast plucked him off the floor and held him up off the ground by his shirtfront, some horrific school bully who wanted his lunch money. Its breath was rank and fetid, and he gagged. Dog breath. Worse. He averted his head and looked at the other.

Looks like . . . dammit, looks like . . .

It cocked its head. Brown eyes sparkled in . . . what? . . . Amusement?

His captor shook shook him sternly, growling, and pain scored his injured leg. The other grinned, slobbering over its pale, hairless chest. It clicked its clawlike nails together in anticipation. He had to find out what—no, who—these beasts were. It was his final obsession. It was all that was left to him in this life as a man. He reached out and grabbed the hairless one by its pointed ear, pulled and twisted with all his strength. "Who are you, you bastard?" he shouted, demanded, sobbed. "Who ARE you?"

The creature worked its jaws laboriously, clicking its jutting teeth, releasing streams of saliva. Then, from deep in its throat, grumbling, tortured, came the words: "Pleesh . . . don . . . mine me . . . John. I . . . m . . . jussssh here . . . to . . . wah . . . sh. To . . . learn."

It was no longer a human voice, but the tone was familiar, the tone was right, the tone of what was left of that voice belonged to . . .

As his captor's shaggy, stinking jaws closed around his throat, ripping it away from tongue to collarbone, exposing the ivory white of his spine, he had time to make that final connection. He had just enough time to say, "Ma—," before his words were cut off by the fountaining of his own blood.

That night Eve and Rudy had watched a number of the infantile offerings the networks had programmed for nighttime viewers. They had turned that off at last, in disgust, and gotten out their worn Scrabble board. This had lasted about two hours until Rudy had gotten a bit disgruntled at his lack of expertise (she was a writer for Chrissake; she's *sup-*

107

posed to know a lot of strange words) and had gone for his nightly walk around Larksboro. As much as he tried to relax, he was too keyed up about his find at the creek to sit still for very long. Eve had, of course, been her usual, logical, wait-and-see self, telling him to save his victory celebration until word came from the experts in Harrisburg that it wasn't just a big sheep dog with fallen arches or something. Well, to hell with that. *He* knew it was some wolf or other, and he'd seen the look on John's face when he'd shown him the pawprint.

Rudy turned the corner back on to Cooper's Point Road and looked up at the clarity of the sky. This never ceased to astound him, as if he had bought his own private Mount Palomar, which brought the heavens so close he could almost touch them, could almost bump his head on the moon. With a foggy sigh he unlocked the front door and walked through, wondering just how long it would take him to lose his city-bred caution. Perhaps never, he thought, and he couldn't see the harm in locking your doors, anyway. Even in a town like Larksboro, there had to be a "shady" element. Then you had the tourists, the kids . . .

He was met by an enthusiastic Godzilla, who leaped up and put his paws on his chest and began lathing his face with his tongue. Rudy laughed and gently pushed the big beast down, where the animal immediately tagged his Nikes as if they were second base and ran pell-mell into the kitchen. Vardon could hear the animal's feet scrabbling against the linoleum as it turned sharply and ran back in to him just to tag up and repeat the process. By the time Rudy got into the kitchen, Godzilla was standing by the back door making sharp barking sounds followed by a whining/growling combination deep in its chest.

The artist knew all the classic signs: There was a rabbit out back or something. Whatever it was, it was in Godzilla's territory, and he would know no rest until he had chased it away. Turning on the outside light, Rudy checked to see that the backyard fence gate was closed and latched. It was, and Vardon couldn't see how anything could get over or under the six-foot wood plank fence to get into the yard, anyway. But the salient point was that his dog was convinced, so he opened the kitchen door to let him repel the intruders, whether they be real or imagined.

In an instant the dog had raced halfway into the yard and stopped, head cocked as if listening, a warning growl making his whole body quake. Then he stiffened and his hackles raised straight up from the nape of his neck to his rigid tail. As an amazed Rudy looked on helplessly, the dog raced directly at the fence barking madly, was up, scrambling for purchase and balance, and over before his master could believe what he was seeing. Even as Rudy scurried out the back door yelling, "Godzilla, no!" he knew it was too late to call the dog back.

They kept ahead of him, but just barely, and he increased his efforts to try to catch up. These things that had invaded his territory smelled oddly, but that didn't give him pause at all. He had encountered many strange new smells since they had brought him here to this new place, but none of these new things were real threats. There had been a few dogs with

109

territories abutting his own to set straight and a few other creatures to dominate, but nothing much different than that other place. And the other place smelled worse and was noisier, and the noise was so bad sometimes that it hurt his ears. He was not allowed out as much at that other place, but here he was out a lot. It was a fine place, and he liked being here.

The ones he chased moved up ahead, and try as he might, he couldn't seem to catch them. He was well out of his territory now, but to have them so close was maddening, and he ran on. When he reached the fields his tongue was lolling wetly from his mouth and he was panting heavily. He had not yet shed his city weight and that, plus his relative inactivity, took its toll quickly. He stood in the tall, dry, waist-high grass with his sides heaving, his senses telling him that his quarry had ceased to run and was close. . .

. . . was coming closer, and now *he* was the quarry, the hunted . . . had been all along . . .

Godzilla stiffened, snarled, realizing his danger, sensing his mistake. He heard the low panting now, could see their shapes as fleeting as moon-cast shadows as they drifted nearer and nearer. Their smell was rich and full around him. They were many, but one he had known before, outside the window of his home, on a summer's night.

One of them rocketed out of the shadows and smashed into his haunches, spinning him around, off balance, biting deeply and tearing. He moved as quickly as he could, managing to tear away a piece of ear from his assailant. The pained yelp and blood-taste infused him with momentary strength and he

110

drove the wounded beast off, but he was exhausted from the chase and the feeling didn't last. As he turned to face the others his will to survive seemed to fold in upon itself until it was no more. He was a puppy again, and there was only surrender to the more powerful forces in life. There was only the offering of the throat. . . .

Godzilla whimpered pitifully, instinctively knowing that there was no submission to these others, there was only death. They fell upon him like the darkness of the grave.

BOOK II

". . . they set upon the houses of men . . . with wonderful fiercenesse, and labour to break down the doors, whereby they may destroy both man and other creatures that remain there."

—Claus Magnus

Chapter 4

The diner seemed filled with ghosts when Rudy
and Eve got there for breakfast. Even the unusual
warmth of the October sunshine couldn't prevent a
chill from insinuating itself into their beings—perhaps it entered through their cheerful morning
smiles—and causing them to shudder in unison.
Dread cast a long shadow in here today, such a dark
one that the golden air just outside the speckled glass
windows couldn't seem to penetrate. Both of them
pressed a little closer together instinctively, sensing
the wrongness in the air. Reiner and Starr were not
engaged in their usual verbal sparring. That old
drunk Ellison Hartmen looked sober, which was
unusual in itself, but he also looked . . . terrified.
Neither one of the Zimmers were present, nor were
any of the local police force. In fact, The Four Starr
was relatively deserted for this early in the morning.

There was Walt behind the counter, serving a couple of truck drivers who shoveled in their food like people tend to do when they live on a schedule; there was Reiner at his usual rear booth with a few of the town's other senior citizens, talking among themselves in whispers; and there was Joshua Gimball sitting in a booth near the middle, facing a man neither Rudy nor Evelyn could place here before. Gimball saw the two and waved them back to join him and his friend, casting them a friendly smile as he did so. He still talked about having them to his place—Moonshadow—for a get-together, but talking was as far as the invitation had gotten as of yet, and Rudy was almost glad. Although they met infrequently—either here at the diner or on the streets— Gimball made Rudy almost unbearably uncomfortable. Vardon didn't know if it was the professor's calm, detached manner or the carefully restrained arrogance and aloofness that seemed to underlie his cheerful geniality. Maybe such traits were the stigmata of genius, which the teacher had a reputation for possessing in quantity. It could even have been, the younger man supposed, that genius itself which, peeking through Gimball's thin veneer of normalcy, caused something in him to withdraw itself in its presence. Or it could simply be the man's sheer physical presence that made him so edgy. The man had the looks and physique of Apollo, Rudy thought with a tinge of jealousy, wondering just what a college professor did to stay in such outstanding shape. Hell, it was probably all natural, and all he ever did was drink beer, smoke some reefer, and letch after the coeds. Just like his superbrain, his superbod was probably God-given.

As he and his lover made their way past empty booths toward the still-smiling blond-haired giant, Rudy saw the man eyeing his woman covetously. It made Rudy angry and proud at the same time. Suddenly unsure, he glanced over at Evelyn, but all was well. He knew her looks by this time, and the look she gave Joshua Gimball was one of honest appreciation, tempered affection, respect . . . but sexual indifference. Vardon smiled then, relieved, and Evelyn squeezed his hand firmly and kissed his cheek. She knows me just as well, Rudy realized. So let her check him out. I check out beautiful women, right? That doesn't mean I want to hustle them into bed, and neither does this. After all, Joshua does have a lot for a woman to appreciate. For his age.

When they reached the booth the other man had moved to sit beside Joshua, allowing Rudy and Evelyn to sit together. Already smiling broadly from his last wry thought, all Vardon had to do was extend his hand to receive the professor's outstretched one. Through the handshake he managed to maintain his cordial expression, even though the hand he held was as solid as a piece of hardwood and possessed of a strength that seemed almost mechanical. He smiled until he looked into the eyes, sensing something there that was as alien as the man's strength. Something wild hid inside this man, something truly wild. Then the smile faded, seemed almost to crumple, as he remembered a triviality he had learned in his college career—one of Apollo's forms. One of Apollo's forms had been a wolf.

The concern in the basso voice reached him.

117

"Rudy. Rudy, are you all right? Don't you feel well?"

He looked at the faces around him; they all wore expressions of concern and caring. They all looked human. What he was thinking was insane, a paranoid fantasy of the highest order. Next he'd be seeing little men from Uranus and wrapping himself in aluminum foil to protect himself from gamma rays, for Chrissakes. He forced himself toward the present. "Yeah. Yeah, I'm terribly sorry. You know how we artists are, folks. One minute we're with you, the next minute we're out in the ozone."

Eve shook her head imperceptibly, rejecting the idea. "Are you sure, Rudy. Artistic temperament or not, it's not like you to float away to dreamland at the breakfast table."

Rudy showed his best apologetic smile. "No, hon. Really. I just spaced out for a minute there, but there isn't anything wrong with me at all." His stomach grumbled obscenely. "Except terminal hunger."

The communal mirth snapped the tension, and Joshua restarted his introductions. "Well, should you ever find that there is something wrong with you, this is the man to see. Dr. Edward Appleby, this is Rudy Vardon, the famed illustrator; and this fair creature beside him is Evelyn Sangellis, an equally famed writer of children's books."

The doctor shook each of their hands in turn, Evelyn immediately reacting to his seamed face and sparkling grey eyes, Rudy noting that his grip was warm and moist and firm—but happily what he thought an old man's should be. The whole of Dr. Edward Appleby seemed what it should be, in fact,

118

from his full head of steel-grey hair to his pencil-thin moustache, and including his ancient blue suit and bowtie. Ed Appleby was a man who would have been impossible to dislike under any circumstances. He was fit, robust, alert, and virile in the understated way of those who have reached old age and wisdom simultaneously. Perhaps, thought Rudy, if Joshua is very lucky, that's what he'll look like when he grows up.

"Well, it's real nice to have two fine-looking young folks like yourselves as members of our community. Although I'll allow," the doctor said, squinting comically, "that neither one of you are going to give me much business."

Eve was captivated. "Dr. Appleby, I'll catch colds just to come to see you."

"And I'll give you a cut-rate just for brightening up my office. Looks like yours, and talent, too? You come to see me as often as you like, young lady. And when you do, you call me Ed. It'll make me feel downright sinful, and it'll give these old biddies around here something to titter about."

"I've heard about you country doctors and your bedside manner," Rudy laughed.

Appleby's eyes sparkled merrily. "Son, I haven't had anything *but* bedside manners for years now, so don't get yourself upset. But if you don't tell anybody, I won't either. It's not good for a doctor to be any less than one hundred percent functional, if you know what I mean." His sly wink included everyone at the table.

"Don't believe a word of that," Gimball protested. "Doc Appleby is widely respected here in Larksboro.

We all think that we're lucky to have him as one of us. Why, he's almost as good with people as he is with animals."

This statement was met with loud guffaws from the assemblage and a disdaining harrumph from the doctor himself. When the outburst had subsided to a manageable level, Rudy asked, "What's the matter with these people in here today? I mean, not many of the regulars showed up, and the ones that did act like their in mourning or something."

"They are." Gimball had turned serious now. "I guess you haven't heard yet. John Scott died of a heart attack late last night. Mack Horner found him this morning up the mountain in his cabin."

Eve lowered her chin against her chest. "Oh my God."

"Are you kidding? I just saw John yesterday, and he was as fit as I am. Fitter. He was running around those damned mountains like a mountain goat."

"Ed examined him himself when they brought him in. That was his diagnosis."

The doctor raised his hand as Rudy started to object. "I was of the same mind as you, son. John had been running these hills for years, I know. He looked fit to live to a hundred. But there was a defect in his heart—a valve didn't close like it should at birth—and it just caught up to him last night. Why, I was his personal physician and I didn't even know about his ticker being like that. It's sad, and I won't deny that, but you shouldn't take it so hard." He reached over and gently patted Evelyn's hand while looking Rudy in the eye. "When you get as old as I am, you'll know it's all a part of life."

120

"All a part of life," Rudy mumbled. "It's just that yesterday he was so . . . healthy. We were running around over by Greystone Creek together. It's just unbelievable. . . ."

Josh's busy eyebrows arched momentarily, then he asked casually, "What were the two of you doing at Greystone Creek, Rudy?"

"I had found a pawprint from one of those . . . dogs that are running loose on the mountain. Well, I thought it was pretty important so I got John to come and take a look."

Now Appleby seemed interested. "What did he say about it?"

"Nothing much," Rudy admitted, a little confused, a little angry. John Scott was dead, and these people—his friends—wanted to talk about dog tracks! "He seemed to get pretty excited, and he said he was going to make a plaster cast and send it in to Harrisburg to get a positive identification, but he didn't really say much about it."

"He didn't tell you what made the print?" Gimball questioned.

"No."

"He didn't even hint at what could have made it?"

"Look, Josh, I know I hardly knew the man, but I don't see how we can sit here and talk about animal track identification the morning after he died. Maybe it was a dog track, maybe it was a damned elephant track! I don't really care at this point, okay?"

Eve put her hand on his shoulder in a gesture of sympathy, but she said cautioningly, "Rudy . . . "

"Right, right. Look, I'm sorry. I didn't mean to jump all over you two. You must be upset about it, too." He tried to smile but it came out as a grimace. "I guess we all have different ways of coping, that's all."

"That's very true," said Appleby. "You're right, son, I'll miss the man. I guess that I just don't question the Lord's will. We do our best to prevent death, even though we know that it's our inevitable destiny. You know, that's my chosen field—preventing death and disease. But when it comes—and I can tell you this from no little experience—we can only accept it as gracefully as we can. It'll come for all of us in time, son. Each of us. What we have to remember is that John Scott was the only one here who died last night, and he sure wouldn't have wanted any of us to go along with him."

"Well, I can tell you something," Eve pouted. "Maybe I'm still young and foolish, Ed, but when death comes for me I'm going to put up one hell of a fight."

The doctor's smile was not one of mirth but one of practiced gentility, and as he spoke, he turned to Josh and they both nodded. "I knew John Scott most of his life," Appleby assured her, "and I'm sure that when death came to call he put up the damnedest fight he was able."

There was something in the old doctor's tone that made them believe he was telling the truth.

The rest of their morning's socializing was less traumatic. By the time the four of them had finished three cups of coffee apiece—with the exception of Doc Appleby, who quit after his second complaining about what caffeine did to his old body—they had chewed over bits of gossip that were more time-passing and by way of introduction than important or even interesting. As Rudy and Evelyn said their good mornings and rose to leave, Joshua asked, "Why don't you two plan on coming to my Halloween party? Say around eight o'clock the evening of the thirty-first. I have one every year, and as they say, a good time is usually had by all."

"You should be honored," Appleby added. "Josh's parties are rather exclusive as well as posh. Many of Larksboro's social climbers would roll over and beg for an invitation."

"It's not quite that bad," Gimball said with a rueful glance at his older friend.

Rudy glanced at Eve, who nodded her head slightly. "Well . . . sure, we'd be happy to come, if you're sure we can make the grade," he said facetiously.

Eve punched him in the small of his back for his impudence, then added quickly, "Should we wear costumes or anything?"

"No, no costumes. Just dress casually. This isn't a grand ball or anything of that ilk. Just a get-together for me and a few of my closer friends. I think you'll really find the company most stimulating."

Rudy breathed a silent sigh of relief. He really didn't want to attend any function of Gimball's, although he didn't really know why. Castigating himself about snap judgments and biased opinions didn't help change his mind. But if he had to go, if Eve wanted to go, at least it would be more bearable to go dressed comfortably instead of in some abysmal bear suit or whatever.

"Well, look," he said, edging away before he could be trapped into something else, "we really have to get going now. Our dog ran away last night, and we want to find him before John . . . before somebody mistakes him for one of those wild ones and shoots him."

"Oh, what a shame," Joshua sympathized. "I know how attached people get to their pets. Well, Ed and I will keep an eye out for him, too, and call you if we see him. I really doubt that there's another dog like him in town."

"I guess not," Evelyn said, "Thanks." Then Rudy waved and guided her out the door and into the bright, crisp morning air.

They walked along slowly, side by side, looking for their missing pet, calling his name hopefully. They were not answered.

"Damn!" Eve hissed when they reached their front door. "Where do you think he got to?"

Rudy put his arm around her narrow shoulders. "Probably ran up into the woods after something. Look, let's go in and do a little work, and if he doesn't show up by this evening, I'll go out and have a look for him at the base of the mountain."

"Good! It's about time we did something other than wish and wait. I'll come with you."

"No, hon, I'd rather you stayed here."

Evelyn looked up at him sternly, shaking off his arm. "Now look, Rudy, I loved that dog just as much as you did and I'm not going to sit around the house like an old maid just because you've got some weird ideas about a wolf or something roaming around the woods at night. Christ! I didn't know you were such a chauvanistic bastard!"

"That's not what I was thinking about, Eve," Rudy said as patiently as he could manage. "What if Godzilla decides to come home tonight and neither one of us is here? What's he going to do then? He'll probably run back up the mountain, and it'll be one more night that he can get himself killed. Now if you stay here and he comes back, you know . . . I think it makes a lot more sense than both of us tramping around in the woods all night," he finished lamely.

"Well then why don't *you* stay here and *I'll* go out and look for him?" She turned and marched into the living room, throwing herself down on the couch and crossing her arms across her chest. Rudy, coming through the open door slowly and shutting it after himself, looked pitiful. "Damn!" Eve hissed, feeling her resolve slipping and knowing there was little she could do to regain it. "Oh, alright. You look for him. But if you don't find him tonight by yourself, then we're both going out tomorrow to look, and I mean it!"

Rudy walked over, bent down, and kissed her lightly on the top of the head, then walked toward the back of the house and his studio. He knew he had only barely won that conflict and wasn't about to say anything to Eve that might rouse her ire and make her change her mind. His excuses had sounded feeble even to him, and only long practice at looking hangdog had saved the day for him. It was the one ploy of his that Evelyn hadn't yet learned how to counter. Thank God.

Rudy was sure the dog wouldn't show up today, nor tonight. And he was fairly certain that Godzilla wouldn't answer his calls tonight either, although he would try until his throat was raw. The fact was that Rudy was certain his dog was dead, but he didn't want to try to explain why he felt that way to Eve or anyone else right at the moment. When Rudy Vardon went out tonight to hunt for his missing dog, he was sure that he would be looking for a corpse.

Joshua Gimball walked through the halls of Larksboro Area Community College like a king walking through his kingdom. Indeed, anyone commenting on the tall, stately man who walked so easily through the milling crowd of teenagers that surrounded him would have remarked that his bearing was rather regal, and they would have been right. Joshua was at home in the halls of academia; it was a game that he played expertly. His voice, his stature, his eyes, his physique; everything about him spoke of dignity and pride and a certain fearlessness—and demanded respect. He was the hero of his male students and the heartthrob of his female ones. The attitude in his classes was one of almost worship. To Professor Joshua Gimball, through no special effort on his part, the whole thing was, as one less literate might say, a piece of cake.

His first class was Philosophy 101, and like the great majority of his classes, it went without a hitch. The students who attended the college were no threat to the continuing legends of Einstein or Michelangelo, but neither were they morons, and occasionally they even entertained some passingly intelligent ideas in their naive little heads. Spending the morning in discussion was not so rare—even though really intelligent questions were—and Gimball passed his days in a stupor familiar to anyone whose job is repetitious but undemanding. Not stimulated, not bored, just there. At least that was how he spent most of his days, but not this one. Today he was going to do something a little different.

Today, after all the other students had filed noisily from his classroom on their way to their various destinations, a girl remained. She was young, about nineteen at most, with short brown hair that she kept trying to shake back off her forehead. This amused Gimball greatly, since he deduced that she must have had her hair rather long for some time and knew that this was how she attempted to look alluring. No, they would call that sexy now, he corrected himself as he watched her move shyly forward from the back of the classroom. His keen olfactory senses could detect her nervousness . . . and her desire. How easily we become aroused when we're young. Turned on. Yes. Ready and willing twenty-four hours a day, unlike any other creature in existence. Perhaps it goes with our brains, he thought. With our ability to fantasize. And he wondered then how many of these humans actually knew anything at all about sex, much less about love. That seemed to be another of man's characteristic traits, to want only what is unknown—they call it novel—and only for as long as it remains unknown. To know is not to love; to know is to yawn.

The girl was almost to his desk now. Her name was Irene Hillman, and she was of medium height, with smallish hips and waist, rather thin legs, and large, full, high breasts that made her look in danger of toppling forward at any moment. Although he had tried diligently, Joshua could not see any rational reason why his friend Alec would want this girl for his mate, but that was exactly the case. He had tried to figure it out until his curiosity had exasperated both of them, but the fact still remained that this was the female Alec had chosen to be his lifelong mate. And if that was Wall's decision, then that was how it would be.

When she reached the professor's desk her heart was pounding, but she did her best to present a calm, collected, suave exterior. This was her big chance, and she wasn't about to blow it acting like some kid. No way! She had to be a woman, had to act like a woman, had to make Professor Gimball want her as a woman. When she let her mind stray to her oft-return fantasies of the two of them in bed, she felt faint. Why didn't he say something? Shit, he had asked her to stay after class, and now he just sat across the desk and looked at her with those incredibly sexy eyes. She tried to return his gaze evenly, but she felt a warmth spreading across her abdomen and down her thighs, and a wetness spreading in her panties. Irene knew that if she didn't say something she'd have an orgasm just standing here looking at him. So she cleared her throat and said weakly, "It was this class you said you wanted to see me after, wasn't it, Professor Gimball?" Oh God, she sounded like an airhead! Great.

Gimball smiled and looked at her from under lowered lids. It was a calculated look meant to fan her obvious fires into a blaze. "Yes it was, Miss Hillman. You don't mind if I call you Irene, do you?"

The young woman only found strength enough to

shake her head.

"Good. And I wish you'd call me Josh, or Joshua if you prefer. First names are quite sufficient between friends, don't you think? I was rather hoping we could become just that. Friends." He learned forward and broadened his grin. "Good friends."

Irene was struck dumb. It was too good to be real. She had dreamed this moment, of course. Many times. But to have it come true, to have it suddenly be real . . . Oh shit! She wanted to be able to sit down. She felt like she was getting a hundred periods and the flu at the same time. Oh God, please don't let me faint or fall down or puke or anything dumb like that. Just let me stand here and be very cool, and then go to his place and ball my brains out. I'll do the dishes for mom, I won't get drunk for a month—or high, I'll go to confession and tell you all about it in case you miss anything. Just please let me do this right. It was terribly hard to control her tongue, but she managed to say, "I'd like that too, Josh. Very, very much." She hoped it didn't sound too corny.

"Good, good. That makes me quite happy." She watched him get up—and up . . . and up—and come around the desk to lightly but firmly take her arm. "Let's go get some lunch, shall we? I know it's a bit early, but we'll call it a celebration. We'll celebrate finding each other and talk about ourselves. There's so much about each other we have to get to know, after all. Don't you agree, Irene?"

At his touch her legs almost gave out, and as he led her deftly toward the door, she thought she had wet herself. Then she knew it was something else alto-

129

gether. Her mind seemed to scatter in a million different directions, although his touch was being relayed to various parts of her anatomy very reliably, and she had trouble focusing her attention on what he was saying. With her fingers crossed for luck, she nodded where it seemed appropriate and tried to make sense of the sounds of his continuing light banter as best she could. But what she really cared about, the only thing, was that she was going out to eat with Professor Gimball—Josh—and, with any luck, would end up in his bed before the day was out. With these thoughts occupying her mind totally, she followed him out with lamblike docility—out of her school, out of her town, and out of her old life.

When they approached the refurbished farmhouse that Joshua called home, he could see the surprise and pleasure on Irene's face. "I thought that we might have lunch here at Moonshadow," he explained easily. "It will be much more comfortable, and we'll be able to get to know each other far better than we would in some crowded restaurant."

"I think that's a fantastic idea, Josh," Irene cooed.

Gimball extended his hand, which she took quite readily, and led her through the front door. The interior was cool and bright, and Irene marveled that a bachelor would keep his place so spotlessly clean. Joshua sat her in front of the large stone fireplace, then disappeared into the kitchen to get drinks. Irene could hear him rattling about out there, humming a strange tune to himself . . . no, singing. She could hear the words now but couldn't make out exactly what the man was singing. It sounded strange, like nothing she could ever recall hearing before. Just another mark of his genius, she thought smugly, and after she got him in bed he would be all hers.

He came out grinning, carrying the drinks on a black lacquered tray. As he handed one to her, he said, "I think you'll find this quite different. It's something I learned how to fix while I was in college."

She cast him what she hoped was a look of aggressive surrender and tasted his offering. It certainly was different, almost tasteless at first, like water. But there was some kind of odd undertaste . . .

She swallowed the mouthful heartily, then quickly drained what remained in the glass. Her stomach revolted, contracted, sent its contents surging up into her throat. Keep a straight face, she advised herself. Smile. Act like it was good. Don't puke! And finally, with no real alternative, her body quit trying to reject this foreign substance and incorporated it into itself. Irene excused herself, asking for the directions to the john. She had to get herself back in line before the big scene. She was sweating like crazy from trying to keep that drink down, she did have to relieve herself, and it was time to get ready. It wouldn't do to have herself less than perfect for Joshua—she was sure he was accustomed to a class trip in bed from his women—and there was the little matter of inserting her diaphragm. It wasn't time for a bunch of rugrats yet. First they had to travel to Europe and the Far East. Maybe Australia. And she would have to buy a few of the newest fashions from New York and Paris, so she could look the part when they entertained the faculty at the parties they would throw at Moonshadow. Winking at herself in the bathroom mirror, she touched up her makeup. What was that her mother always said. "The worm has turned." That was it. Worms. Yuccch! But still, the . . . worm . . . was turning. Big things were going to start to happen in her life, she just knew it.

She exited the bathroom flipping her hair over her shoulder, even though it was far too short to flip anywhere. She would grow her hair long again and to hell with what her parents said. When Josh saw how she looked with her hair hanging down to her ass cheeks, he'd never leave her for sure. She wet her lips. Moist lips turn a man on, she had learned.

The floor tilted suddenly to the right. The room brightened as if it were a star going into nova, all the details fading into a blinding white light that seemed to be burning awareness from her brain. She lurched forward and started to fall, but caught herself on something soft and warm. She couldn't see it; didn't know what it was. Her mind wouldn't work at all; there were no thoughts that stayed long enough to gather words around them. She tried to force them to stay, but the world she couldn't see started to spin around her like a whirlpool, a tornado. Even though she could see nothing but blinding white, she could feel it, pulling her down. Her left knee struck something hard, painfully, and panic flooded her. What was happening? Was she dying? Where was she?

I'm at Joshua Gimball's, she remembered. I just had a drink with him. We're going to walk into the bedroom soon and make love. He'll take my clothes off slowly and kiss me all over, then he'll . . . It hit her again, like vertigo. She trembled. Her bones were turning to smoke; she was floating away. Her bones were turning to lead; she was sinking down. I'm changing, she thought with a rush of awareness. I'm changing, but what am I becoming? I'm changing, but I don't want to change.

Irene Hillman toppled forward to the floor. She didn't see the wood rushing up to strike her forehead; she just felt the jarring impact when the two met violently. The spikes of hurt that pierced her cleared her mind slightly, and she thought that she would never get him to make love to her now, not after acting like this. Then a chilly blackness spread toward the center of her self from the corners like a smothering syrup, and just before it engulfed her she realized she was going to pass out. There was no more inside to Irene Hillman, no more outside. No front opposed to back. No up distinguished from down. No dream less real than reality. There were no distinctions like that anymore. Her mouth moved and formed a word just before her mind was blotted out. That word was, "Shit."

The two of them looked at her as she lay on her back, her short hair in disarray against the white sheets. She was in the guest room, on a small cot, naked.

"I still don't know why it is she that you chose," Joshua said quietly from the doorway.

Alec Wall stood beside the young woman's prone form, running his hands over her as if mesmerized, feeling the softness of her skin. His eyes drank in the large, firm mounds of her breasts, coursed down her length to her shapely legs and the patch of darkness

133

between. "I want her because she is beautiful." The statement was simple but packed with quivering emotion and desire.

"I'll admit that she is comely, Alec. But to base the selection of your life's mate on physical beauty alone seems folly to me." His tone was amused but gently edged. Alec Wall was his friend, and he didn't want him making a mistake about so serious a subject. "You have only a few days to reconsider, my friend. Once you two have mated, the law of the pack is quite specific. I could not change it even should I want to."

Alec kissed the warm lips that lay before him, caressed the breasts whose nipples rose instinctively. He looked over at his friend and thought how sad it was to live only by the tenets of the mind instead of by the dictates of the heart. It was the only sphere in which they differed. "We love the flowers because they are a pleasure to behold, Joshua. We love art for the same reason. Man loves beauty for the sake of beauty, and now I want *her* because of her beauty, her warmth, her softness. I want to share her body and soul. What better reason, Joshua? What better reason?"

"You can turn and walk away from the flower or the painting. You don't expect understanding from them, Alec. Nor compassion, nor love in return. But, Alec, as beautiful as she may *look*, or *feel*, she may be hideous at her core. You cannot equate roses with a woman. The beauty of a rose *is* the rose and lasts only one season. And you can't compare the beauty of fine art with a woman: The beauty of art lasts only as long as the work itself, is a property of the work, inseparable. You mate with this girl, Alec, and you mate for life. Only her death or yours can release you from bondage. Her form is one of pleasing beauty, I'll grant again. But what is her heart like? Will she be a companion to you? Will she hunt by your side and be as one with you? When the two of you are in human form, will you be able to get along for all the coming years? I don't think you've given thought to these questions, Alec. I hope that your infatuation for the beauty and youth of this creature is not causing you to abandon your intelligence and common sense."

Alec had heard it all before. "Joshua, I want this woman. You know how much I've thought about it; you've been through this with me again and again. In my mind, my choice is final. Unfortunately, we can't really take the time to know our women before the coupling, but we just have to live with that. I feel good about this, Joshua. That's enough for me, okay?" He walked over to his friend, clasped his arm, and led him from the room.

"Now," he said, changing the subject while he had the chance, "when are you going to claim that Sangellis woman as your own. You wait such a long time before you ever act on these things, Joshua. Sometimes I think you get trapped in your own head and can't find the way out."

Gimball smiled at him. "First I have to insure that the spell I cast on your woman is binding. And she will need our support unsparingly the first few times she changes. But I have invited Eve and that man she's living with to our Halloween gathering. I'll take her for myself there and then. Are you satisfied with

135

that, Mother?"

"What about the male?" Alec laughed.

"Oh, don't worry about the male. I have some rather interesting plans for Mr. Rudy Vardon."

Charlie McQuire shifted his excessive bulk around in his chair and tried to get himself comfortable. He could see the sun being extinguished by the mountains outside his window, and it was not his habit to stay at work this late. Right now he should be at Robin's having his second or third cold brew and trying to make time with that new blond waitress they had there. Damn! What was her name? Couldn't hardly impress a woman if you couldn't even bring her name to mind now, could you? Martha, he thought. Probably Marty. Well, if Gimball ever showed up, he'd sure as hell hurry over there and give her a try. He threw his thick legs up on the corner of his desk, leaning back into his protesting swivel chair. He'd like to be over there now—the early bird, and like that—but he knew that he'd either wait for Joshua Gimball now or regret it later. And it was all so damned dumb. Hell, Mack was right in back and he could take care of a thing like this just as well as McQuire himself. But the professor liked the man in charge to *be* there, whether he was really needed or not, and it wasn't too smart to argue with the professor. The last time Charlie had tried to face him down, the mayor had called to ask him if he didn't like being chief of police. Shit. What did that asshole Cooper think, that he wanted to *work* for a living? So he'd just have to wait and hope Martha—Marty?—would, too.

Mack Horner walked into McQuire's office without knocking and sat across the desk from him. Charlie raised his eyebrows questioningly.

Horner was tall and angular, with a look in his eyes that made most people dislike him instantly. His hair was lank, greasy, and thinning, and his mouth twitched nervously when he talked. "That pimp downtown says he ain't got the full price this time, Chief."

Charlie sighed and lit up a cigarette. "Well, then, you just send Astin down ta help the boy look for it, Mack. That nigger got to have misplaced it or sumpthin'. I know the bastard's got the shit somewhere, an' he sure as hell can't tell me he ain't. Yeah, you jus' send ol' Astin down to help that coon look, an' maybe you should go along to make sure they do a good job, eh? After all, we pride ourselves on e-ficiency here, don't we?"

Horner tittered ratlike, nodding at his boss. If there was one thing he loved to do in this world, it was roust people around. He liked to see folks cry and holler and scream in pain. He liked to hurt people and have them beg him to stop. He never did stop, though.

He had killed a man once, and he'd liked that, too.

The deputy sat across the desk from Charlie McQuire, picking his nose and nodding in moronic agreement, the glee of what he was supposed to do already suffusing his face. Although the man disgusted Charlie on a personal level, he had to admit that Horner had a certain "talent" for getting things from people. He did his job right to the letter, enjoyed it, never complained. He probably would've done just as good a job without Charlie putting that little extra in his pay envelope every two weeks but, what the hell, it sweetened the pot and kept him even happier. Besides, what McQuire gave out was just a fraction of what he took in and placed in his safe-deposit box down at the bank. He had quite a roll stashed down there right now, and in a couple more years he'd ask Gimball if he couldn't just retire—he had Horner and Astin Chubb now, anyway—and spend the rest of his life relaxing and hunting. He did really like the hunt and had to thank the professor for getting him into that, even if the blond-haired man did seem a little uppity to him.

He looked over and saw that Mack was still there, and slammed his hairy fist down on his desk with a resounding thud. "Dammit, Horner," he thundered, "will you get the fuck out of here and do what I told you to do." As the deputy scuttled for the door he added, "And will you take care of your fuckin' eyebrows, you stupid shit? You tryin' to give all of us away or what?"

It was fully dark when Joshua and Alec pulled up and parked in the alley that bordered the police building adjacent to City Hall. McQuire, whose anxiety had grown in direct proportion to the hours he had waited, opened the side door to the building before they had a chance to knock. He tried valiantly to hide his ire at the lateness of the hour. "I was gettin' a little worried. It's pretty late."

Alec brushed past the fat officer as if he wasn't there, but Joshua stopped in front of his beer barrel stomach and pinned him to the wall with a hard stare. "It's only nine-thirty, Charlie. That is not that late, and it's not as if you've put in a hard day of police work now, is it?"

McQuire lowered his eyes in submission. "Well, you don't have to get all huffy about it, Professor. Damn. It's just that I been waitin' since about six an' here it is, like you said, nine-thirty. A fella gets a little worried after three and a half hours of waitin'."

"Not if the 'fella' hasn't been given an exact arrival time, Charles. And especially not you about me. There will be plenty of time after we conclude our business to romance that bleached blond whore at Robin's Bar. Now, shall we get this over with, Chief?" As he turned and walked into the building, he threw over his shoulder, "I see your ear has healed up nicely."

McQuire touched his ear. That damned big dog of Vardon's had ripped a healthy chunk out of it and it was still touchy and pink, but it *had* healed up real nice. He still was amazed at how fast his wounds healed now that he was one of Gimball's group. Fingers grew back on, wounds closed, sight was restored, bones mended, ears grew new pieces. Not of a moment, mind you, but real fast. Damn fast. The professor called it regeneration so he supposed that was what it was, but he called "the change" transmogrification or some such shit, too. Well, he could use his high-powered words if he wanted, but Charlie McQuire just knew that he healed and he changed, and that was the long and the short of it. So fuck your big words and damn you anyway, Professor Gimball Bigshit. You'll get yours someday, too. With

139

that he turned and followed Gimball to the jail.

Justin Marks knew he was in trouble when he saw
that big mother standing at the cell door sizing him
up. Marks had never seen him before and wasn't the
type to be afraid of bigger men, but this dude gave
him chills. He wasn't a cop, but that fat fuck of a
police chief was doin' his fair share of bowin' and
scrapin' and kissin' ass, and the other dude that was
with him was mindin' his manners, too. This fucker
didn't take charge—it was given to him without him
even askin'—and Justin could see why. This cat was
BAD. It was written all over him. The way he
walked, the way he held himself, in the quiet thunder
of his voice. And in his eyes. His eyes were crazy
damned things, and Martin couldn't seem to look
into them steadily, no matter how hard he tried.
Those eyes said all there was to say about the man,
and what they said made Justin Marks sorry he had
ever looked into them. This dude was one bad, one
dangerous motherfucker, and Marks didn't think he
was gonna' like what old dead eyes was thinkin'.
Man, the prisoner thought, I hope this bastard ain't
nobody but my lawyer.

"His name," said Charlie McQuire officiously, "is
Justin Marks. He's thirty-four years old, Caucasian,
male, five feet nine . . ."

Gimball made a cutting motion with the flat of his
hand. "If you don't mind, Charles, please refrain
from stating the obvious and tell me why he's in your
jail."

"Oh. Yeah. Okay. He knifed a man down by Twin

140

Willows at that sleazy little beer joint along Main. Cut him up all kind of ways, and the man just croaked this morning. We got him on manslaughter at least, no problem. Fucker's guilty as sin. Lots of witnesses."

"Does he have any friends or family in town, or anyone who knows that he might be staying in our community?"

"Nope. I checked all that out, Professor. No living relatives, no next of kin, no friends. He's only been here a coupla' days, been in there mosta' that. Just drifted into town from upstate, and they want him real bad up there on a parole violation. He's a runner, is all."

Joshua looked at Marks and smiled. "Not a very loveable sort of person, are you, Marks? A convicted criminal, a parole violator, and now a killer of your fellow man. What do you think waits for you back home, Marks? Or here, for that matter?"

Justin Marks sat quietly, waiting, seeing just where this was going to lead.

"And not a very sociable type either, eh? Well, that suits me just as well, sir. I know that you're probably wondering, so I'll get right to the point of my presence here today. I've come to offer you a sort of deal. I will offer it once and once only; you may take it or leave it as you see fit. You are not permitted to ask for any more information than I care to give you; in other words, no questions will be answered. Do you understand this so far, or should we give you some time alone to go over it in your mind?"

Marks spat once on the cement floor.

Gimball's eyes flashed with anger at this show of

impudence, but the leering grin never left his lips. Beside him, Wall growled once low in his chest and started to move toward the cell, salking. Joshua extended his arm to block his way, holding him back.

Mark's heartbeat quickened. Adrenaline shot into his bloodstream, and bile rose simultaneously in his throat. Without giving it any thought, he knew that his life was being threatened, that his future was being decided here in this poorly lit wing of cells. These men were crazy, more wacko than any of the bastards he had run up against in his many years in prison. He balled his scarred, calloused hands into fists. That fucker *growled*, for Christ's sake. He thinks he's a goddam dog or somethin'. Marks put his back firmly against the rough cinderblock wall. Well, man or dog or fucking rhinoceros, if he came in here to get Justin Marks, he was going to get his head busted.

"Relax," Joshua ordered Wall, tersely. Then he turned back to the iron bars. "You too, my friend. We mean you no harm. My friend here just gets a little upset when people don't show the proper respect for their fellow man. He forgets how little you must know of such things as respect. Now, as for the offer. It is this: You allow me to come in there and bind your hands. I will then lead you out of here by the side door into the alley, where I will put you in my car and take you up the mountain to my home. Once there, I will have you perform certain tasks that only a man of your abilities could complete for me, and when these have been carried out to my total satisfaction, I will release you into the forest to go where you will. That is my offer. As I said, there will be no discussion as to the nature of the tasks to be performed or anything else to do with this little deal. All I require from you is a simple yes or no so that I can be on my way." Gimball stopped speaking for a long moment and held the other man's eyes. "Well, man," he said finally, impatiently. "What is it going to be?"

Marks needed no time to consider the proposal. No matter what would become of him if he stayed here in the Larksboro lockup—and he knew that it would be a long time behind those state penitentiary bars, at least—it had to be better than what a man like that could ask him to do for him. Freedom waited after his work was done—if you could trust what the dude said—but there were some things that even a man like Marks had become wouldn't do. That was the kicker; that was what Mr. Cold Eyes hadn't figured out. There were things that Justin Marks wouldn't do, even to be a free man. Like what? he argued with himself. What is it that you wouldn't do to be back on the road? And he didn't know. That was the scary part. He had done damn near everything that had ever come into his head: kinky sex, robbery, murder, cruelty to animals, rape, bestiality, prostitution—everything. He couldn't think of anything that he hadn't done. . . .

"Sorry, Mr. Clean. I kinda' like it here. It's real homey, you know. I think I'll just stick right here and take my licks like a good little boy. So why don't you just go fuck off, huh?"

Before he could be stopped, Wall sprang. He hit the steel bars with a thud and hung there, his eyes wide and red-rimmed. Justin realized that the guy on

143

the other side of those bars was growling steadily now, sounding like an outboard motor or a chain saw. And as Marks looked on, he was sure he saw the lean man's face darkening, his eyebrows growing closer together, his lips thinning and pulling back over teeth that seemed to be growing impossibly long and very pointed. If it wasn't a trick of the damned shitty lighting, his ears had gotten pointy and his hands were hairy and his fingernails were lengthening . . . and in his hands the steel bars that separated them were making the weirdest sounds as they began to pull slowly apart from each other, making a hole that wouldn't let him out as soon as it would let that crazy bastard in. Marks moved back along the wall, shaking his head. He couldn't be seeing what he was seeing. He must be going crazy.

Gimball and McQuire both darted forward, but Joshua was much quicker than the overweight chief and got to Alec first. He reached out and grabbed his friend by his corded, straining arm, pulling Wall around easily to face him. Gimball's hand whipped out and contacted Wall's shifting features with a resounding slap, which rocked the younger man's head back on his shoulders, stunning him. Then he was handed quickly to the chief of police, who escorted him rapidly into the next room and out of sight. When Gimball finally turned to look at the man in the cell, trapped, cowering in a far corner, he had some control of his seething rage.

"As you wish," he said with his jaw quivering. "You will stay here and await your just punishment, then." So saying, he spun on his heel and quickly left the room.

144

Justin Marks was left alone in the cell block, his back firmly wedged into the corner furthermost from the door to his cell. He slid slowly to the floor and squatted there, staring at the two misshapen bars just five feet away from him.

At eleven o'clock, Deputy Mack Horner woke his only charge up and acted sympathetic when the man jumped and whined with fear. He held out a cup of steaming coffee and produced a flask from his back pocket, adding some to the brew. Then he offered it cautiously to Marks. "Here," he soothed, "ain't nothin' to be afraid of now. I got somethin' that'll take them shivers outta' ya an' make ya' sleep like a fuckin' log. Well, whaddaya say, Marks? Guaranteed to fix what ails ya, boy."

Marks accepted the cup and stared deeply into the dark liquid, his eyes searching for any telltale signs of drugs added to help him along to slumberland. When he saw nothing, he put the rim of the cup under his nose and tested the aroma, finding it to be safe, too.

"Not a trustin' kinda' guy, are ya?" the deputy asked amiably. When his prisoner issued a hostile harrumph and began to cautiously drink the coffee without saying any more, he chortled, "Nor real sociable, neither."

Marks examined his situation over the rim of his mug. There was only one guy in the room, and the door was open as all hell. He was sure that he could give this shithead hick a shot in the head, then get through that cell door and out into the street before anyone could stop him. *If* the main door was open,

145

too. And *if*—this was the big one, man—*if* that big cocksucker and his wacko buddy weren't just waitin' out there somewhere in the shadows for him to try something like that.

Horner saw Justin Marks tremble, saw the coffee overspill the lip of its container and flow down around the white knuckles of the man's hands.

"Can't hardly stand ta drink with a guy that rattles on so," he mocked. Then he cocked his head toward the outer hall—Marks caught a glimpse of the tufted hair that filled the deputy's ear and felt his bowels loosen—harkening to some noise, some movement, something. Weasellike eyes sparkling with their own light, he leaned to Marks and asked in a whisper, "You hear somethin' just now?"

"No." It was terse, like a handclap or a pistol shot, spat out rather than said. He *HAD* heard nothing, but still he watched the hall, concentrating on the shadows, fearing any movement toward that open door. "Close the door!" Then, softer, almost pleading, "How about closin' the door, man? Okay?"

Sighing, Mack Horner rose to his feet, putting his cup of laced coffee on the floor. "Well, boy, if you're gonna be so worried about the damned thing, I'll close it." He turned and walked away, and Marks noticed something about the way he moved that just didn't seem right. At first he couldn't think what it was, but then he thought that it might be that the man, tall and angular as he was, moved with an almost hypnotizing grace, a looseness, a coordination, which the criminal had seen somewhere before. Where? Where?

"So, Marks, why don't we just sit and drink and

146

you tell me just what happened 'tween you an' Mr. Wall?"

Justin jumped, startled, and just managed not to scream. His eyes flew immediately to the cell door, but it was closed now. Deputy Horner was seating himself on the cot, picking up his half-empty drink and the threads of the one-sided conversation at the same time. His eyes kept wanting to focus on the deputy's hair-packed ears. Marks put the drink in his hands to his lips and drained it, then held the cup out toward his companion for a refill. It quivered in the air.

"Well, now, decide to get friendly, did ya? That's nice, 'cept I ain't got any more coffee." The deputy's voice was a taunt. "Then again, you look like ya probably don't need coffee 'smuch as you might need a little taste a' this." He pulled out the flask from his back pocket and waved it around in the air—a miracle of prestidigitation—before uncapping it, pouring a healthy dollop in the proffered cup, and adding a little freshener to his own.

"Thanks," Marks managed as he drank half of the new.

"Sure, Marks. I can see where you might need a little steadyin' up." The wiry man folded himself forward and placed his elbows on his knees. "Now," he said expansively, "tell me just what happened in here, ol' buddy. I don't really know the whole story, so I come right to the source, as they say."

Silence for a second or two, then, "Nothin'."

"Nothin'. Come on, boy, who you tryin' to bull-shit? Nothin' always scare you this bad?"

"He . . . changed."

"Changed?"

"Yeah."

"Changed into what, for Chrissakes?"

Marks couldn't say what he couldn't let himself think. "He just changed, goddammit! He just . . . changed." He finished his drink in one pull, raised his eyes beseechingly, and held the cup out again. He saw Horner's eyes widen and his jaw start to slacken. He saw that the deputy was staring off toward the front of the cell, toward the pooling shadows.

He heard him say, under a hitch in his breath, "Inta THAT?"

Justin Marks whirled about to face the enemy, readying his empty cup instinctively as a weapon, shifting his weight forward as he started to get to his feet. He was ready to run, he was ready to fight—he was ready to cry. But he saw nothing at all until pain welled up in the back of his head and flooded front to drown his consciousness.

What Justin Marks had *not* been ready for was Mack Horner's pocket flask of whiskey, which the deputy had used to bash his prisoner soundly across the head, collapsing him into a loose pile of bones and flesh on the concrete floor. The blood from the wounds on the back of the fallen man's skull dropped wetly down to mix with the puddles of liquor that had escaped from the broken bottle. Horner licked his fingers and looked at the pinkish pool sadly. "Damn," he said. "Now I ain't got no more until tomorrow mornin'."

Before he hoisted the unconscious man to his

148

shoulders and carried him out past Charlie McQuire, sitting impatiently at his desk, and into the side street where Joshua Gimball and Alec Wall waited with even less patience for his delivery into the back of their four-wheel drive pickup, he kicked the fallen form resoundingly in the ribs and said petulantly, "I hope it takes a long time with you. I hope you wake up in the middle of it."

Charlie McQuire said, "It's about fuckin' time, Mack. I wanta get the fuck outta' here tonight!"

Joshua Gimball said, "Throw him in the back, Mack, and cover him over with the blanket you'll find there."

Alec Wall looked at his blond friend and asked, "Tonight?"

Gimball's group was well prepared when he and Alec reached Moonshadow. Astin Chubb, another of the town's deputies and a confederate of Horner's and McQuire's in most of their endeavors, met them as they parked the truck and helped them to carry the moaning prisoner into the barn. "I don't like this part of it," Chubb confessed sheepishly. "I don't see why they have to be alive for this."

Gimball gave him a warning look that silenced him immediately. "Are you questioning my knowledge?" he intoned deeply. "My leadership?"

"No, no. Nothing like that, Joshua. Nothing like that. I guess I'm just a little nervous or something, you know? That last one . . . God! The way he screamed, it was enough to . . ." He couldn't think . . . To what? Wake the dead? Freeze your marrow?

149

Yes and yes, but more. So much more.

I must remember that they are new, they are pups, Joshua thought. They do not see the reason nor the logic yet. They think it unnatural, even horrible. And yet they will hunt. They will quite willingly hunt.

"Have the block and tackle been erected?" he asked, breaking away from his musings. The paradoxes and contradictions of the ongoing transformation of the psyche provided him with hours of quite fulfilling mental exercise, but now was not the time.

"All set to go," reported Astin. "Is there going to be anybody else with us tonight?"

"Only the girl."

Alec, startled by this revelation, spoke for the first time. "Irene?" he questioned. "Are you sure that she's ready, Joshua?"

Gimball thought that this surely must be his night for impertinence. First there had been McQuire, then this criminal they carried, then Chubb, and now his best disciple. He knew that Wall was simply concerned over the welfare of his chosen mate, but he was still disappointed in this lack of faith. None of his pack were naturally of the wolf, as he was. It was he, Joshua Gimball, who had to change them all; and it was he who had to, after making them of his blood, teach them to control rather than be controlled by. He had done all these things, given these gifts, and now the scent of a little female musk, the prospect of mating, could make even the best of them forget. It was the human in then, he knew. The wolf would trust the dominant male explicitly.

"She is ready," he reassured his friend. "Do you think I would let her see this if she were not?"

Alec shook his head, embarrassed.

"I don't know," Chubb tried, for comic relief. "I've seen this kind of thing before, Joshua, and I don't know if *I'm* ready to see it again."

"You," said Gimball without a trace of humor, "are not the best of students."

The reprimand stung, and Chubb got out, "Well, I'm a lot further down the path than she is," before a tensing in his leader's muscles persuaded him to fall silent.

The barn was well lit. They laid their burden down on the floor amongst a covering of straw and sawdust, Joshua and Alec readying the block and tackle while Chubb undressed the criminal at his feet. When all was ready, the man was carried into the center of the floor, bound hand and foot, and raised off the floor like an animal ready for butchering, head down. He groaned louder and his eyelids fluttered rapidly.

"Bring the ladders and the pail," Joshua ordered.

Chubb hurried to a dark corner and dragged out two stepladders of medium height and a galvanized five-gallon bucket. He carried all three over at once, with no sign of exertion.

"And the rack?"

Chubb snapped his fingers and spat, "Damn!" Then he moved soundlessly to the same corner and retrieved a stand some four feet high and five feet long. It was constructed out of wood and looked to be a relation to those folding clothes hangers that were used extensively to hang clothing indoors before the invention of dryers. Astin carried this over and set it down decisively, saying, "Here we go," and folding

151

his arms across his chest, puffed up like a pink balloon.

"My God, Astin," Alec chuckled. "You look like the Pillsbury doughboy."

Chubb opened his mouth to reply when Gimball asked impatiently, "And the tools, Astin? Would you kindly bring the tools also?"

Muttering about being a wolf and acting like a fucking gopher, Chubb returned to the corner again and came back with a small trunk. Setting it down he asked indignantly, "Is that all, *sir*?"

Joshua, who couldn't keep a straight face, shook his head in amazement. The man was more clown than wolf, but he was loyal and did what he was told. Even a wolf pack needed its lackeys.

Opening the chest, Gimball withdrew a metal stake, which he drove into the ground under Mark's head. He then took a length of rope and secured one end around the hanging man's neck and the other around the stake, loose enough not to cut off the man's breathing or circulation but tight enough to keep him from swaying or bending. The tall blond then took out two ornate knives wrapped in silk, handing one to Wall. With the other, he carved into the dust on the barn floor a large circle, which encompassed the ladders, the rack, the pail, and the three of them. Leaving one area of the circle open, he walked its interior, drawing strange figures and chanting to himself, his voice so low that it was unintelligible to his two companions only a few feet away.

Astin Chubb moved closer to the second in command and said, sotto voce, "What's he saying, anyway, Alec?"

"We are not advanced enough to know," Alec replied, dismissing his inquiry.

Chubb made a long-suffering face.

"Go and get the female," Joshua ordered. "Alec and I will finish here."

Astin came back into the barn a few minutes later, leading a girl that looked almost like Irene Hillman. Almost, except for the strange light in the eyes—a coldness, perhaps—and the flowing way that she moved, loping out of the night darkness into the bright light, alert, aware.

Despite his foppishness, Astin Chubb could be observed to walk in the selfsame way.

"Hello Irene," Joshua said. "Are you ready?"

Irene took in the whole of the barn in one casual glance: the dust in shimmering motes raised by the two men's feet; the circle on the floor, complete save where she would enter; the victim hanging upside down at its precise center, groaning, alive; the bucket under his head; the stepladders on either side of him; the rack standing near. She snuffled, testing the air, and thought she could smell the strange man's fear. Certainly she could tell of Alec's worry, she knew him that well.

"Hello Joshua," she said. "Alec. Yes, I'm ready."

Alec said nothing, simply holding out his hand, and Irene went to him, feeling a charge in the air as she crossed the circle's perimeter. She touched his hand and their lips met briefly. While their faces were close they smelled each other's breath, each other's body. "Irene . . ." Alec began.

153

She touched her fingers to his lips. "Don't worry."

The hanging man moaned more loudly and his eyes flickered open. "Wh . . . wh . . . wh . . ." Saliva fell out of his working mouth and ran down into his eyes and hair. Some of it dropped off of his nose and cheekbones in elastic strands and fell dully into the bucket. "Wh . . . wh . . . wh . . . wha. . ."

Joshua motioned Astin Chubb into the circle. The short, pudgy man had a greenish look on his greasy pig-face that intensified every time Marks tried to speak. Gimball could afford to throw the poor fellow a bone so, though it mattered little to him personally, he pointed to the hanging head and said, "We are ready to start. If you wish to save this gentleman some misery, I suggest you do it now. It is your last chance."

The deputy slid his nightstick from its holder and raised it over his head. Then he hesitated. "Look, Joshua, do we have to? I mean, why don't you just teach her them first spells and forget about this shit, huh?" His watery black eyes said, "Please."

"Astin," Joshua started with barely restrained impatience, "you know as well as I do that the girl has got to have the girdle at the beginning. Without it she cannot change herself. Without change she cannot know. You know this, Astin. You had to wear a girdle at first."

"Yeah, yeah, I know. It's just that, well . . . I wish there were some other way, you know."

"We do what we must, Astin. I am going to close the circle and proceed. Please move to the barn door and stand watch."

"Oh, alright, dammit! Just let me . . ." He

quickly smashed his nightstick across the hanging man's forehead with a thunk. Immediately the stammering, sputtering moans stopped. The body convulsed once, giving up its hard-earned consciousness reluctantly, and then hung still. Because of the upside-down position, the mouth hung open even farther, spittle cascading down to plunk into the bucket with regularity. The eyes hung open, tearing, the salty liquid joining the saliva in streams that spawned rivers. They hung open and stared at Astin Chubb, and he stared back.

Gimball pushed the squat man out of the circle and said simply. "The door." He closed the perimeter, mumbling under his breath, then stood, looking first at the woman who joined him there, and then the man.

"As we hand you the strips of skin, Irene, you will lay them carefully on the rack to dry. Be careful of them; they tear much more easily than you might think." Gimball nodded to the bucket beneath the unconscious man's head. "Most of the blood will run down the body into that, so hopefully the floor won't get too messy as things proceed. Alec and I will do the skinning, so you needn't worry about that part. You just take the strips of skin and *carefully* hang them up to dry. Each strip will be about three fingers in breadth. That's . . . oh, about two inches. They will be as long as we can make them, but that usually isn't over three or four feet at best. Just hang them up, Irene, that's all. Oh, and adjust the position of the bucket if the blood flow seems to be missing it too terribly, right?"

Irene nodded her head in understanding.

Gimball climbed one ladder and Alec the other, knives in hand. At the top, where they could easily reach the man's feet, they stopped. Both held their knives at arm's length over their heads, pointing them ritualistically in each of the four directions, then straight up, then down, as they muttered an identical incantation. Alec finally opened his eyes and stared at his friend, who nodded, satisfied. As he held his knife poised for the first cut, he looked down at the expectant woman at his feet and said, "This may take some time, my dear. Relax."

Astin Chubb watched the two men making their first cuts, then he turned his back to the proceedings and stared out the wide barn door into the darkness. Somewhere out there the rest were hunting, and he wished he were with them. He didn't mind the hunting, not even the hunting of men, because then they were prey. It was sport, just like when he used to hunt with a rifle and shotgun. Of course, that wasn't nearly as much sport as what he could do now, running them down until they tired, catching them, biting through hamstring and tendon until they fell or faltered, and then sinking his teeth into their throats, feeling the warm sweet blood well up into his mouth, fountain down his throat until he felt he was going to choke on the joy of it . . .

From behind him, he heard Irene Hillman gasp. It was not a sound of horror or shock, he knew. It was a sound of pleasure. That Irene was one stacked lady, but he sure wouldn't want to spend a night in the woods with her. Nor anywhere else, for that matter. There was a meanness in her that scared him—a pure, heartless coldness. She would make a great wolf, though, and a fitting mate to Alec. She would be the dominant female of the pack until Joshua took a female for himself as well. Then that would have to be worked out, and knowing the hateful viciousness of Irene Hillman, the solution would be something to see. Joshua Gimball's wife would have to be one hell of a balls-up female.

The woman gasped again, but this time it was husky, almost sexual. A part of Chubb wanted to turn and look, but he denied it. This was not sport, not even natural. This was butchery. This was what *men* did, and not all men at that. Just evil men. Bad men. The thoughts were leading him somewhere when he heard the first hesitant drops of rain. He tried to cock his ears forward, but the pain that shot up over his head reminded him that he was in the wrong shape to do that. Having two shapes was confusing, especially when you only had one set of senses. His ears were canine sharp, but he'd have to move his whole head to zero in on the sound.

It came again, harder, more insistent.

He realized that the sky was clear and star-filled, the corpse-white moon waxing toward full. How could that be? He stepped outside and extended his arms toward the sky, hands turned palms up to catch the falling droplets of water. There was nothing.

But still the sound came, harder than before, the sound of a heavy rain hitting a roof and running off the soggy ground. The sound of a broken pipe spitting water into a puddle. The sound of . . .

The sound of . . .

He didn't want to turn, for he already knew, but his senses prompted a reaction too quick for his much

157

slower thoughts to check. He about-faced and stared into the barn. Astin tried to slow his gaze, to make it stoppable by attaching it to Hillman's face, but the eyes he saw beaming there simply shoved his own toward what they were not anxious to see. They jumped toward the loft, the roof, trying to escape, but latched onto the massive form of Joshua Gimball up on his ladder, and he was cutting, cutting . . .

And there is the body, and it must still be alive somehow because it's glistening, oozing. And the glistening, the oozing stuff is flowing down and down, obeying the commands of gravity. It's flowing down and down the still-twitching form until it reaches the bottom.

It reaches the bottom and flows over this big red thing that looks like a monster tomato. It's the man's head, yes, but it's all red, solid red, and the hair's sopping red and hanging down. It looks just like some tomato grown incredibly huge through exposure to nuclear radiation or something. (Hydroponics, Astin my boy. The wave of the future, you know.) Just like some fucking giant tomato. And under it is that shiny bucket, and into the bucket drips a steady fusillade of heavy, thick red droplets. When they hit . . .

When they hit, they sound just like rain.

The sound of Astin Chubb wretching violently just outside the barn door didn't seem to bother the other three at all. In fact, Joshua took time to look at the smiling pretty face of Irene Hillman and chuckle.

"God, how disgusting," grimaced Irene.

Astin had not yet reached a point where he felt quite himself, so he had failed to clean himself of the

158

vomit that splattered his shirt front and caked the lower half of his trouser legs and shoes. Joshua waved a hand in front of his nose. "I'm forced to agree, Astin. Not only do you look terrible, but you smell . . ."

". . . gross," Irene finished.

"Crudely put, but true. Please, go and clean yourself up and then go back to town. We'll have no more use for you tonight. It won't be light for a few hours yet, maybe a little hunting would put you in better spirits. You still look a little pale."

"Yeah, you might be right," Chubb said in a subdued tone. His jowls still quivered pitifully. "I think I'll clean up and just go home and watch some TV." He walked away like a man caught in a dream.

"Joshua, I don't see why you insist on keeping that man around," Alec confided. "Some day he's liable to cause us a lot of trouble."

Joshua grinned. "It isn't his fault if he isn't quite what he wishes he were, or even if he's not what he thinks himself to be. There are few of us who could not be accused of that. Astin is quite harmless to us, believe me. And it never hurts to have friends with careers in law enforcement, does it?"

The other two were forced to agree with that last point, although Alec still had a few reservations that remained unvoiced.

"Good!" Gimball concluded. "Now, let's move on to the more pleasant aspects of our evening, shall we?" So saying, he walked over to the drying rack and removed one of the longest strips of peeled human flesh, bringing it over to the woman and placing it in her hands. "Now, dear, I want you to

159

take this strip of flesh and wrap it around your waist. I realize it's a little shabby, but it will do until we can make you a more fitting one. This is your girdle, made, as it must be, from the skin of a convicted criminal. When you wish to transmogrify, you simply place the girdle around your waist and concentrate very hard. When you wish to return to human form, you simply take it off. Do you understand?"

"Yes, Joshua."

"Good. Soon, with the help of myself and Alec here, you will be able to dispense with the girdle altogether and use other, more convenient means. Until then, however, this will allow you to get some experience in your other form until you can accomplish a complete change. Now, Irene," he finished, "if you would be so kind?"

The woman tied the skin girdle clumsily around her waist and thought of the change. She had never done it herself; either Joshua or Alec had always put her under some type of spell to induce it. Alec called it "enchanting" her into it, and she guessed that was as good a thing to call it as anything else. She fixed her mind on an image of what she wanted to become . . . and she felt it. Her blood felt as if it were boiling, her skin as if it were stretching, her heart pumped so madly that the sound seemed to fill her being. Dimension after hidden dimension of sensation washed over her as her perceptions jumped far beyond canine levels. She could feel herself being reworked, remade, as if she were nothing but clay. But the artist who used it was insane. He was malevolent. He did not create her gently or kindly but instead ripped and tore her, broke her, crushed her in a hateful grip. And the rage of the creator seeped into the creation. As the pain of this became unbearable, she came in long racking shudders, throwing her head back in a scream that was a howl from the ravaged, raped, and damned center of her soul.

From deep within the shadows of the far mountain, she was answered by one, then another . . . still more. Her new family. They came.

By the time the others had reached Moonshadow, Joshua was sitting on a crate just outside the barn door, flanked by Alec Wall and a naked, hirsute shape that was clearly female, but not so clearly human. The face was wolfish, but of a type only seen before in hell and the minds of those who spun legends. Or by the eyes of those who had, down through the centuries, made the acquaintance of her ancestors. The neck, shoulders, back, and rump were all covered with longish black hair, as were the breasts. The hands were darkly furred, taloned, but for it all, still human in semblance. The feet were far more like paws, causing her to lean slightly forward as she stood, panting. Drool slid from behind her bestial dentation and slimed her black lips. As the others approached, her grotesquely large, pointed ears rotated forward to catch the soft sound of their footfalls. Her wet black nostrils twitched as she caught the smell of more males and began to squirm. Then she caught wind of female musk and growled challengingly. Her claws clicked together nervously. From within her new body, Irene Hillman sized up the opposition and began to plot her ascendency.

Alec Wall thought she was the most beautiful thing he had ever seen. Irene was so wild, so free, so noble. He caught the scent of her and became immediately aroused. As his penis grew to massive proportions, he realized that he had lost control, was changing himself. Before he could stay it, his shirtfront ripped with three muffled pops and a whooshing. His watchband tore at the new hairs growing in the few already on his wrist. His Adidas became almost unbearably tight, and an embarrassing whimper escaped his throat.

Joshua glanced at him and smiled. The impatience of the young. Even after all of his rigorous training, show him a female and he was making a fool of himself. Perhaps that was not that bad, though. Gimball grew wistful. How would he, himself, act if the female beside him were Eve Sangellis rather than this slatternly Irene Hillman? Not that Irene would do badly. On the contrary. He could see where she was going to make quite a name for herself in the pack. The dominant female, no doubt. Ms. Hillman would make a fine werewolf, of that there was no doubt. And she could be the dominant female until the very day that Gimball claimed his mate from the swarm and thrust of the humans that surrounded them. Irene Hillman could be number one until he took Evelyn to himself, and then she would have to step down. Or die.

Joshua stroked the fur on Irene's back, stood before the others, and pointed to the pinkish, glistening form that lay on top of the old blanket he had placed on the barn's floor. Beside it sat a bucket glinting in the artificial light.

"It is nearly dawn," he said. "Come. Eat."

Rudy Vardon walked through the chill shadows, staring up occasionally at the waxing moon, whistling halfheartedly for his lost dog. He was trying to follow, to the best of his ability to reconstruct it, the path the animal had taken when he had run off. The trail had led him across yards and fences, skirting gardens and flowerbeds buried beneath brown leaves, to the wild, brown-weeded fields that skirted the base of the mountain. If the dog had gone into those woods, he might never be found. God only knows what lived up in those hills or what it would do to poor Godzilla, alive or dead.

He heard the snap of a twig and froze in terror moments before it lay beneath his feet. He was sweating heavily despite the cool autumn weather, and he wiped his face with his hands.

"Paranoid," he mumbled.

But, didn't he have a right to be paranoid? First there were all those reports of wild dogs—and they were still going on as far as he knew—then those two backpackers disappeared, then John Scott died suddenly like that, then Godzilla disappeared . . . and don't forget that fucking huge canine Peeping Tom. Don't forget that. It wasn't like Charlie Manson or the Hillside Strangler were committing mass murders in these woods or anything, but shit! He knew what Eve would tell him. One man dying of natural causes and a few dogs disappearing—even if you considered those backpackers—did not exactly make for a murder spree or even a crime wave. In fact, she had told him this afternoon when he had castigated her for her lack of imagination (My God, Eve, you're a writer. You're supposed to have an imagination. Hell, you're not even just a writer; you write books for kids, for Christ's sake. That's supposed to take even more imagination. You write fairy tales.), she had told him that, being a writer, she knew that what they had for a plot wouldn't even make a decent horror story.

Well, what the hell do writers know, anyhow?

He walked on, watching the tree line get closer and closer, watching the shadows that capered beneath the pines in case one should disconnect itself from the rest, maybe howl, and spring for his throat. The closer he got to the trees the lower his voice became, until he was taking baby steps and whispering, " 'Zilla, here boy. Come here, baby," with his hands formed around his mouth as if he were screaming his lungs out. He had to either talk himself out of his fear or turn around and go the hell home. He started to turn.

And fell flat on his chest, his nose furrowing up dead leaves before it met more persuasive resistance against the hard-packed soil. It was too sudden to frighten him. He sat up stuttering dried pieces of leaf and branch out of his mouth, turning to look at his feet to see who had reached out to grab him. For just a moment he wondered for the thousandth time why a person will blame the cracks in the sidewalk for tripping him before his own clumsiness, but then he sneezed hard and felt a trickle of moisture run across his upper lip. When he licked it, he found it was blood.

"Shit!"

He stood and dug a red bandanna out of his back pocket, applying it to his nose to try and stop the bleeding. Trying to remember exactly what to do with a bloody nose, he first tilted his head backward, but his throat filled up with blood quickly, so he tried it the other way.

When he lowered his head, spitting blood, he found his dog.

Godzilla lay at his master's feet in the exact spot where he had died the night before—and where they had feasted upon him. All that could be said to remain were various sized tatters of his black fur and his paws. Even the skull had been cracked open by some hellish force, the brain consumed, the eyes, the tongue. The skull had been gnawed clean of meat, then splintered into dust, as had the rest of the skeleton. A few feet away lay his collar, chewed but discarded, intact. It was thick and black and studded like the collars of the cartoon dogs on Saturday morning kiddie shows. Rudy and Eve had gotten it for him when he was still young, when they had learned the only strong emotion that had lurked in his huge black body had been love. They had gotten him as a guard dog and hoped that the collar, along with his deep, playful barking, would make him seem fearsome to people who were unacquainted with him. It had worked rather well, unless you stood your ground long enough for him to reach you, jump on your chest, and begin to lathe you with his tongue. The two of them used to joke that the only way Godzilla would stop a burglary or a mugging was if the criminal had a weak heart. Seeing his two-hundred-pound-plus bulk bearing down on you unsuspectingly was enough of a shock to capitalize on that weakness.

The collar lay mutely in the stiff brown weeds. Rudy bent to pick it up, tears mixing with the blood on his face. This had been his dog's disguise, a scary mask to prevent others from seeing his warm heart. Now that heart was cold and still, and this was the only bit left that recalled him. Rudy sank to his knees and tried to wipe away the mist that blurred his vision. He clenched his teeth, gritting them hard, but the sobs broke through despite his efforts, and he beat impotently on the earth and cried like a child.

The shadows looked on silently.

After forever the tears stopped, but the grief continued. The tears were just the streams and rivers, and he sensed that, long after they had dried up, the fullness of the ocean that was his grief would still be with him. He wiped his eyes and lip and then, not thinking, blew his nose. It started the bleeding again.

"Damn," he whispered, daubing off the new track of blood.

Rudy was calm now, his eyes were clear. Whatever it was that would do this, it had overstepped itself when it had killed his friend.

"You've gone too far, you bastards," he hissed toward the swaying trees, and they rattled bare branches back at him, shook fists of leaves. I sound like a hero on the late show, he mused. Maybe that's why you hear these things so often; because that's really what people say. Then wryly, or maybe that's why people say them; because they've heard them so often. He decided he didn't care. If there were a bunch of wild dogs out there and they had committed this atrocity, then he would learn to hunt and shoot and he would kill every one of them. He would find them and he would kill them, he promised himself. The act was unspeakable; it would be avenged.

Starting now.

He had to find tracks, to track them, to find out where they lived. First he bent over at the waist, bandanna to his nose, and looked for anything that looked like it belonged to a wild dog. Spoor, he thought. I've got to find Spoor. But after a few minutes of searching the ground he saw nothing; no tracks, no dogshit, not a damned thing.

"The fucking streets of New York aren't this clean," he moaned as he straightened his aching back. Well, he sure as hell wasn't any kind of a great woodsman, so he might have missed seeing something, not that he even knew what he was looking for. Damn! John Scott, where are you when I need you? The thought sent a chill down his back. Scott had found a track, hadn't he? And that same night he had turned up dead. Vardon looked down at Godzilla's remains and wondered what the game warden had really died of. Had he ended up like this dog, mangled, pulped, destroyed? Had his body been ripped apart and chewed and swallowed? Did whatever did this know that Rudy Vardon was here, now? Was he watching right now, maybe, ready to fall upon him in the dark and shred his guts for him? Is he?

Is he?

Rudy turned to leave, almost breaking into a panicked run. He did, in fact, shamble a dozen steps before he forced himself to halt. He looked down at the thick leather strap, lined with gleaming studs, that he held clenched in his sweating fist. He let out his breath in one sorrowful moan. Then he turned and walked back to the scene of the slaughter, got down on his hand and knees, and began to look for clues.

Hours later, he had found nothing. He knew he had to get back soon; Evelyn would be waiting up for some word, worrying herself into a breakdown. He got to his feet and brushed the dirt off the knees of his jeans. How could something like this happen? A pack of dogs attack and kill—and eat, for God's sake—an animal the size of Godzilla, an animal who must have put up some kind of struggle to save its own life and not leave a single pawprint? None at all. It was as if the whole area had been swept and raked, policed, like those men the parks hired to walk around with their sticks and pick up all the litter they saw, placing it into their little over-the-shoulder bags. But dogs wouldn't do that. Not even Lassie would do that. So what was going on here, anyway?

"If I'm not being too nosey, Lord," Rudy said, looking to the heavens, "just what the hell is going on here?" He waited for an answer.

He heard them coming.

It was just the smallest of sounds, not more than a scuffling of something through the dried leaves that coated the forest floor. He thought he heard it, then was sure that he hadn't, then heard it again. Just a scuffling, like a squirrel rooting for nuts, but it was past midnight. He never remembered learning if squirrels came out at night, but he didn't think they did. What moved in the woods at night? What was nocturnal? Raccoons, he thought. Possums. What else?

It came again. And again. It came from different parts of the mountain. There was more than one of them, whatever they were. Slowly, as the sounds came again, he started to back away from the trees, his eyes scanning the shadows for any movement. The darkness was pooled like motor oil around the slightly lighter trunks of the trees, and there were still enough leaves on the branches to create illusions in the wind. Had something moved there? He couldn't be sure. The hair rose on the nape of his neck and he broke out into gooseflesh. There was a sudden comotion to his left and a shadow separated itself from the rest, bounding out of the woods in graceful leaps. Rudy braced himself to run, trembling as he saw the creature running away from him, waiting for it to turn toward him and attack. Then he saw the bobbing rack and caught a glimpse of flashing whitetail in the moonlight. A deer.

The air in his lungs whooshed out of him in a rush. His head spun and his leg wobbled crazily. Feeling like he had aged fifty years, Rudy kneeled on the ground, lowered his head, and tried to pull himself together.

The howl, long and mournful, drifted down from the top of the mountain like a bird of prey, gripping his unsuspecting heart in talons of ice. His head snapped up and he looked far up into the forest. So that's where you are, he thought. That's where you are.

Then the answering howls came; first one, then another, then many. They did not come from the top of the mountain. These howls came from creatures that had spread silently along the edge of the forest in search of their prey, spooking a slumbering white-tailed buck as they came. They came from the stalkers of Rudy Vardon, who sensed that he was unaware, caught in an unguarded moment, and who howled in answer, in triumph, in jest.

Vardon was up and running before the first low shadow broke from the trees to pursue him. He ran with a speed fueled by pure terror. There was no need for thought; the intellect was shunted aside as a deeper, older portion of the mind took over. It was the part that was responsible for our escape from pterodactyls and saber-toothed tigers thousands of years ago, and it had done its job quite well enough then, thank you. To it, the logical, rational portion of the brain was an upstart that would rather think about acting than act, that would lose the moment weighing the alternatives. It knows there are no alternatives to a dead man. Some religions would have you spend years cultivating its favors but, for most of us, mortal danger brings it to the fore. Under its influence, Rudy Vardon ran as he had never run before.

He could hear their panting as he reached the first street. When the headlights hit him he almost froze like a spotlighted deer, but instead he doubled his efforts. The slapping of his feet against the asphalt was drowned out by the squealing of tires behind him as the driver of the approaching vehicle slammed on his brakes. The car turned sideways in the road, slamming broadside into two of the pursuing beasts. The creatures were not hurt, rolling to their feet and disappearing back into the field before the driver could regain his senses. As he looked through his windshield, badly shaken and confused, he saw a man clamber quickly over a high wooden fence and disappear from view, followed soon after by something that looked like an enormous dog, which took the obstacle in one vaulting leap. Shaking his head, the man left his car and walked to the passenger side, where he ran his hand over his badly stoved-in door and rear quarter panel.

"Be a son of a bitch," he said, spitting blood from his split lip onto the damp asphalt.

He walked to the rear of the car and bent the fender away from the tire, then walked around to the driver's side, shaking his head mournfully, and got in. Even as he started the engine he was thinking about how he was going to explain *this* one—it being the third company car he had wrecked in fifteen months—when he got to Pittsburgh. Throwing the car roughly into drive, he pulled away.

As Rudy threw himself against his backyard gate, he could hear his pursuer's claws scrabbling for purchase as it rounded the corner twenty-five yards down the street. He fought the latch for a second but it wouldn't open, yanked harder but still without effect. Rudy thought for an instant of climbing the fence, but the panting of the creature behind him let him know there wasn't enough time. He fumbled with the latch again and again, yanked on it with all his strength, and then, punching it in futile rage, found he had been opening it the wrong way. There was no time for embarrassment. He rushed through, slamming it behind him, hoping to slow the beast. But as he ran for his back door, he knew that the creature had jumped over, could hear its claws gouging the wood as it pulled itself up.

He thought, Oh, my God, if Eve's locked the door . . .

As he grabbed the brass knob there was a soft thud behind him; the creature was in the yard. He collected himself and turned the cold lump of metal, pushing inward frantically as he did and rushing into his own kitchen. Rudy thrust the door shut behind him, heard the lock click into place, and felt, just a second after, the door shudder violently in the frame as the creature threw itself headlong into it, but too late.

Look, he screamed at himself. See it.

He rushed to the window above the sink, looked out, but saw only a thick grey tail waving above his fence as it sunk below his line of sight. The neighbor's back lights were on and someone was saying, "My God, Aaron, did you see that? What was that?" Aaron answered, "I don't know, Mary, just get my damned rifle and shut the hell up."

From the living room, Eve asked in a worried voice, "Rudy, is that you? Rudy? Alright, I've got a gun, now who the hell's out there?"

Rudy tried to laugh, then tried to answer, but his

172

throat ached terribly, and he realized he had been
screaming for blocks. His head spun and everything
got so far away. And that was fine with him as long
as THEY were far away too, so far away . . .

When Eve finally got up the courage to enter the
kitchen, brandishing a Stanley hammer she had
found in a closet, she discovered her boyfriend
sprawled in front of the kitchen door, a small red
puddle spreading from under his nose and a thick
studded dog collar in his hand.

Chapter 5

Working as a plumber had its bad moments, Ben Griswold reflected, but when he finally got here to his cabin in autumn, it all was worth it. He and Lynn finished pulling the dead tree Ben had felled off their property into the woods, dropping it among the other boughs and branches and twigs that the two of them, with a little help from their children, had cleaned off of their property so far today. They walked back toward the hunting cabin hand in hand, as comfortable with the silence and with each other as they had been for the past seventeen years. There had been rough times, sure: at first, when the jobs were scarce and the money scarcer and they were trying to support their oldest son, Wade; then, later, with the arrival of the twins, David and Margarette. But they had both adjusted. Like some of the kids were saying now, they had learned to cope, and now life flowed along nicely for all five of them. Ben thought there was a lot to say about describing life as seasons; he could see it from spending so much time in the woods. The twins were one season, spring. They were young, like the first sprouts in the garden or the first

174

leaves of grass poking up through last winter's cloak of decaying leaves; tender things, easily hurt, but amazingly resilient at the same time.

Wade would soon be growing into the summer of his life. At sixteen, he was tall and strapping, much as Ben had been himself. He wore his hair a little long for Ben's taste, but his father knew that was the style nowadays and didn't think it really hurt, anyway. Where it really counted, in the heart and in the soul, his oldest son would soon be a man, and Ben was pleased and proud. His body was strong, though not as resilient as the twins'. Wade could use the intelligence that he had strived so hard to develop to avoid being broken by the gusting winds of misfortune. Yes, it was early summer for Wade Griswold, but he wouldn't really worry about it for quite a few years.

Ben and Lynn sat silently on the porch in the twilight, he throwing his arm lovingly across her shoulders, and she smiling and scrunching in closer to him, looping both arms around his waist. He regarded his wife tenderly for a moment before looking off across at the slopes that surrounded them, the trees that colored them in various stages of nudity. Some already stood naked against the oncoming winter, while others were fleshed with leaves of the brightest yellows and reds, the last arboreal vanity before the long silence of winter. They're dressed in their finest for their going-away party, Ben thought, and squeezed his wife tightly.

Ben and Lynn were in the summer of their lives, the late summer for himself, Ben thought. At thirty-seven, he was a full three years older than his wife, and though the gulf in numbers seemed barely mentionable, the gulf in actual time seemed to be staring him in the face at every turn lately. She was starting to appear so damned young to him. When people eyed her appreciatively as they walked together downtown, then looked at him as if to say, "I wonder what he's got," Ben had to admit that he felt real good. God, but when he looked at her as she slept at night or when they made love or sometimes when he'd just surprise her and she'd turn to him not yet realizing she wasn't alone—at these times she looked so very very young and he wanted only to protect her and always keep her from harm. He grinned wryly at his foolishness, and when Lynn turned her head to look up at him, he kissed her softly. She knew he was in one of his philosophizing moods; she would say nothing until he did, respecting his need for silence.

The kids. Ben could hear the kids arguing around back. If you were going to have kids, it was best to have them early. That way you didn't get wild with that taste for freedom and doing. You couldn't just take off if you were a working parent; you couldn't just up and go here or there without first getting babysitters, arranging for this and that. It all got really complicated, as well as expensive. So, better to have your kids young, help them to grow into themselves, and do your roving after they've left. You don't have to be a young man to enjoy, after all.

And he wasn't young, though maybe Lynn still was. He was entering the autumn of his life, with his hair starting to turn like the trees—and fall off, too—and his joints getting stiffer and the body he had always taken such pride in starting to wither, just a little, around the edges. The autumn, and the Lord had been good to him. He had spread his seed and had lived long enough to see it take and sprout and grow into strong young ones. Soon winter, but he didn't know what that was yet. Was it when your hair turned white, like your head was covered with snow? Was it when you died and they placed your rotting husk so reverently in the ground, acting like it made you special and not the other way around? Sitting on the cabin's porch, with his arm tightly around his beloved wife, Ben Griswold had to shake his head and admit he didn't know. But he knew he'd find out, given time. Everyone does.

He kissed his wife softly on top of her head. "Look at that," he said, pointing across the tops of the mountains to the far horizon. The sky was clear, and it was one of those evenings when you could see the moon rising ghostly in the sky before full dark. It was waning now, but Ben could tell that there was more than enough of it to make a brilliantly moonlit night if no storms moved in.

Lynn nodded, sighed, hugged him tight, briefly. "It's beautiful, isn't it, Ben?"

"Yeah. It sure is."

The children's voices drifted around the corner of the cabin and over the roof, starting low and then rising to a crescendo as each tried to outshout the others and get control of the conversation for himself.

"Jesus," Ben murmured. "Those kids'll scare away all the wildlife for thirty miles."

"Sounds like they're having a disagreement, doesn't it?"

"Disagreement? Sounds like they're having a riot back there." He rose stiffly, pulling reluctantly from Lynn's arms. "Guess I'll go back and find out what's going on. I wanted to take Wade out and see if we can spot anything before it gets completely dark, anyway."

"Okay," Lynn said, stretching languorously. "I'll keep the other two busy out here finishing up the yard, then I'll go in at dark and start fixing a late supper. You want anything special?"

"Naw, anything'll be fine, hon. Surprise me." He disappeared around the corner for a second, then stuck his head back around and added, "Just make a lot of it. I'm hungry."

"You've been hungry a lot lately, Mr. Griswold," she quipped, patting her stomach.

"It shows, huh?"

" 'Fraid so, sweetheart."

"Humph," Ben responded, ducking back around the corner out of her sight. Time to break out the old jogging shoes and sweat suit, Griswold grimaced as he walked toward his children, who were presently engaged in a dried leaf battle. "Hey," he shouted. "You guys are supposed to be cleaning that up, not spreading it around again."

Wade looked at his father with a mixture of pride and embarrassment. Pop was only a father, after all, but he guessed the old man was a lot better than some others that he had seen, even if he was a little rednecked about some things. He wanted his father to be proud of him as a man—Cheryl said he was *all* man—or even as a friend. And now his little brat brother and his little snot sister had conned him into

178

this leaf fight and he had been caught, acting as if he were six years old instead of sixteen. He looked at his father with chagrin.

"I was just telling them that they'd better start cleaning this mess up, Dad."

"Oh?" Ben said with a poker face.

"Wasn't not!" David piped up indignantly, soon joined by the other twin Margarette, who poked her brother and said," It's *was not*, stupid," before joining his call. "Was not, was not, was not . . ."

"Can it!" Ben screamed to be heard over the ruckus, and the noise stopped immediately. Both of the twins suddenly found something very interesting on the toes of their shoes. "Now look, you two," he continued. "Wade and I are going to take a walk in the woods for a while. I want both of you to help your mom finish cleaning up the yard. You stay around the cabin, do what she tells you to do, and be good, okay?"

Wade, learning about his impending escape from his brother and sister for the first time, cast his father a glance that conveyed both thanks and relief. He loved the two of them dearly, but there is just as real a generation gap between a sixteen-year-old and his six-year-old siblings as there is between a thirty-seven-year-old and his sixteen-year-old son.

"If that's alright with you, Wade?" his dad asked.

"Oh, you know it's fine with me," Wade answered lightly, but he was already trying to edge his father away.

With a final admonition to the twins to behave, Ben and Wade moved around past the front of the cabin, giving Lynn a fond wave and promising to be

179

back shortly, and traipsed into the woods. Ben picked up his binoculars from the tree stump where he had left them this afternoon, and they walked deeper, trying desperately not to sound like a parade as they crunched their way under the boughs of partially denuded oaks, picking up the pace a little in the softness of the spongy floor of a pine stand. There were enough signs to indicate to both of them that the venison was as good as in the freezer this year, so they stopped just before dusk to sit on a promontory of rock that overlooked the deep creases between the upraised mountains surrounding them. The view was breathtaking. The two of them sat, in the way fathers and sons do, talking about the small, unimportant things in each other's lives directly and circling around the big things, coming close enough that a piece of the problem might be knocked off here and there, making it smaller, more manageable. It was the kind of stumbling, faltering, groping, falsely light banter that leaves the participants with a surface feeling of affection and closeness, and a deep knowledge of separateness; a certainly that they will always be strangers to one another. Only when much older does one realize that this is the human condition.

Ben leaned back on his rock seat, lighting one of the few cigarettes he permitted himself, and stared off into the sky at the deepening dusk. Out here he knew an inkling of the vastness of life; that it contained answers he would never want to know and questions he would never think to ask.

Wade, too, was silent, looking to the far horizon as the reds faded to violet and purple. Birds appeared as black specks winging their way to their roosts in trees and caves, some calling noisily to one another in flight, some moving in total silence. The young man drank the solitude in like a draught of peace itself, thinking that the old mountain men must have had very little need for alcohol or drugs or even religion, for that matter. The thought stunned him slightly, and as he ran it over and over in his mind, wondering why he would dare to think such heresy, he heard the noises.

They were faint, carried to his ears by the day's dying breezes, but Wade could tell the sounds were made by people and, although he found such a thing a little hard to believe up here, apparently by people who were having a real good time. A party, maybe. But they were miles into the boondocks, and it was a trifle damned cold to be running around outside at a barbecue or something. He listened closer and could hear the lower range voices of men counterpointing the alto and soprano of women. It sounded like they were singing or laughing. Has to be laughing, he though. Can't hear any music. But where the hell were they, anyway? He looked over at his dad, but he was lost in the maze of his own thoughts, his cigarette a long grey ash that broke off under its own weight and fell away, down the steep drop to the floor of the forest. Wade followed the ember reflexively, bending over the slight overhang and watching it until it disappeared in the low-lying gloom and mist. He sighed, realizing it was getting dark and that the two of them would soon be heading home, hoping that whoever was partying out here had nice warm sleeping bags because it was going to get cold. . . .

And as he righted himself, he saw them.

They were in a clearing, surrounded by mostly naked oak trees, low down on the slope across from where he and his father sat. It was pure luck that he saw them at all, luck and the time of the year. In spring or summer or even the early fall, their clearing would have been completely camouflaged by the surrounding woods. The teenager leaned far forward, straining his eyes to make out just what they were doing. Were they dancing around in a circle? It sure looked like it, but who danced around in a circle other than little kids? Hell, punk rockers didn't even dance around in one big circle, and punk rockers did some really weird shit! He leaned forward some more and saw that every one of the dancers was naked as the day he was born. Oh my God! Wade recoiled. A nudist colony!

The boy reached over and grabbed his father's arm, shaking him abruptly, gasping, "Holy SHIT!"

Ben, shaken out of his reverie and almost off his perch, heard his son's pronouncement with a little bit of awe. All kids swore, he assumed, remembering when it had been a very macho thing to do in his own early years, but the least the boy could do was cool it around his own parents, for God's sake. He started, "Wade, you know I don't like . . ." but saw the rapt look on the boy's face and stopped, puzzled. There was surprise written there and awe and just a trace of something else . . . lust, he realized at last. This, more than the continued worrying of his arm, made him understand that something out of the ordinary was going on here. He reached out and gripped his son's shoulder to stop the shaking, turning him slightly as he did but noticing that the boy's head and eyes never budged an inch, and saying, "Wade, what's the matter? What do you see?"

Wade extended a long arm in front of his face, pointing to the spectacle in progress across from them. "Dad, check this out. There's a bunch of nudists down there dancing around in a circle like a bunch of kids. Really. Look at 'em, Dad, just look at 'em."

Griswold looked along his son's extended arm, sighting as he would down the barrel of his deer rifle, searched for a few minutes, and there they were. The boy was right. A bunch of people, naked as hell, dancing around in a circle in a clearing in the middle of the mountains. His face went slack and he gasped, "Holy SHIT!"

"Dad, the binoculars." Wade punched his shoulder playfully to get his attention.

Ben said, "Huh?"

"The binoculars, Dad. Use the binoculars." The boy pointed at the Zeiss binoculars hanging around his father's neck and grinned devilishly. He bet a lot of this story would be left out when they told Mom—if they told her at all.

"The binoculars?" Ben asked, looking to where Wade's finger pointed. Then a sheepish grin crossed his face and he said, "Oh, yeah. The binoculars." As he raised them to his eyes the boy tried to snatch them out of his grasp, but he was quicker and chuckled, "Me first."

"Why? Just cause you're older, right?"

"Right. There might be something down there that would warp your virgin mind. I'll risk mine first, just to keep you safe from harm. Besides which"—it was Ben's turn to flash a wicked grin—"I got the binoculars. It's nine-tenths of the law, you know." The man busied himself adjusting the focus, cutting it down finer and finer.

"Yeah," Wade said disgustedly. "Nine-tenths. Nine-tenths my . . ."

"Wade!"

". . . elbow."

Then the focus, the resolution, everything fell into place as if by magic, and Ben could see these nudists as if he were standing ten feet away. For a second he marveled at the excellence of the small bit of technology that he held in his hands. Perhaps the twentieth century had few heroes, fewer dragons, and even less magic. Progress had displaced the old rites, but it had brought a magic of its own; not so romantic, perhaps, but just as useful. Then he comprehended what he saw, and all thoughts of the death of ancient myth and spells and monsters were burned from his mind like a morning mist. Unless he was dreaming, unless he was tripping, unless he was crazy, he was looking at—

Ben lowered the binoculars and rubbed his hand across his eyes hard, trying to scrub away this illusion. Wade made a grab for them, yelling, "My turn!" playfully, but Ben tore them from his young hand with surprising violence and bellowed, "NO!"

The mountains answered nonononono . . .

And Ben heard the echo as it rebounded from slope to slope to slope and back again. In his head he screamed STOP IT, PLEASE, STOP IT! but the mountain paid no heed. Quickly he raised the binoculars again and stared down into the clearing, fully knowing his mistake, hoping desperately he could cover it. There was a large man down in the clearing, tall, wide-shouldered, broad-chested. The way he stood spoke of command carried easily; Ben had seen it before in Viet Nam, where he had served in the Green Beret "advisory" unit from 1963-1964. The man looked carved out of wood or rock—a sculpted god, an icon. His hair was so blond it was almost white, and he turned and looked directly at Ben Griswold through the opposite end of his binoculars. Ben whimpered, "Ohmygod, no. He can't see us. He can't." But he knew that he could.

Griswold looked again. He saw the man point a finger directly at them. Quickly he scanned the others in the clearing and saw that they were looking, too. He wondered if Wade could hear his heart pounding through his Woolrich hunting coat. He wondered if that naked man could.

As he spread his attention over the group of them, Ben saw something else. He saw some of these "nudists" dropping to their hands and knees and rolling in the leaves. He saw them get darker and darker until he realized what he saw was hair growing on their bodies. Fur. He saw them changing, and then he saw them coming.

As he jumped up from the seat and ran back through the trees toward the cabin, pulling Wade roughly along behind him, ignoring the boy's worried queries of, "Dad, what is it? What's the matter Dad?" he heard them howling. As Ben Griswold ran, dragging his son behind him, he started to pray. Wade Griswold heard this and the boy, who had

185

never before heard his father pray, who thought religion was for women and kids and weirdos, hearing his father calling on his God thought that he had never heard a more terrifying sound in his life than that. The fear overtook him then and swept him away, and he had soon outdistanced his father by yards as the two of them raced madly toward the cabin.

Lynn stopped raking when she heard the dog howl and pushed a tuft of her mousey brown hair up under the bandanna she wore over her head. Margarette and David worked along with her as best they could, picking up far more sticks and pieces of broken branch than they could possibly carry and dropping most of them on the way to the trash pile. It occurred to her that a mother can only use so much help, no matter how well-intentioned, and she had just turned to order the six-year-olds into the cabin to wash up for supper when she heard an oncoming clamor in the trees. Shaking her head at the childishness of grown men and the mannishness of young boys— racing each other home, no doubt; how terribly macho, how positively tribal—she returned to her raking, deciding to leave the children play until Daddy and Wade arrived.

Wade broke into the small clearing they called their front yard first, his breath coming in asthmatic gasps. Lynn smiled when she saw him pounding out of the murkiness under the trees, frowned when she heard his stentorian breathing, and saw him trip and roll six feet over the ground. When she saw the bottomless terror reflected in his eyes and the slackness of his face, her blood froze. She ran to him as he tried madly to scramble to his feet, pulling him up and enfolding him in her arms. Wade, in turn, clung to her so tightly that she thought he might break her ribs, but she held him, crooning, feeling him tremble like a small, terrified bird in her grip. Then she thought, My God, where's Ben? Something's happened to Ben!

She pushed her son away hard, shaking him, panic seeping into her voice. "Wade, what is it? Is it your father, is he hurt? Wade? Wade. What is it? WADE, WHAT THE HELL HAPPENED?"

Hearing his mother scream and swear snapped the boy out of the dementia, brought on not so much by fear as by the uncertainty of not knowing just what was to be feared. "I—I don't know," he stammered. "Dad just looked at those nudists, and then he screamed and jumped up and . . ."

"Nudists?"

". . . and he grabbed me and started running. He was running and—and he was praying." He grabbed Lynn hard and pulled her to him. He was crying. "He started praying, Mom, and I just got so scared. Jesus, Mom, I got so SCARED . . ."

Lynn stroked his head, feeling his tears soaking into the shoulder of her flannel shirt. "It's alright, honey. It's okay now. But where's your dad, Wade? Where's—?" She felt a pull on her pant's leg and started, gasping. Then she looked down into David's curious face.

"Why's Wade acting like a baby?" the child asked. "Where's Daddy?"

"Wade isn't acting like a baby, David. He's crying.

187

Big people can cry too."

"I'm not big, Mommy. I'm little. When I cry you tell me to act like a big boy and stop."

"David . . ." But he was gone like a horse out of the starting gate, smiling ear to ear, yelling, "Daddy, Daddy!"

If the sight of her son stumbling out of the woods had frozen the blood in her veins, the sight of her husband dried it up. He was cut and begrimed from falling and running into the lower branches of trees. There was a tear almost three inches long in the sleeve of his red and black checked hunting coat, and both the knees of his jeans were ripped out. His cap was gone, and his sweat-soaked hair hung lankly in his eyes as he staggered toward her across the clearing. He looked like a man on the verge of a stroke or a heart attack, with his pale face and deep-set, shadow-rimmed eyes. He looks like a man who's seen death, Lynn thought. Maybe his own. Or a man that's gotten a look into hell.

David stopped dead in his tracks, took one look, and started walking backward toward his mother.

When Ben reached his wife he fell to his knees, his head sagging forward until his chin bounced off his chest. He was drawing in huge, ragged lungfuls of air that sounded as if they hurt him badly, but a few seconds later he struggled to his feet and looked into Lynn's worried face. "Into . . . the . . . house," he managed, making her trip over David who had hidden between her legs and was starting to cry silently.

"Ben, what—"

188

"Into . . . the . . . HOUSE!" her husband commanded, shoving her again, more roughly than before.

"Ben, DAMMIT! What is the matter with you?"

The weary man took the child from between his wife's legs and shoved him against her chest. "GO!" he commanded. "NOW!"

He turned and walked away from the retreating forms of his angry, confused wife and his crying child to his oldest son, placing an arm heavily across the boy's shoulders. "Not as young . . . as I used . . . to be," he confided with effort.

"Dad," Wade pleaded, "what was the matter back there? Why did you act like that?"

Griswold wiped a hand down his face to squeegee off some of the sweat. "You'll see," he promised. "Too soon." He started to walk toward the cabin hurriedly, his breathing slower and less painful. He motioned to Wade to walk beside him. "I want you to make sure your mother, brother, and sister are all locked up tight in this cabin. You too. Take the .308 and load it, keep some extra shells handy. If anything comes in that cabin that isn't me, blow it away. Do you understand me, son? Blow the fucker away!"

Wade shuddered. "Sure, Dad, I understand but, Christ, what's going on? What am I supposed to shoot? Where'll you be?"

"I'm going to take the Winchester .30-.30 and the Ruger .44 and get on the roof by the chimney. I'll have a good field of fire from up there. We'll be shooting . . . I don't know, Wade. Monsters. We'll be shooting monsters."

Wade stared at the man in front of him. This man

189

had raised him. This man had brought him up and sent him to school and bought his food and clothing for sixteen years. He didn't exactly trust this man, it went deeper than that. He felt he *knew* him and that he cared. And now his father was crazy. Wade looked at Ben Griswold closely. No, no, he's not crazy. He turned to do as he was told. But, Christ, I wish he were.

They both heard Lynn holler crossly, "David Wayne Griswold, you better come here this instant!"

A small form shot between their legs as they walked over the threshold, shouting, "Catch me, catch me, betcha can't catch me," in a singsong voice that diminished startlingly as the child got farther from the cabin and closer to the trees. Just when he hit the first pine David stopped. He had orders not to go into the woods alone and he knew it was a law. But no one seemed to want to play and he did, and he had to figure how to get somebody to chase him. But when he looked back he smiled broadly, because Daddy was coming. Daddy would play with him even when the others were too tired, and he was coming to play with him now.

"Bring the guns," Ben ordered over his shoulder as he started walking briskly across the clearing. He heard Wade hop behind him and was proud of his son once again. Whatever they were, those beasts, those monsters, would not get his family. He would kill them all if he had to, kill them with his bare hands. For a moment he doubted, wondering if he could still do it. He had done it in Nam, not liking it but doing it well because he believed in his cause.

Now he wasn't too sure about the good he had done in Viet Nam, but he had a new cause that was probably the oldest of man's causes—his family's survival. He saw David standing near the tree line holding his groin. For a moment he was tempted to ask if the boy had to pee or to tell him not to put his hands there, that it wasn't nice. But he thought he saw a tree move or a shadow float across an open space like a cloud, and the thought died like autumn leaves and fell into his subconscious. He increased his pace. He had to hurry, grab the boy, get him back to the safety of the cabin, button it up. Hurry, man, those things are getting closer all the time. Halfway there.

"Dad!"

Something touched him lightly from behind and he dropped and spun around, fists clenched, prepared to strike.

It was Wade with the rifles.

"Dad?" The boy drew back, afraid, until Ben relaxed his fists and stood straight. This was a new father, one he had never seen before. He couldn't say yet if he liked him or not. "I brought the rifles." He handed Ben the .30-.30 and dug a box of shells out of his hip pocket. "Here's some shells, and the rifle's already loaded, but I couldn't find room for the Magnum, Dad. Sorry."

Ben worked the lever on the Winchester to get the shell into the chamber. "That's okay, son. Now go back in with your mom and sister while I get David." The boy nodded and smiled good luck and love, and Griswold was just turning away from him when he heard two things that deadened his heart.

191

Lynn, standing in the open doorway of the cabin, screamed.

Something behind him, something near the edge of the clearing, roared.

Something monstrous, something hairy and monstrous beyond Ben Griswold's wildest imaginings, had stepped from the forest not ten feet from where David stood. The child stared at it, petrified and quaking, easy prey. An easy kill. The boy whispered, "Daddy?"

When Lynn screamed her disgust and terror to the stars the thing turned toward her for just a moment, roaring its challenge. Ben could feel his muscles stiffening, his joints locking with paralysis as his brain fought to shut out this abomination. But he screamed at himself, "NOT NOW, NOT NOW!" and raised the rifle to his shoulder, squeezing off a shot that raised dust on the creature's pelted chest, knocking it backward into the bushes and out of sight. He took a step toward David, who was running toward him now as fast as his small feet could carry him. The child seemed to be fairly skimming over the ground, screaming, "Daddydaddydaddy," when another shape, thin and grey, seemed to appear out of thin air beside the six-year-old. Even as Ben raised his rifle to fire, it grabbed the child around the back of the neck with its jaws, just as a dog grabs a cat or a cat a mouse, and shook the small form viciously. The cracking report of the Winchester came too late to disguise the pop of the small boy's neck.

The first bullet hit the grey thing low on the side and staggered it, but did not put it down. Screaming in pain and rage, the father charged toward it, firing again and yet again, both shots hitting the creature high on the back between the shoulder blades as it dragged its prey toward the cover of the trees, the third shot finally making it pitch forward on to its chest and face. But before Ben could fire again the creature was gone, crawling on all fours into the shadows with its victim hanging grotesquely by its tiny neck from between the beast's slavering jaws. Wade was wretching loudly somewhere behind him. He could hear a popping and tearing but refused to think what it might be. Ben Griswold thought, Oh God. Oh dear God, they've taken my boy. My baby boy. Somewhere within him a door closed with a muffled click. It had taken him years to open that door after Nam, years and love and Lynn. No matter what happened to him now, he knew deep inside the door had closed this time for keeps. Suddenly, he felt very cold. It was all a dream. A dream.

Turning. Reloading the rifle on the run, no time to stop. There were more of them, many more. Grabbing the boy and pulling him up, slamming the rifle into his chest, screaming at him to run for the cabin. Lynn, in the door crying, telling her to get in the cabin, in the cabin. Turning back to the woods to provide cover, but nobody home. Why? There were so many more of these animals, these things. Turning again, toward the cabin this time. The boy running ahead, fast, wary. I know. I know what it is, son. I know. But the boy's stopping, turning, firing. Firing. Firing. Oh my God. Oh my GOD. Outflanked. We've been outflanked.

Wade heard the low growling as he ran all out, pinning all his hopes, his life, on reaching the cabin door. But something growled like a street rod with glass packs, and he turned to see them loping easily toward him along the side of the building. He put the .308 to his shoulder and fired just like his father had taught him. Aim, breathe, squeeze. Aim, breathe, squeeze. Five rounds, all raising dust from their hairy bodies, all causing gouts of blood and gore to spray from their chests and stomachs and shoulders, all good hits. But they wouldn't die. They would stumble and stagger and fall; but then they'd get back up and come at him again, panting and growling like dogs. The boy squeezed off shot after shot until the rifle was empty. There was no time to reload. The last thoughts he had were tied intimately to emotions, but they were simple enough: He felt disappointment that he had let his family, and especially his father, down and thought, God, Dad, I'm sorry. I'm so sorry. Then he felt in awe of these creatures, understanding the meaning of the word "awful" as it was meant to be, and thought at the last, What *are* these things? At that, they took him.

Ben ran forward desperately, watching his son fire, firing himself. He didn't wonder about the nature of these creatures that were murdering his family. He wanted only to kill them, to tear them, to rend their bodies apart piece by piece and make them feel a small part of the pain that gouged at his very soul. He watched his son fire and he watched him fall, and he was proud even then as he thought what a fine man the boy could have been, what an outstanding boy he had been. If only he could have grown up, gotten old enough that they could have become friends. But that could no longer be.

It could no longer be because the creatures had hit Wade like the front line of the Philadelphia Eagles, three of them, maybe four, and driven him to the ground not fifteen feet from the cabin door. Before the body had hit the throat had been torn out by the first beast to take him, gobbling it down greedily as the young man's blood fountained over its head. The others contented themselves with wrenching off arms and legs and disemboweling the corpse to get at the preferred organ meat. The largest of the creatures, a mangy, overweight animal, was trying desperately to crush the skull and get at the brain. Griswold felt the gorge hot and sour in his throat. The rifle was reloaded. He stopped and raised it to his shoulder, the feasting beasts ignoring him totally. He would try a head shot or two. All he wanted was to kill one, just one, before they pulled him down. Just one dead . . . THING, to make up for the loss of his past and his future, and the hideous befouling of his present. He started to squeeze the trigger slowly, exhaling calmly, sighting on the ugly head of the big bastard that had mutilated his son. He looked around briefly to assure that nothing would get him from behind or from the sides before he got his shot, and that's when he noticed his wife standing just inside the still-open cabin door, hands hanging limply at her sides. Her eyes were wide and unfocused, in shock. Behind her on the cabin floor lay Margarette, balled into the fetal position, eyes tightly closed.

"Dammit, Lynn," the man hissed. "Damn."

He carried the rifle at high port as he ran around the things clawing around Wade's remains. They seemed to take no notice of him at all. He reached the door and grabbed his wife roughly, shaking her until her head was bouncing front and back like a metronome, whispering her name over and over and glancing always over his shoulder. When she failed to respond, Ben slapped her hard with the back of his hand, feeling the sting of the nerves as he realized that this was the first time he had ever hit her. The pain seemed to call her back. She said nothing, but her eyes cleared and stared into his. "Get in there and shut everything you can. Lock everything. Don't come out no matter what, not even for me." Her eyes lost focus and he shook her again. "Dammit, woman, listen to me! You can't do this to me! Load the shotgun with buckshot. Don't let them . . . don't let them take my daughter." He was crying, but he heard the low snarl behind him, caught a blur of movement off to his right. Desperately he shoved Lynn back inside as hard as he could and slammed shut the door. An instant later he heard the inside bolt ram home.

He had his back against the door now; there would be no sneak attacks. If he could only get himself enough time to climb on to the roof he might still have a chance.

One of the creatures, thin and wiry with chocolate brown fur, raised up on its hind legs from beside the corpse and started to stalk him. The thing's mouth was flecked with blood and bits of flesh, and fresh tears rolled down Ben's face when he realized that was Wade, little bits of Wade around those black lips and clinging to its wiry facial hair. He snapped the Winchester up and fired, but the thing dodged adroitly. As he was levering another round into the chamber he only caught a glimpse of the silver-blond rocket that flew at his head from the blind side, catching it in great yawning jaws and tearing it from the shoulders with a single flex of its thickly furred neck.

Inside the cabin, Lynn Griswold rushed around madly, shuttering and locking windows, bolting the back door. The house, once a fortress against the "wilds," seemed almost frail now. Would it keep them out? They had killed David and Wade, and she hadn't heard her husband out there for a long time. Oh God, was he dead too?

Me? Just me? What can I do? What can I do alone?

Save Margarette, Ben had said. The shotgun. Buckshot.

Lynn walked to the gun cabinet and pulled out the twelve-gauge over-and-under. Then she rummaged through the drawers until she found the right load shells, broke the gun open, and stuck two in the chambers. Two shots. Only two. How could she save her little girl with only two shots? She collapsed on the couch and started to sob. If only she could grow wings and fly her away from here, take her high up and far away from this nightmare. Then she grinned in triumph: the crawl space.

There was no basement in the cabin, no attic, and only one real closet, but there was a crawl space that you entered from that closet in which they had put whatever small things would fit. Neither one of the adults would fit through the opening, so the job had gone to Wade until he grew too large. Then the responsibility had passed on to the twins. They loved the place. It was secret and quiet and just their size. They had played there all the time. Now she would put Margarette there for a more serious reason, to try to save her life.

Crooning to her gently, Lynn picked her daughter off the floor and rocked the child in her arms for a few precious moments to try to reassure her. She would have liked to have brought her fully back into reality gently, lovingly, but the increasing frequency of grunts and growls outside convinced her that there was very little time. Instead she carried the child to the closet and, holding her with one arm, unblocked the opening.

"Margarette," she explained, "I'm going to put you up in your special place, and I want you to be very, very quiet. If you are, the bad things outside will all go away after a while and you can come down again and not be afraid, okay? Will you go up there now and stay very quiet for me, honey, for as long as you can?"

"Say please," the child whispered, looking up at her timidly.

Lynn hugged the girl to her breast. "Please," she sobbed.

Something thudded against the door.

"Will David come up, too?"

"No," Lynn whispered harshly, hurrying to lift her up, to hide her away. "David is . . . with Daddy and Wade." The tears trickled down her cheeks. She had cried so much today. So much. How many tears can one person shed before she goes dry? Just dries up and blows away like so much dust. She tucked the child into the opening and started to replace the cover. "David and Wade and Daddy are together now," she choked through the sobs that make her chest heave.

"Don't be sad, Mommy. Daddy won't be mad if we go see him then. And Wade won't either. David might," Margarette flipped her hand haughtily, "but he's just a kid."

"Yes, yes, you're right," her mother breathed. She could hear them clawing at the door, tearing it to pieces. "Now you put this over the hole and be quiet and don't come down for a long, long time. Not even if you hear scary noises. You just stay up there and be quiet and those bad things won't get you, okay?"

"Okay, Mommy." The child slid the cover over three quarters of the hole. Then her voice came from behind it. "Mommy?"

"Yes. sweetheart?" Hurry, please hurry.

"What if I have to go pee?"

Oh God! Lynn fought back the hysterical laughter that was building in her throat. "If you have to pee or poo, you do it right up there on the floor in the corner. Don't come down here for that."

"Really?" the child asked. She was plainly shocked.

"Really."

"Well," she said, still disbelieving, "okay." The cover slid over the whole way.

There was an ominous tearing from the front door, then a resounding crack, like a gunshot.

"Margarette," Lynn whispered dryly as she moved to the closet door.

"Yes, Mommy?" came the faint reply.

"I love you."

199

"Love you, too," Margarette responded in her best cloak-and-dagger voice, but Lynn didn't hear it. The closet door was tightly shut, and the woman who had shut it was drying her tears as she walked steadily to the living room, to the twelve-gauge, and to her death.

One final stroke applied to the already shattered door and it split into tinder and fell. At first nothing came, then something did, and it was hideous.

Lynn backed away from it as it advanced stealthily across the wooden floor, claws ticking and scraping. It was not a man and not a dog, but it looked like the worst of both thrown together willy-nilly by some madman. It walked on two feet unsteadily, hunched slightly forward, taloned hands flexing hungrily. It panted, doglike, and spittle flowed from behind its massive yellow teeth, across its rubbery mottled lips, and down its wire-haired chin. The stench of it made her gag until the hysteria nearly claimed her again and she started to giggle. A second later, she was crying.

She looked behind it, in the dark doorway, and saw a female. It was more woman, less dog. She wondered why that should be, but it didn't really matter. She had two shells. In a kind of dance the beast advanced and she retreated, step for step, give and take, until her back hit wood and she was stopped. IT was not. It came on slowly, and as it came she saw something that finally broke her hold on herself. Between the thing's legs something red and glistening was poking its way out of the hair, getting longer and longer and longer . . .

(Good old Uncle Charlie had a dog he called Hector. You'd go to his house for a visit and sometimes Hector—he was a German shepherd—would get all scary and come up to you and jump on you and move funny until Uncle Charlie would come up and be real mad and slap his butt and curse at him. And the whole time he moved funny this red pointy wet thing would grow between his legs and after Uncle Charlie would slap him Hector would go off somewhere and lick it until it disappeared like a popsicle. And if you asked Uncle Charlie what that red thing was he'd tell you it was . . .)

She screamed. She screamed until she thought her throat would bleed. She screamed until she thought her lungs would rupture. She screamed . . . until she remembered that Margarette was in the crawl space and might hear her screaming and come down. Then she stopped. But she watched as he came closer, and she moaned softly, "Oh God. Oh sweet Christ."

She saw the thing flinch as if she had hit it with something. "God," she said, but nothing happened when she said that, so she tried, "Jesus Christ."

And the thing yelped in pain. The one at the door turned tail and ran off into the night. It hurts them, Lynn realized. It hurts them. Maybe it'll kill them.

At the top of her lungs she yelled, "JESUS CHRIST!"

The thing in front of her didn't die, but it did something else. It started to shimmer in her view, to become unfocused. At first Lynn thought that it must be her eyes, but then she realized that, no, it wasn't her eyes. Something was happening to it. It was getting smaller and shorter and less bulky. The hair was vanishing, leaving pinkish skin. The skull reshaped itself, the snout shortened, the teeth changed. In a few seconds more, she was confronted by a naked man standing in her living room. A small, skinny, oldish naked man that she recognized from somewhere. From . . . the Larksboro Western Auto. The naked man was Fred Zimmer!

Lynn was shocked, but no longer either afraid or intimidated. She pointed the shotgun at the man's flabby stomach. Later she would worry about what had just happened. Later, when she and Margarette were safe somewhere far away and she had time. Now she gave the gun a shake and said, "Mr. Zimmer, if you take one more step I'm going to blow your balls off."

Fred Zimmer reached instinctively to cover his genitals, but then figured, what the hell! So he extended his hands toward the lady in front of him in supplication. He wasn't sure what had happened, but he didn't feel any too brave any more. The shotgun looked big and the lady looked serious besides, and, it was never wise to take unnecessary chances.

"We're going to back up," Lynn hissed. "You're going to take me to my car and we're going to drive back down the mountain, and if you give me any shit, I'll kill you, you bastard, and I'll love it. You got that?"

"I certainly do, ma'am," Zimmer assured her in his most dulcet tones. "You seem to know me, but I don't seem to know you. You're Mrs. . . ."

"Shut up," Lynn ordered between clenched teeth. What was she going to do? Whatever he had been before, Zimmer was a man now, and she couldn't just murder him. What would Ben do, she asked herself silently, and the answer came. He'd blow him in half.

"Now Mrs., ah, I'm sure we can talk this over sensibly," the aging storekeeper assured her.

"I told you to shut up!" Mrs. Griswold raged. Then she smiled a tight little smile and commanded, "Sit."

"Beg pardon?"

She motioned toward the floor with the gun barrel. "Sit."

"As you wish," Zimmer answered demurely. He sat.

"Now lay down." This was almost fun. (And what can your dog do, Mrs. Griswold? Oh, he can sit, he can lay down, he can bag, he can turn himself into an old flabby man. The usual thing.) A laugh started to bubble in her chest and crawl up her throat, and she decided that if she didn't let it out she'd crack up. So her lips curled upward, though it looked more like a snarl, her eyes sparkled from the tears that coursed down her cheeks in freshets, and a burbly laugh started to slide between her clenched teeth.

And Fred Zimmer shook his head sadly and reflected that the poor woman was totally deranged.

And with a roar and a crash that merged together and deafened like nearby thunder, one of the creatures outside thrust his massive fist through the window and the wooden shutter against which Lynn Griswold leaned, raking her across the chest and throat with its four-inch claws. The force of the blow spun her around, her nearly severed head laying over flat against her shoulder, and her pumping blood spray painting the kitchen red.

And the force of the attack startled her as it pulled her backward and around, causing her arms to drop automatically. Her finger twitched on the shotgun's double triggers, and the loads of "OO" shot in both barrels spewed across the room in a shattering belch, intersecting the floor precisely where the naked and cold Fred Zimmer lay shivering, shredding his body from the waist up and spreading the remains throughout the living room.

The pack cleaned up around the Griswold cabin in a state of shock. The wounds that had been suffered in their wolf-forms were many and painful, but they would heal quickly and leave no marks. They were invincible in their wolf-forms; although they could be hurt, they couldn't be killed, and though the wounds transferred to their human shapes, they healed quickly, spontaneously almost. There was a little remaining pain and stiffness, that was all. A reminder, Joshua told them, to be more careful next time.

But Fred Zimmer was dead.

That fiend of a woman, that witch, had found a weakness. She had thrice called out the name of the Saviour, turning all werewolves in earshot immediately back into their human shapes. In a human shape, a werewolf is just as vulnerable as any normal man. As Fred Zimmer had been as he lay naked on the kitchen floor. Human. When two loads of buckshot had ended his lives, both man and beast.

The pack cleaned up what remained of the Griswold family. They carefully removed the blood and gore from the kitchen and the living room. They swept and cleaned and buried. They mourned.

Mattie Zimmer was inconsolable, but they understood. She went off by herself, laid her ears back along her head, and spat her grief at the faintly brightening sky. Then she transformed and had herself a god old-fashioned cry. Irene Hillman conforted her emptily.

Joshua Gimball stood off by himself under a pine. It was the first loss to the pack, and he wondered what it would do to their collective spirit. Would it bring them even closer together? Or would it make them lose faith in him, themselves, the change? Too soon to be sure, he decided. It was a hard thing to learn, that you could be all this and still not be a god. But that was the truth of it. They weren't gods, just a new species, a new race, a new form of being. What a god was and how to become one, well, he guessed only a god knew that.

Mack Horner finally found the keys to the Griswold's Bronco and gave them to Charlie McQuire (They were right there on a peg by the kitchen door, Charlie. They were just a little mucked up, is all. Hey, d'ja see me dodge when that fucker took that shot at me? Pretty fancy footwork, huh?). Charlie, in turn, brought the keys over to Joshua and said desultorily, "Here's them car keys, Professor."

"Yes?"

"Well, I thought you might want them."

"For what, might I ask?"

The fat, balding man shrugged, then belched. "'Scuse," he muttered. "Guess I ate too much."

"Charles," Joshua intoned as if he were talking to a rather dense and disgusting child, "take what's left

205

of the bodies, put them in the truck, and have a nice little traffic accident with them, yes? Make sure it's a nice fiery one and no one puts it out too soon."

McQuire nodded his head knowingly.

"Now, Charles," Gimball prompted. "Do it now."

The chief turned and wandered off dumbly. Joshua shook his head. It must be my cross to bear that I need such people.

A few minutes later, with the cleanup mostly over, Agatha Cooper and her husband walked by within earshot. The woman was limping badly and walking like a two-by-four was strapped to her spine, but her mouth was in fine shape.

"Really?" she groused at her husband. "Well, *you* only got shot in the chest. That bastard shot me in the back three times! Shit. I won't be able to walk by ten o'clock, and I have to unload that whole shipment of costume jewelry they're delivering at noon."

Martin Cooper said nothing, nodded frequently, and yawned. As the pair walked into the woods, Joshua marvelled at the people whom other people choose to spend their lives with. He was sure that Aggie Cooper would drive the Pope to drink.

The Bronco was loaded with its grisly cargo and driven away, with Astin Chubb at the wheel, to meet its fate. Doc Appleby and his daughter had left sometime earlier, Charlie and Mack were catching a lift to the foot of the mountain from Astin, and Irene and Alec were walking Mattie Zimmer home. Doc would take care of that alibi, forge the death certificate, whatever. Right now, Joshua Gimball was alone . . . and tired. He wanted to go home and get a few hours sleep; after tonight he felt like he could sleep for days.

As exhaustion elbowed its way rudely into his limbs, the prospect of the long walk to Moonshadow seemed more and more distressing. Well, there were other ways. The tall, massive professor walked a few steps into the trees. There was a brief rustling, then a short bark, and scant seconds later, an enormous pale wolf with glittering grey-green eyes floated quickly, wraithlike, down the forested slopes toward its home.

Leaving a six-year-old orphan named Margarette Griswold in the crawl space of her father's hunting cabin where, curled into a tight ball and sucking blissfully on her fist, she slept the sleep of the innocent. She was even spared dreams.

Chapter 6

The bright morning sun spilled in a golden fall through the kitchen windows, over the stainless steel sink, cascaded down the front of the pine cabinets, and pooled at Rudy Vardon's feet as he sat at the kitchen table grumbling into the morning paper. He could hear Eve rustling around upstairs as she dressed—warmly, he hoped—for their daily walk to Walt Starr's diner for breakfast. Some of the magic was taken this morning, though, by his foreknowledge of the gossip topic of the day: There had been a horrible traffic accident up at Stuckey's Peak, the bold black headlines informed him. A fiery crash, which had killed an entire family named Griswold. Man and wife and their three kids, the way the article read. Drove right off of Stuckey's Peak Road and plunged down the sheer one-hundred-foot embankment to burst into flames on the road below.

Rudy folded the paper and stared out the window into his backyard. Well, the road was a damned bad one, and he couldn't really say it was that hard to believe some tourists or whatever could drive right off of it, especially at night. For a moment he visualized a vehicle out of control, running off the road, crashing through small trees and bushes and bursting out into thin air. He could almost see the faces of the passengers, but he shied quickly away from that, focusing instead on what it must feel like to plummet over one hundred feet in an automobile—the gut-wrenching, roller-coaster drop, your stomach knotting and your heart flying into your throat as you realized just what was going on, what was going to happen. The fall would be over in seconds, but those seconds would take forever to pass. Rudy felt mildly sick and oddly empathetic. He tossed the folded paper into the trash.

"You don't mind if I read that, do you?" Eve asked from close behind him. He had been so wrapped up in his morbid imaginings that he hadn't heard her come downstairs.

"Oh, no, I'm sorry. Go right ahead," he replied, gesturing to the trash can. "Help yourself." Then he fell silent.

Eve walked over to the trash and picked out the paper, seating herself finally at the table across from her boyfriend. "That's so very kind of you. God. Which side of the bed did you get out of this morning? It should be exorcised."

"Look at the headlines."

Evelyn shook the paper open and read for a few moments. "Oh, I see. You're feeling bad for these people, huh?"

"Yeah. It just seems like a shitty way to go, you know? And two of the kids were only six years old."

"Well, look," she said, patting his hand, "I know this sounds kind of coldhearted, but I think you're overreacting a little, don't you? I'm sure this was a pretty quick death from the way it sounds, hon, and there're a lot of kids that die worse ways than this every day. C'mon. I see why you're upset and I love you for it, but I think you're going a little overboard here."

"May I speak frankly?" Rudy asked. "Without us getting into some goddam big argument about it?"

"Sure."

"Well, sometimes you really amaze me. I mean, you're a woman, a writer—a writer of children's books, yet—and you come out with something like that. How can you be so callous? My God, five people died last night. They burned to death or got blown apart or smashed against the pavement or a little of all three. They were people, Eve, just like we are, and our parents, and our friends. Can't you see what I'm getting at?"

Eve sat back in her chair and nodded grimly. "Yes, Rudy, I do see what you're getting at. And I feel for them, too. But they weren't the only ones to die in this world last night, and they weren't the only ones to suffer. Christ, you knew what was happening during Viet Nam, didn't you? Did the fact that all those human beings—people, Rudy, no matter what their color or what their beliefs were—were being napalmed and shot and gassed and God-knows-what-all, did your knowledge of that stop you from eating or going to football games or enjoying a sunrise or sunset or getting laid? Did it? I'll bet not, and you were right. Recognize the bad things, Rudy. Realize them. Go out and do something about them. But if you just sit around wailing and weeping and feeling sorry, ultimately you're just feeling sorry for yourself. Don't turn away from reality when it gets bad, baby, or you won't notice it when it gets good."

Vardon rose silently and walked to the window, squinting his eyes into slits against the brilliant sunshine. The sky was dazzlingly blue between a collage of clouds, which flowed smoothly across its length and breadth for as far as he could see. And all the time they moved you could see, if you looked seriously enough, that they were constantly shifting, changing shapes, changing. Change. Early October, and the whole world was changing. Perhaps, if he were smart enough, he could find some meaning in that.

"Is the lecture over, Dr. Sangellis?"

"Yes it is. I'm sorry. I got a little carried away."

Rudy walked to her and smiled softly down into her face. "Yes, and so did I. Maybe I'm still on edge over that monster that chased me home the other night. I don't know. Anyway, thanks for the piece of your mind." He leaned down and kissed her languorously.

"I think," Eve said, breaking away from the kiss breathlessly, "that you have another kind of piece in mind entirely, sir."

"You are wise beyond your years. You did say not to let it stop me from, ah . . ." His hand slid to her breast.

She grabbed his hand primly and placed it against his own chest. "Then I shall have to prevent you, sir, since I am famished and eager to breakfast, you see. A good breakfast," she winked, "is rumored to supply a body with quite a bit of vigor."

"Ah-ha," Rudy exclaimed, chivalrously helping the damsel from her seat and ushering her toward the door. "Then let us, by all means, make haste to dine . . . as fully as needs be. Ah-hum." As she slipped through the door ahead of him, his hand on her rump made her squeal in surprise.

"You know, it's odd, come to think of it, Walt. The paper said the accident happened late last night, but I didn't hear a siren or a horn or a bell, nothing."

"Me neither, Rudy," Walter Starr replied as he leaned on the counter in front of his young regulars. As Vardon had guessed, the diner was almost electric with the news of the car crash. "Course, that is pretty far outta' town, ya know."

Evelyn felt another conspiracy theory coming on. She had never seen her man act as oddly as he had since they had moved to Larksboro. First there was his thing with the wild dogs, then his suspicions about those people who disappeared over the summer, and now he insisted that the creature that had chased him home the other night *wasn't* a dog, but some kind of monster or beast from another planet or some such nonsense. Even he admitted that he didn't exactly know just what he was talking about, but that didn't stop him from jumping to some quite irrational conclusions and becoming generally paranoid. If it got any worse, Eve thought that she'd suggest the two of them visit some friends in New York City for a change. She almost laughed out loud at that: Going to the Apple to cure your paranoia just didn't seem like the everyday thing to do.

"*Now* what are you getting at?" she moaned, making her displeasure evident in the tone of her voice.

"Well, dammit, I'm not really sure yet," Rudy admitted irritably, and Eve rolled her eyes skyward. "Now just wait a minute, love. First, we have all those weird things that happened this summer . . ."

"We've already been over that a jillion times."

"I know, dear, and I won't go over it again . . . right now. But, second, we have that what's-it that tried to have me for supper last month . . ."

"Thought you said that was a dog?" Walt interrupted.

"*She* said it was a dog. I said it was a—"

"Rudy, our neighbors saw it. They said it was a dog. They scared it off, for Chrissakes. They said it was a dog. A big dog, an ugly dog, but a *dog*."

"Well, fuck them. What the hell do they know about it? It didn't chase them across town. It didn't try to turn them into a late night snack. Hell, it didn't even try to break their door down, now did it? No. So enough of that shit. Now, third, we have this mysterious car accident that nobody sent any emergency vehicles to."

Eve looked at him peevishly over the rim of her coffee cup.

"Just because you didn't hear them doesn't mean that there weren't any sent out."

"She's got you there," Walt refereed.

Rudy turned to Starr and silenced him with one sour look. "I didn't hear any, you didn't hear any, Walt didn't hear any." He swiveled on his stool and shouted loud enough to be heard throughout the eatery, "Did anybody hear any sirens or anything last night?" The question stirred up a lot of mumbling, but no one came up with an answer either way.

"Oh God," the young woman beside him moaned to herself, trying to become invisible on the stool.

"Nobody heard anything," Rudy continued. "Plus, you just heard that the Griswolds had their cabin on the other side of town. The Pittsburgh side. And they came in from Pittsburgh, that's where they lived. So what were they doing over on this side of town, huh? Tell me that."

"The man's got a point there," Walt admitted, not wanted to seem biased.

Evelyn gave him her best sour look and he turned and walked quickly back to his grill.

"Maybe they were taking a ride or something, Rudy," she whispered, trying to control the volume of the conversation, which had gotten increasingly louder and was now drawing some stares from the nearer booths. "Maybe they were spotting deer. Maybe they were going for a pizza. Who the hell knows why they were driving around on Stuckey's Peak . . . and what does it matter, anyway? God, you act like they were murdered or something!"

"Well, it just seems damn strange to me, that's all," Vardon pouted. Then his face grew a little darker, although his eyes seemed to glimmer slightly. "I wonder why anyone would want to murder a whole family like that? . . .

"Charlie Manson did." The voice was as grating as a rusty hinge and came from just behind them. It was Reiner, on his way out.

"Say what?" Rudy asked, startled.

"I say Charlie Manson did. Just up and slaughtered a whole family for the hell of it. Ya 'member?"

Vardon rubbed his chin thoughtfully. "Yeah. Yeah, I remember."

"Je-sus Christ!" Evelyn grimaced. "Just what does that have to do with anything, Mr. Reiner?"

"Just seemed to fit in with what your husband was sayin', is all," the old man shrugged. Then he turned and walked out the door without another word.

"Wasn't Charlie Manson into Satanism or something, Walt?" Rudy asked interestedly.

Eve was becoming more incensed by the moment. To her, this was just some silly macho game-playing. These men needed dragons to protect their damsels from . . . or something like that. She hadn't thought that her boyfriend was into such . . . chauvinism, but she was not about to stand for it. It was going from ridiculous to absurd and, frankly, she was starting to get concerned about Rudy's sanity.

"Walt," she said firmly, "I forbid you to answer that." She turned to Rudy, who was just starting to open his mouth to speak. "You be quiet," the lady ordered quietly, and his jaws clamped shut. "We are not going to talk about this any more, do you two understand that? I don't care what else we talk about, but we won't bring up this subject again. Right? Now, Walt, why don't you start us out on this *new* conversation."

"Sure," Walt stumbled. "Sure. Well . . . ah . . ."

"C'mon Walt, isn't there anything else of local interest that happened last night?"

Starr was hit with a revelation. "Yeah, sure, Eve. I just didn't think about it, what with all this about . . . I just didn't think about it. Y'know Fred Zimmer, runs the Western Auto downtown? Well, damned if he didn't up and die of a stroke late last night."

Rudy Vardon jumped to attention so hard that his coffee cup landed at Walt's feet, spilling cold coffee all over the yellow countertop.

"Well, I don't care," Eve said as they walked home through the center of town, arm in arm. "I think that we need to get away from here for a while until you calm down. Rudy, do you know what you sound like when you get started? God, it's spooky, that's what it is. I keep expecting to see a butterfly net drop over your head."

Rudy stopped walking and turned her toward him. "Okay, so I sound wacko. I know. But I really believe there's something weird going on around here, hon. Something really weird. And probably dangerous, too."

"The only thing weird going on around here is your thought processes, pal. And if you don't calm down, or at least shut up until you've got something incontestable to tell me, what's dangerous is going to be the rap I give you in the head to straighten you out." Her face softened and she stroked his cheek. "Really, Rudy. Just hang loose for a while, okay? Go with the flow, and all that."

"Alright," he conceded. "But if I find

216

anything . . ."

"*If* you find anything . . ."

"That's what I said: If I find anything, I'm going to say "I told you so" for a long, long time."

"Good enough," Eve grinned, stood up on her tip-toes, and kissed him firmly. "Now," she whispered throatily, "don't we have an appointment somewhere?"

"Indeed we do. Shall we?"

At the end of the block they both waved a greeting to Mayor Cooper and Aggie, who were walking in town from their home to go to work. The mayor looked in his usual good health, but his wife was walking very strangely.

When they had walked up to meet them, Eve saw that the older woman was frightfully pale and obviously in a great deal of pain.

"Aggie," she gasped, grabbing the old woman's hands in a gesture of silent concern. "Are you alright? You look terrible. Are you sick or something?"

Martin Cooper put his arm around his wife protectively and drew her toward him. "She'll be alright," he assured the younger couple. "She was changing lightbulbs at home last night and fell off the stepladder. She seems to have twisted her back and bruised her ribs. Dr. Appleby said she'd be just fine in a couple of days."

"Silly of me," Agatha winced. "Martin's told me time and time again not to get up on that ladder, but you know how bullheaded you get as you get older, dear. You mustn't worry."

"Oh, but you look like you're in such terrible

217

pain . . ."

"Come now, dear. That's just an old woman's way of getting sympathy from you youngsters, don't you know? I'm fine, really."

"Well," Martin said, "we really must be going. I've got piles of work to do at the office, and Aggie has a shipment of jewelry to come in at the Emporium this morning, so—"

"Sure. We'll see you around Mayor. Aggie," Rudy smiled, thinking it sure sounded like a brush-off to him. Then he noticed, through the mayor's open jacket, a pinkish, dampish-looking spot on his pale blue shirt, just to the right of his tie. "It looks like you spilled something on your shirt," he pointed out.

The mayor acted as if he had been slapped. His head jerked down to look, his eyes widened. He placed his fingertips against the spot and felt it with a degree of gravity that struck Rudy as out of place. "Damn!" Cooper cursed. Then he seemed to recover a little of his politeness and blushed. "Sorry. I must have dropped some marmalade on it this morning at breakfast. Thank you for pointing it out, Rudy. I'll have to change the shirt. Can't have the Mayor of Larksboro running around with stains on his shirt, can we? Give us a bad image, and all that. Well, we'll see you around, folks. And thanks again."

Martin Cooper walked off zippering his jacket front hurriedly, his thin, greying wife limping along at his side.

"Christ," Rudy muttered. "They look like they've been through the wars." As he looked after them, he saw Charlie McQuire's cruiser pull alongside of them. Cooper walked over and bent in the passenger side window, which the chief had cranked open. After gesturing a few times toward Rudy and Eve, casting subtle glances in their direction, the mayor straightened up and continued walking toward City Hall with his battered wife. The police cruiser moved off also, but Rudy had seen the man inside fix him with a covert stare.

"Rudy," Eve asked, "are we going to stand here all day, or what?"

"We might as well stay here a few minutes more," Rudy answered. "I think we're going to get company any time now."

Before Eve could question the artist further, the black-and-white pulled around the corner a block down and rolled to a stop along the curb in front of them. McQuire touched his hand to his forehead in greeting, then reached over and rolled down the door window.

"G'morning, folks."

Evelyn looked at him oddly, but Rudy answered, "Good morning, Chief. I just had a feeling we were going to see you this morning."

" 'Sat right?" the officer grinned at him. "Well, you must be one of those psychics or somethin', then, Mr. Vardon. Didn't know it myself till I saw you two standin' here. 'Charlie,' I says to myself, 'you ought to go on down there and say hello to those young people; see if everything is okay.' So that's just what I'm doin'. Just that." He pulled out a cigar and worked the flame of a kitchen match under it until he was satisfied it was lit properly. "So. Is everything okay with you two young people?"

"Why, sure," Evelyn hesitated, her voice expressing

the subtle mistrust of the young and intellectual for such blatant authority figures. "Should there be something wrong? I mean, what could be wrong, anyway?"

"Oh, now, I didn't have nothing specific in mind, miss. I just heard that your boyfriend here seemed a little upset over at the Four Starr a little piece back." He exhaled expansively and watched the blue smoke as it funnelled out the open window. "Guess it wasn't anything important, then, Mr. Vardon?"

Rudy was amused by the officer's little game, realizing that McQuire was both hinting and questioning. "As a matter of fact, Charlie," the artist said, leaning through the open window conspiratorially. "You don't mind if I call you Charlie, do you?"

McQuire shook his head, jowls quivering.

"Good. As a matter of fact, Charlie, there is a little something bothering me this morning, and you might be just the one to clear up my thinking on it. That family that . . . drove off of Stuckey's Peak Road last night—what were their names? . . .

"Griswold."

"Griswold. Right. Well, the way I hear it, the Griswolds have a cabin out to the west of town. Now, the peak is off to the east of town. What do you think they were doing out there, even the small children, in the wee hours of the morning, Charlie?"

Eve squeezed his hand hard, but he smiled and ignored her.

"Well, now," Charlie considered, picking bits of tobacco from between his fleshy lips, "I don't really know what those poor folks were doin' out there. Probably never will, either. Guess it was just their own personal business, Mr. Vardon, and it ain't my job to know folks's personal business less they start causin' trouble. That Ben Griswold been comin' up here for years, nicest guy in the world, never caused a bit of trouble for us. Same with the wife and kids. It's a damned shame they had to go like that, but these things happen all the time, son. Real nice people just up and die and there just don't seem to be any sense to it. Maybe there ain't. Maybe their number just came up, like some folks around here say." McQuire gave the younger man his best paternal look. "But, son, I can tell you this. I've seen a lotta' accidents in my day, and there ain't many of them that ever makes a whole buncha' sense. Not many at all." He shook his head sadly and reached for another kitchen match. His cigar had gone out during the lecture.

Vardon looked thoughtful. "You might be right, Charlie, you might just be right. Well, we've got to go home and get to work now, so I guess we'll be seeing you around." He casually took Eve's arm and steered her past the front end of the cruiser and into the street.

As the two reached the driver's side and waited for a car to go by so they could cross, McQuire stuck his head out the window and summed up, in his friendliest down-home voice, "Sure, see you folks around. Mr. Vardon, hope our little talk's put your mind at ease. I'd hate to see you lose any sleep over this."

Rudy knew he should keep his mouth shut, but the temptation was too great. He turned back to the police chief and said wryly, "Oh, I sleep just fine, Charlie. In fact, I sleep so sound that last night I didn't hear a single ambulance or fire truck or police car going out to the wreck. I didn't hear a sound and, you know, those emergency vehicles had to pass within three or four blocks of my house on their way out there. Now that's some sound sleeping, isn't it, Charlie?" He didn't wait for an answer. Instead he waved casually and, turning nonchalantly, walked across the street with his woman on his arm, mounted the far curb, and headed for home.

"What the hell are you doing?" Eve hissed.

"Walking home, what do you think I'm doing?" There was a suppressed chuckle in his voice.

She punched his arm. "Back there, dammit. You baited the chief of police, for Christ's sake. You did everything but laugh in his face. Rudy, this paranoid delusion of yours had gone far enough, don't you think? Try to be rational for a minute. Be logical, adult, whatever. There are no monsters running around these hills. The Mafia or whatever is not conspiring to knock off innocent campers and hunters . . ."

"And game wardens. Don't forget game wardens."

"Oh shit! John Scott died of natural causes, Rudy. Doc told you himself."

"And dogs."

"Rudy . . . what the fuck is the matter with you!" she screamed. An old lady walking past them winced and walked to the other side of the street. "Godzilla was killed by a pack of wild dogs. The other dogs just strayed off and starved or something, or maybe the wild dogs got them, too, but there isn't anything *sinister* going on in Larksboro that you have to ferret out. No monsters. No conspiracies. No murder or mayhem. Good God! I think you're suffering from some weird cultural shock or something. Jesus!"

A few blocks later, a spotted mutt of indeterminate origin but overly aggressive character charged out to greet them as they walked past. It slid to a stop at the chain link fence that marked the boundary of its kingdom, barking madly to turn back any possible attempt at trespass. The onslaught was so sudden that Evelyn, deep in worried thought, didn't hear it until the dog was only a few feet away. Then she reacted so violently that she literally shoved Rudy into the street as she yelped and tried to get out of the way of her attacker. Rudy stifled a laugh and choked off a biting remark, but was too weak to prevent the grin that spread across his face like a brush fire. When he extended his arm, the woman yanked him to her and pressed on down the street as quickly as she could, not daring to look her companion in the eye but muttering, "Oh my God, I think it's contagious."

They walked into the morning in silence, each engrossed in their separate thoughts. Rudy could guess what his woman was thinking; the worry was written in shallow lines across her forehead and around her eyes. If she knew what I'm thinking, he told himself, she'd get a gun and shoot me. Or else have me committed.

As soon as Evelyn had settled down to the business of writing, he quietly put on some old clothes and snuck out of the house. Since he couldn't take the car without alerting Eve to his departure, he walked five or six blocks, found a phone booth, and called a cab.

The ride to the western end of town didn't take long at all.

As he walked steadily up the mountain, panting lightly already from the exertion, he went over his plan of action mentally. Actually, it was more like this: He discovered that he had no plan of action. There had seemed to be a choice to make that was reasonably simple. The Griswolds had been involved in an accident at Stuckey's Peak while they were in Larksboro, presumably staying at their hunting camp. If one wanted to find out something about them, then, one would either have to go to the scene of the accident, which was probably cleaned up damned near spotless by McQuire and Company, or check out the cabin for . . . what? Clues? Bloody fingerprints? Large dog prints, perhaps? The fact was, other than where he was going, Rudy Vardon didn't know what he was doing on his way to the Griswold's camp this sunny October afternoon. He didn't know what he was doing, why he was doing it, what he was looking for, or even if he'd know what he was looking for if he found it. But at least he was doing something. At least he was taking action, right?

It seemed to take forever to get to the top and the cabin, and the sun seemed to have dropped a mile more toward the western slopes each time he looked at it. If he had to, he guessed he could stay the night up here—just imagining what it would be like trying to go back down in the dark made him groan at his own stupidity—but that would mean explaining to a very upset Evelyn Sangellis just what he had been doing out all night, and that wasn't a very attractive prospect, either. Just as he was about to give up and turn around, while there was still plenty of time to find his way back, he walked suddenly out of the trees and into a well-tended clearing—Ben Griswold's "yard."

The cabin and its grounds said more about the owners than he could have read in any biography. The area was tidy and well cared for, but its place as a part of the mountain had not been usurped by that compulsive organizer, man. Trees grew as they would, and the low bushes that dotted the cleared ground were untrimmed and growing in the ways that it was their nature to grow. It was obvious that the grounds had just recently been raked, and Vardon could see a pile of dead leaves and branches just inside the tree line at the front of the cabin.

The cabin itself was made of rough logs; expensive looking, but not pretentious. It looked sound and tight. As Rudy approached, he could make out carved wooden shutters at the windows, which he could see from his vantage point. What he could see of the roof looked good to his untrained eye, and the brick chimney that roosted at an end was as picturesque as the rest of the structure. He drew closer, examining the place with an artist's eye for detail. The place was idyllic, yet there was something wrong. The building, the grounds, all reflected the owner, who had built and maintained them with love and pride; there was continuity. Yet somewhere that sense of pattern was lost, interfered with, dissembled. There was something that was out of harmony here, Vardon noted with growing excitement and apprehension. He stopped, looking, letting his gaze wander over all he could see, letting his mind drift so it might intuit what he could not see. Something.

Something.

There was no door to the cabin.

The rest of the building was neatly buttoned up, but the front door was missing completely. Heart pounding with discovery, he ran to where the door should have been and looked inside. Where was the door? At first he thought that it might have been left open, but now he could see that even the hinges were gone from the jamb, leaving only a darkened outline and tiny wormholes where the screws had been turned into the hard wood. The door had been carefully removed and not long ago. The color of the wood that had been under the hinge plates was still unweathered. So it had been taken down recently. He looked closer and saw that a number of the small screw holes were misshapen, as though someone had wobbled them back and forth while taking them out. Some were even noticeably larger than others, as if two different sized screws had been used. Rudy couldn't imagine why anyone would do that, but he couldn't think of any other explanation for the difference.

Right. So much for where the door was. Now, where is it?

It wasn't resting outside against the wall. He would have seen it when he walked up, but he rechecked anyway. No.

It wasn't to the right of the door when he looked there nor was it to the left, but he saw that a large chunk of the jamb had been ripped away just where the latch would have been. That's when it struck him

226

that someone had broken the door down.

And then calmly unscrewed the hinges, taken it down, and carted it off somewhere.

Sure.

He looked into what must have served as the living room, dim and shadow-haunted in the fading afternoon light. It was too dark to really be sure of anything, so he stepped inside and began to conduct as thorough a search as he could think of, coming up with zero until he noticed the gouges that spaced themselves across the polished wood floor. Lowering himself to his knees, he examined them minutely. They were fresh, like the gouge in the doorjamb and the marks where the missing hinges had been. So, someone must have taken, or broken, the door down and dragged it across the floor toward the rear of the cabin. He followed the trail into the next room, where it petered out on the new linoleum floor to be replaced by something instantly recognizable and much more frightening in its implications: the unmistakable pitting that a load of shot makes when it strikes a smooth, soft surface. Like linoleum. Big shot, from the chunks that had been destroyed even in the areas farthest from where the most damage was concentrated. Rudy got down and looked at the disfigured surface, running his hands over it as if it were braille. In the next few minutes he found five rather small round bits of lead that he managed to dig out of the floor with his penknife, and he knew his first impression had been right. What he held in the palm of his hand looked like buckshot to him, and it probably was just that. He got to his feet slowly, perplexedly, and looked around at the walls, the cabinets, the sink—all the appliances and surfaces that make a kitchen what it is. They were clean, spotlessly so. For a moment Rudy had the crazy feeling that if he ran outside he would be able to see the Sears delivery truck just pulling away.

"Just calm down and think. Calm down and think. Put together what you have so far."

Well, that should be simple enough. Someone came to the door of this nice little cabin in the woods and broke it down, then they took out a screwdriver and unhung it, dragging it through the living room and out into the kitchen, where they laid it on the floor and shot it full of buckshot. Great.

Just fucking wonderful. Officer, arrest this man for unlawful carpentry and the murder of an unhinged door. How did I figure it out? Oh, elementary . . .

"SHIT!" he spat at the immaculate room around him.

Well, don't just stand there, asshole. Look for more clues.

There was another doorway off the kitchen so thinking, What the hell, he walked through it, across a narrow hall, and into the first of two bedrooms. Apparently it was a child's room; there was a single bed across the far wall, and across from it a bunk bed hunkered beside posters of Miss Piggy, Strawberry Shortcake, and the Incredible Hulk. Rudy remembered the two six-year-olds and felt on the verge of tears, their reality made even more evident by this display of their heroes and heroines. The sadness mixed with his confusion and formed rage. There had to be something here that would help to explain why this had happened, but what he was finding was only adding to the uncertainties he had felt for months. He stomped out into the hall and into the master bedroom.

Again, he could read the personalities of the people who had lived here. An old-style canopy bed was tucked along one wall, aligned so that whoever lay in it had only to turn his or her head to look out on the forest beyond. These people had been romantics and they had been in love. Rudy hoped that he and Eve would have a relationship like that when their oldest child was almost grown. He saw the two strangers in each other's arms, faces toward the window, contentedly gazing at the world transfigured by moonlight.

He indulged himself a few moments more, then wiped his eyes roughly and returned to his investigations.

Nothing seemed unusual or disturbed. Nothing even seemed dusty.

Nothing . . . even . . . seemed . . . dusty.

That was it! That was exactly what had been bothering him the whole time he had been here. The place was not abandoned or unused; it had been cleaned quite recently and quite thoroughly. Some of it would be due to the Griswold woman—he knew the family had been here, he could sense it—but then some of it might not be. In the kitchen, though the flooring had been gouged and split by a shotgun blast, there were no fragments of linoleum to be found anywhere. There were no wood splinters around the front door, no chips, nothing. There was no disarray anywhere, and that was wrong. No matter how neat, a family with two six-year-olds and a teenager would leave something out of place.

Something. But this place was so clean it was almost sanitary.

He walked back out of the bedroom, toward the kitchen, and froze in midstep. Another door. A closet, by the looks of it. He pulled the door open quickly and gasped in surprise. A shape dropped heavily out of the darkness and thumped to the floor, partially covering his feet. He could feel his bowels loosening and a scream building up momentum in his throat.

It was a sleeping bag.

Jesus Chris. He leaned his forehead against the wall and took a few needed deep breaths. Oh wow.

When he had recovered sufficiently he opened the door again, slowly. It was a closet, and it was stuffed with all the things a family of five might need for an outing in the mountains. There were more sleeping bags, backpacks, another bundle that might have been a tent, boots of varying sizes and shapes and degrees of cleanliness, a square piece of plywood that reminded him of a hatch cover on a ship . . .

It was a cover. A cover for what, though? Without really thinking about it, Rudy looked over his head and saw the dark rectangular entrance to the crawl space. His heart leapt. He was just about to try to squeeze up into the opening, when he checked himself.

There might be someone up there, he thought. There might be some*thing*.

Or some bodies.

"Oh, fuck it."

He gave a little hop and grabbed the edge, chinning himself as best he could into the darkness. The head fit, but even his relatively unathletic shoulders were too wide. It was very dark and musty. He sneezed three times in a row before he could call hoarsely, "Anybody up here?"

Nothing.

"Hey!" Is anybody up here? It's okay, I won't hurt you."

He yelled once again, "Anybody home?" and got no answer. By this time his knuckles were white, his hands hurt, and his biceps and shoulders were complaining in no uncertain terms about the unaccustomed strain. He dropped to the floor with a groan and stood, trying to shake the cramps out of his hands. Well, nothing in the closet but some camping equipment and the entrance to a crawl space under the roof. Not even a skeleton, he tried to joke.

Still, he wondered why whoever it was that had tidied up the rest of the place had not put the cover back over the hole. That was pretty sloppy, considering. He looked back into the closet, shook his head, and closed it firmly, walking across the short hall and back into the kitchen. There he looked around, sighed, and shook his head again. It had been one hell of a long walk for nothing. The door had either been broken down or taken down, or both. Something had been shotgunned on the kitchen floor. The door? That couldn't be right. Not even he would shoot a door, and he was beginning to seriously doubt his own sanity. Maybe it didn't have anything to do with the door. Maybe the man was just cleaning the shotgun in the kitchen or something like that, and it had gone off into the floor accidentally. That sounded logical. Things like that happened all the time. The problem was, if that were true, it left him with even less than before. Also, it didn't jive with what he thought he had learned about these people. It wasn't consistent.

He started to return to the front door—where the front door should have been—his eyes downcast. Eve had told him to be rational, logical. Well, damn it, he was trying. But this just didn't seem to be a problem that required a rational, logical solution. This seemed to demand something different. Like what, he didn't know. He needed a pattern.

Like the pattern of the scratches on the floor. Not continuous, like something had been dragged. Regular, yes, but intermittent, like Morse code. Dash dash dash. Dot dot dot. Scratch scratch scratch. One right and one left, and repeat. A pattern. He looked very close and noticed something else, wondered how he could have missed it before: They were not single scratches, but four separate grooves that seemed to get closer together as they got shallower. A pattern.

It occurred to him in a rush that left him dizzy with relief and triumph. He sat back unceremoniously on the floor with a thud. Of course there was a pattern here, and he knew what the pattern looked like, he knew what these scratches were.

"Claw marks," he whispered to himself. "They're claw marks. Footprints." Nothing had been dragged across this floor, no indeed. Something had walked across it after battering down the door. It had walked into the kitchen and someone had shot it, or at it, and ended up tearing up the floor. Just like it had torn up the living room floor when it had walked across it.

On two clawed feet.

Rudy's hands dropped loosely, the knuckles rapping painfully on the floor. He mouthed the words, Oh my God, but no sound emerged. Before he could fully regain his feet he was scrabbling for the empty doorway and the woods beyond.

He had reached the tree line when he heard the engine purring behind him and tires crunching over bits of twigs and rock that were laying strewn over the dirt road leading to the clearing in front of the structure. Panicked, he dove quickly into the bushes for cover. Then, scratched, bruised, and curious, he peeked out between the branches to see just who had come to call.

It wasn't long before a black and white car bearing the markings of the Larksboro Police Department scrunched its way over the last few feet of the rubble into visibility and stopped. Charlie McQuire extracted his bulk from behind the steering wheel, slammed the car door with a resounding thunk, and stood looking toward the empty cabin. A few seconds later he was joined by Doc Appleby, who climbed out of the other side and walked over to stand in front of the chief of police. After talking and gesturing for a few minutes, they walked up to the cabin and went inside.

Rudy decided that he wasn't nearly skilled enough to creep up to the cabin to eavesdrop on the goings-on, but damned if he was going anywhere until the two of them came back out and he had some idea of just what the hell was going on. He settled down to wait.

"We're going to have to sand the scratches out of

this floor and replace the linoleum in the kitchen," Appleby said.

McQuire sat heavily on the couch and looked at him morosely. "Seems to be one hell of a lot of work to go to when I can think of at least one easier way, Doc."

"The easier ways aren't always the best ways, Charlie."

The smell of cigar smoke filled the air. "C'mon Doc. Don't give me that shit, huh? You know damned well we could burn this son of a bitch down, blame vandals or lightning or somethin', and nobody'd ever know the difference. Or care, for that matter."

The doctor coursed through the house, making note of anything and everything that would have to be corrected to make the cabin look as if it had just been shut up for the summer and never reopened. Charlie was right about one thing: It was going to be a chore to set things to rights. Maybe he was right about the fire, too.

"Hey, Charlie," the old man's voice floated in faintly from the bedroom hall, "Did any of you fellows check this closet last night?"

"What closet's that?"

"Right. Well, that answers that, doesn't it?"

"What closet you talkin' about, Doc?"

"Never mind," Appleby hollered. Then, much lower, "Never mind." He opened the single pane door, saw the hatch cover, and looked immediately at the ceiling. something heavy gathered in his stomach, and he turned and walked quickly back to stand before his partner, who sat leisurely on the couch

234

engulfed in shifting blue smoke. "How many bodies did you pack in that truck?"

The question required a little thought, but McQuire muddled through. "The old man," he ticked off on his pudgy fingers, "the old woman, that little snot kid, and the teenager. Stringy fucker he was, too."

"That's four."

Charlie looked at his outthrust fingers. "Yep. Right. Four."

"Only four."

He waved the fingers under the doctor's nose. Shit, the old boy must be gettin' senile, couldn't remember what he'd just been told. "Four, Doc, four. One . . . two . . . three . . . four." He helpfully folded his fingers down into his palm as he counted them off.

"Charlie . . . what happened to the little girl?"

"What little girl? What're you talkin' about?"

"The Griswolds had a little girl. The boy's twin sister. Dammit, Charlie, there were five of them. Five of them," he breathed, collapsing into the easy chair, "and we've only accounted for four."

What the doctor had been saying finally registered with Charlie McQuire. "Holy shit," he exclaimed. "What happened to the girl, Doc?"

"The mother must have hid her up under the roof, in the crawl space. The opening is in the ceiling of the closet in there by the master bedroom. We missed it completely. Damn!"

McQuire rose ponderously. He smiled. "Hey, no problem, Doc. I'll just jump right on up there and give the little bit a surprise. I was gettin' kinda' hungry, anyway." So saying, that chief's features started to blur and waver and the words he muttered lowering gradually into a growl. "Why, grandma, what big teeth I have," he burbled.

Appleby rose and pushed him backward stoutly into the soft cushions of the couch. "Forget it, Charlie, she's gone. Use your nose, idiot. The scent's old. We'll have to track her down now or hope she gets lost and dies of exposure before she can find her way down the mountain."

"Shit!" McQuire spat, fully human again. "My mouth was all set for a tasty little snack, dammit!"

"C'mon, Chief," the doc said, rising wearily from his seat and heading for the door without waiting. "Let's get going. We've got to let Joshua know what we found so he can decide what to do about it."

"What a fuck of a spot to be in," the fat man nodded to himself as he followed his companion out the door. "I could be just as good a leader as that fancy-ass faggot college professor. Hell, you'd think they'd at least give me more rank than the doc. Shit, the one of them ain't got a woman and the other don't screw nobody but his own damned daughter. They're both of 'em perverts, and then they tell me that I don't have what it takes!" He slammed his marshmallow palm against the vacant doorjamb, asking, "Ain't that a crock of shit, though?"

Just as Vardon was trying to ease his cramped legs into another, more comfortable position, Doc Appleby walked into the waning sunlight followed closely by Charlie McQuire. The doctor leaned into the cruiser and pulled something to his mouth, talking into it momentarily, listening, talking again.

Chief McQuire waddled up and leaned his fat rump against the fender of the car, jamming his hands deeply into his trouser pockets and managing to look quite miserable as he watched Appleby hold his conversation. Rudy tried to listen, tried to read lips, tried even to see the looks on their faces, but it was to no avail. He felt like screaming with frustration.

Finally the grey-haired man replaced the radio transmitter and, motioning curtly to the rotund policeman, walked around to the other side of the cruiser and got in. McQuire soon followed suit, and within minutes the car had disappeared behind a screen of pines.

Rudy levered his aching, stiff body off the ground, joints popping and cracking, and cursed his luck. He had collected nothing but a good scare today. There was no concrete evidence of any wrongdoing, even though there was much to be suspicious of. The theories that were fluttering around the corners of his mind would get him no further than the psychiatrist's couch at best.

Thinking, finally, that some light was better than no light at all—both on the mystery and on the mountain—he turned and began the long trek home through the glooming trees.

Not quite dark, and not quite dawn. The trees had become containers of darkness, overspilling and pouring shadows on the ground to pool liquidly at their roots. Bushes seemed to gain a mischievous life. They shifted and squirmed when he could only see their movements out of the corner of his eye; they shook their brittle stick arms after his clothing and hide, and rattled their dried leaves shamanistically behind his back. Night in the forest seemed much more alive, more populous, than day. Rudy could hear the crackling of the brittle leaf carpet under the spidery trees as creatures of little size—and occasionally the crunch of one of some size—bobbed, scuttled, bounded, and ran away from his path. He tried to quell his unease by thinking of how fearsome and huge he must sound, stumbling around in the near-dark, to the animals that called this woodland home. It was a noble attempt at rationality, but it only made him wonder just what type of creatures those might be. Did some of them walk on two clawed feet, snarling and growling, strong and ferocious enough to burst through sturdy doors and withstand the impact of a close range shotgun blast? Were those creatures like that out here with him tonight, and were those scrabbling sounds retreating in fear . . . or were they stalking in hunger?

A roosting grouse was startled into flight by his clumsy approach and reared out of a pine only a few yards in front of him. Rudy veered, raising his arms over his face in an instinctive gesture to protect his head and neck. His feet caught under an exposed root and he fell forward, bouncing off the rasping back of a pine trunk and rolling some fifteen feet downhill until he came to rest with a resounding thud at the foot of an arthritic old oak. There he lay, exhausted from his nervous fear, dizzy from his fall, shaken by his collision with the two trees. Asthmatic breaths rasped in and out of his lungs until, starting to regain some composure, his respiration began to slow to normal.

When he heard the rustling, he stopped breathing completely.

At first he thought it was a rabbit or a possum, maybe a raccoon. But it was too steady, and it was too loud. And it was coming closer. He thought about Doc Appleby and Charlie McQuire, and then his mind's eye gave him a glimpse of something big and hairy, which looked like a dog (No . . . a wolf) but walked on two feet like a man. The bushes whispered to him that THEY were coming now. Coming for him. And when they found him they would bear their yellow fangs and . . .

. . . Godzilla had been unrecognizable, shredded, scattered in a million chewed pieces of meatless hide. As huge as he was, the dog had been pulled down and killed, torn to shreds and. . .

. . . devoured. They would find him and kill him and feast upon his flesh, gnaw his bones, drink his warm blood.

The sound got louder. Closer.

Vardon whimpered and moved across the forest floor like a crab until he was partially hidden by the double trunk of another oak. He searched around him frantically, using his sense of touch for sight on the leaf-strewn ground, looking for something he could use to defend his life. Alright, they were coming, and perhaps they would have him in the end, but he would make them pay as high a price as he could for this meal. This was Rudy Edmund Vardon, and Rudy Edmond Vardon was prime meat.

His hand brushed something hard, ran along a satisfactory length, clasped a stout breadth. He rooted out the length of oak branch and tested it as one might test the balance and rigidity of a baseball bat. It wasn't a gun or a knife—or a tank or a hand grenade—but it felt as if it might do. It had to do. It was all he had.

The shuffling in the leaves drew very close now.

As silently as possible he snaked his way up the trunk to a standing position, trying to move in such a way that the oak would stand between himself and . . . it. He tried to pierce the darkness until the tears streamed down his cheeks. Then the high bushes not ten feet away from his shook and the scuffling feet came within range. He jumped out from behind the tree trunk, oak club high above his head, whooping and screaming like a demon from hell.

Just before he brought the branch down with all his strength on the head of his hunter, he saw it clearly. It was small, not nearly as tall as he was, and bedraggled. It wore a yellow mane of tangled hair, and green Grranimal slacks with a color-coordinated top. There was a green ribbon-shaped barrette in the hair. The small head tilted up at him in shock and fear and, yes, resignation; he saw it was a little girl. She had blue eyes, and dirt was smudged and smeared over her clothes and every inch of exposed pale skin. The only clean spots on her face were the twin lines that ran from her eyes, down her cheeks, and ended at the jaw line. The tracks were still glistening and moist.

The little girl was the most beautiful thing Rudy Vardon had ever seen. He lowered the club slowly and felt that his heart would burst from relief. He didn't even reach out to hold her, to comfort her. He was afraid that she was a dream. He was afraid that she would run away. He wasn't really sure that she was real.

Of course, there were a lot of things that Rudy Vardon didn't know, the very least of which was that he didn't yet know he was looking at Margarette Griswold.

Chapter 7

He carried the child the rest of the way down the mountain in the darkness, stopping only briefly to rest his aching arms. The thought came to him that a woman seemed to be able to carry a child around all day long with no trouble, and he wondered how they did it.

The darkness fell quickly in the woods on a fall night, as did the temperature. Neither of these facts had contributed to their sense of well-being at all, and they had clambered down in the dark as quickly as their tired bodies would allow. There had been little attempt at conversation, and what there had been had been more to assure each other that each was real, friendly. Human. They had clung to each other as if they were the only two survivors of Armageddon.

By the time they had come to the outskirts of Larksboro, he felt that he could carry her no farther. She told him she was okay. She could walk by herself.

She told him, when he got around to asking her, that her name was Margarette, but Rudy had either missed her name in the newspaper account of the accident or was too upset to make the connection. They were walking toward the downtown section, only minutes from home and Evelyn.

When she said the name "Griswold," he thought that he must have heard her wrong. As calmly as his excitement would allow, Rudy stopped and knelt in front of his small charge, smiling into her wide eyes and caressing her cheek. "Margarette," he said softly, "I don't think I heard you right. What's your last name again?"

"Griswold."

For a second the artist's mind reeled and he was nowhere, not here nor there nor anyplace else. There was just a spinning blackness where his sense of self had been, almost as if he had gone catatonic. Then reality, or what might serve to pass for it, rushed into his head and he grabbed the child by the arms before he could think, his voice shaking when he asked, "Griswold? Honey, did you say Griswold?"

The girl tried to pull away, nodding shyly.

Her eyes told him what he looked like to her and he let her go as gently as he could. "Oh . . . oh, I'm sorry, honey, I didn't mean to scare you. I thought . . . I read that—" What the hell! How could he possibly expect her to understand what had come over him? Should he tell her that everyone thought she was dead, burned to death and smashed against the blacktop like her mother and father and two brothers? Should he tell her that she was his proof, his evidence that all wasn't right here in Larksboro, that he wasn't mad? Maybe not.

He looked at her thoughtfully, a small child in tattered clothing standing under a streetlight on the

243

main drag in Larksboro, Pennsylvania. She was shaking from the cold, and as he took off his jacket to drape around her shoulders she looked up at him with trusting eyes. She trusted him instinctively as an adult and protector. He marvelled at the adaptability of children. With her mother and father gone, she had done the only thing that made any sense: She had found another grown-up and placed herself in his care. There was fear in her eyes, true, but perhaps children were always just a little afraid of these mammoth beings called adults. Maybe that's why they grew up to fight them so vehemently as teenagers. Rudy held out his hand and she took it, and together they walked east.

"Where's your mom and dad?" Rudy asked softly.

"Dunno."

"What were you doing alone in the woods?"

Margarette looked up at him measuringly. "My daddy has a wood house up there. We were cleaning it up for him."

"And did you get lost?"

"No," the girl said softly, knuckling a tear out of the corner of her eye. "Some big monsters came. They were going to eat me, so my mommy put me up in my secret room and told me to be real quiet and not come down. I waited a long, long time."

Rudy reached down and picked her up. "I can carry you for a while. Your mommy told you to stay in your secret room? Where's that?"

The child measured him again. "You won't tell?"

"No."

"It's way up high in the ceiling in the closet. Mommy said the monsters wouldn't find me there."

244

"And how long did you stay in your secret room?"

"I said, a long, long time." She buried her head into his shoulder and muttered, shamefacedly, "I even peed up there. But Mommy said it was okay. She did!"

"I believe you, Margarette," Vardon reassured her. "Why did you come down, then?" She looked at him and he caught the glint of something in her eyes. My God, she thought he was going to punish her for coming down. Her mother had told her to stay up there and she had come down, and now she thought he was going to spank her for it or yell at her or something. "I'm not going to punish you, sweetheart. I just want to know, that's all."

"Well . . ." She cocked her head. "Mommy didn't give me even a san'wich or some Kool-Aid. So when I woke up, I had to come down an' get something to eat."

"Then there wasn't anybody there, so you went into the woods to try to look for them, right?"

"Daddy always said if I got lost to walk *down* in the woods. He said that would make me get to town. So I thought that the monsters must have chased Mommy and Daddy and David and Wade and got them all lost in the woods, and then Daddy would walk *down* in the woods, too. I tried to look for them. But it got dark . . ."

She started to sob again, and Rudy held her tightly into the hollow of his shoulder. His arms were blazing with pain, but he hated to put her down. He didn't want to leave her even that alone after what the child had been through only yesterday. God! To see what she must have seen. What would it do to an adult, a grown man like himself, much less a six-year-old girl? And she keeps talking about monsters. What's a monster to a child? A bad man? Wild dogs? Or could she mean *real* monsters? He remembered the scratches on the wooden flooring and shuddered. The girl would have to be asked, but later, and maybe by Eve. She had a way with children and with words. Maybe she would understand the girl's emotions better and be able to phrase the questions more gently.

He turned the corner and saw his car gleaming dully under the pooling light of the streetlamp outside his house. Thank God, he breathed inwardly. Safe! With a suddenness that was paralyzing, his arms cramped rigidly and he was forced to admit he would have to put his young burden down. He did so as gently as possible, groaning, and straightened up with relief. For a second he simply stood massaging his arms in turn, trying to push the blood back in and the pain out. He heard a door slam and refocused his attention.

It had been his own.

In the feeble yellow glow of the streetlight, he saw a tall man walking down his front walk toward the street. The figure looked naggingly familiar, but he couldn't seem to place it. Too tired. Got to get home, have a drink, and make some sense of this mess.

But he didn't move.

The tall shape moved gracefully off the curb and into the street, almost seeming to float above the concrete as if disdaining to walk on such a mundane thing. Whoever it was moved to a spot just outside the circle of falling light and stopped, gazing around as if he were looking for muggers.

And I thought I was getting paranoid!

The humor stopped quickly.

Something was happening to the light. The shape of the man seemed to blur, flowing into and around itself like a summer thunderhead. As Rudy watched, hardly able to credit what his eyes told him he was seeing, what had once seemed to be a man's solid shape turned to shadow, seething, shifting, billowing. Like watching a photograph developing, but reversed. Gradually the shadows got smaller, squatter, closer to the sidewalk. Then they began to elongate, coming back into sharp focus again slowly, tortuously. Sweat ran from Vardon's armpits in the chill night air, his heart pounding a drum solo against his rib cage. Margarette drifted to his side without seeming to move and grasped his fingers so tightly that her grip nearly made him cry out. He bit down on his tongue until he tasted the salt of his own blood.

"Look!" Margarette whispered in awe. "That's one of the monsters!"

Before him, on the periphery of the light, where a man had previously stood, sat an enormous, panting, slavering wolf.

There is a place beyond fear where one simply acquiesces; you go along with the inevitable. There are things which, if fought, would herald the death of consciousness and of sanity. Children seem to know this; all things are possible to them. They believe in magic. Rudy Vardon believed in magic, too, in his own way, and what sat not one block from him— what he had seen—was simply that. It was his unconscious willingness to believe the reports of his own senses, rather than strength or sense or manliness, which prevented his reason from falling in upon itself and making of itself a black hole of madness. Often this is true: The ability to suspend reason preserves it; the willingness to give one's life saves it. Why this is true neither Margarette nor Rudy could have explained. If proof be needed, however, they were it.

Vardon stared at the beast with something that approached reverence. "Oh . . . my . . . God," he realized. "He . . . it came out of my house!"

"The monsters want to eat you, too," the child panted, and started pulling on his hand, trying to drag him back the way they'd come.

The creature stood and stretched, then loped off, passing briefly into the light before passing out of it again to disappear into the night. In that brief instant Rudy saw its color—silver-blond. And he thought about the tall human shape that it had been, broad-shouldered and athletic, and knew who it was.

Looking around carefully and seeing nothing, he swung the child with him up into his arms and ran down the last block to his front door. He was afraid to think about Eve. If she was alright. If she was alive. Don't let her be like this girl's family, he prayed. Don't let her be like my dog.

He tried to walk inside, but the door was locked. Putting the girl on the porch, he breathed a sigh of relief as he knocked. "It's going to be okay," he told her.

Footsteps echoed within the walls, growing louder as they moved toward the front of the house. A few seconds later the door was opened and relieved-looking Evelyn asked him crossly, "Rudy Vardon, you bastard. Just where the hell have you—"

Vardon pointed to the girl.

"Who is that?"

"Margarette Griswold," Vardon said, slipping past her and pulling the child inside in tow behind him. "If you don't mind, my friend and I would rather talk inside." Turning, he removed her hand from the doorknob and shut the door, locking it. Then he walked into the large living room and seated himself and the girl on the sofa. The child drew close to him, holding tightly to his arm.

Evelyn walked in slowly after them. "Margarette *Griswold*, you said? Come on, Rudy, that little girl died. . . ."

Her boyfriend shook his head.

"She didn't?"

"No."

"And this is her?"

"This is her."

"Well, Rudy, where did you find her?"

"In the mountains by her father's cabin."

For a moment the woman was enraged. Would this man ever behave rationally again? She slapped her forehead in dismay. "Oh great. Turn my back and you sneak out the door like some little kid and start playing Sherlock Holmes. Christ, Rudy, why don't you let the police handle this? They're getting paid for it, you know?"

"I don't trust the police. Especially the chief of police."

Evelyn slumped on the loveseat. "Grand," she said in exasperation. "Just grand. So what are you going to do in general, and with her in particular?"

"First, we're going to feed her and get her cleaned up. In case you haven't noticed, she's in a bad way. Then we're all going to get the hell out of here as fast as we can until I can figure out just who'd believe me if I tell them what I know."

The woman's face softened and she came over to kneel in front of the girl, who was sleeping with her head on Rudy's arm. In sleep her face was guileless and innocent, devoid even of the fear that had etched itself into it so sharply. "I'm sorry. I was feeling sorry for myself, I guess. I'll go get her some soup and crackers or something. Then we'll give her a bath. But I don't think we should take her anywhere tonight, Rudy. We should just put her to bed and let her get some rest. Tomorrow we can figure out what we should do about her other than having Doc Appleby check her over."

"No!" Rudy hissed. "Not Appleby."

"Oh, Jesus. Now what is wrong with an old man like Doc Appleby? Is he some kind of mad doctor or something, do you think?"

"He could just be something like that," Rudy mused. "I'm not sure. He might be a werewolf, too."

Evelyn stared at him in shock. "He's a WHAT?!"

"A werewolf. A wolf-man. Was Joshua Gimball here just a little while ago?"

For some reason the writer felt she wasn't following this conversation very well. "Well, yes. In fact, he just left a few minutes before you came, but what about this were—"

"What'd he want, did he tell you?"

"Well, of course he told me. He came over to be

250

sure that we were going to attend his Halloween party. I told him I'd have to check it out with you, first, but I was pretty sure that we'd be there. It'll probably be fun. Aggie says his Halloween parties are famous around here. Why the sudden interest in Joshua, Rudy? And what'd you say about were—"

"Yeah, right. Halloween party," Vardon smirked. "I'll just bet. I was pretty sure it was him I saw changing out there, but I wanted to be sure. Damn! He probably knows I know by now, too." He laid the child down on the sofa and started to get up. "C'mon. We'll pack a few things and get the hell out of here tonight. Right now. We can get her something to eat when we reach another town or a motel or something. A few more hours without food isn't going to kill her."

Eve grabbed his belt and pulled him back down. "Whoa, whoa. What do you mean leave? What do you mean change? Rudy, if your going to act like a madman, you could at least tell me what you're talking about so I can act crazy, too. Maybe we can get adjoining rooms at the asylum."

He grabbed her shoulders and stood, pulling her up with him. There was a feeling of calm growing in him that he didn't understand. He was thinking more clearly than he could remember ever doing before, experiencing each detail of reality with a clarity and single-mindedness that was awesome. "Leaving," he explained, "as in getting the fuck out of town. As in pack a few things quickly and boogie. Shag ass. Change as in grow hair and claws and teeth and howl at the moon. As in become a werewolf, Eve. A wolfman. The whole Lon Chaney Jr. number. Joshua

251

Gimball is a werewolf. I just saw him change. And there're more than just him, because a bunch of them killed Margarette's family. I bet they killed those campers, too. And John Scott. They probably have been killing the deer and dogs around here right along. Shit, Evelyn, there must be a whole *pack* of werewolves in Larksboro." He walked to the fireplace and leaned on the mantel.

"Rudy, look . . ."

"No, dammit, you look. Gimball's one, I know that. Doc must be one, too. That's why he falsified those death certificates. And I'll bet that Charlie McQuire is one, and probably a couple of others on the police force, too." He saw Mayor Cooper leaning into the squad car and talking to McQuire. "Maybe the mayor . . ." And Agatha Cooper limping down the street with her bad back and bummed-up ribs. Her too? Didn't Appleby have a daughter? Didn't Gimball have someone who lived up at that place of his to tend it? "Jesus Christ," he said, alarmed. "They've got a fucking army. My God!"

Eve walked over to him and stroked his arm. "Maybe we could talk about this more calmly in the morning," she said quietly.

"No goddammed way." He shook her off, spun her around, and pushed her toward the stairs. "Humor me, I may get violent. Go up and pack a few things for both of us. We're leaving. Now."

She shook her head sadly, but she obeyed.

The car keys. Where are the damned car keys? He found them in the pocket of a jacket hanging by the door and, taking a deep breath, walked out of the house and into the night. The door closed with a click of finality. They had to get out of here now. They had to get away before it was too late. If he was right, there were way too many of them to fight—even if he did know how to fight werewolves. Which he didn't.

He tried to hurry down the walk to his car, but he seemed to be wading through molasses. He couldn't remember the walk being so goddamned long.

When he reached his car and tried to unlock it, his hands shook so badly that he dropped the keys and had to retrieve them from under the car before he could try again. Which way do you turn the damned thing to unlock the door? Shit, he'd had the car for five years, he should know by now. At last he did it. The lock clicked, the door opened smoothly.

As he got in, he knew it was too late; there were dozens of hairy shapes milling in the shadows, and they would take him now. Just now, when he was so close to escape. Just now, when he was almost back to muggers and rapists and flashers and a sane, orderly world. He could feel their claws shearing his flesh, actually tensed his back in anticipation of the bitter pain and the knowledge of defeat.

It didn't come.

He settled against the cracked and worn vinyl and slid the key into the ignition with a minimum of fumbling. As he turned it he thought some crazy half thoughts about the sexual symbolism of keys and locks, but shook them aside with a grimace. Psychology 101 will ruin you for life.

They key rotated fully forward, but nothing happened.

He tried again, disbelieving. I just had it tuned up,

he pleaded. The battery's only a year old!

Nothing. There was no grinding, no lights, no noise, no shaking. The car was dead.

And so, he thought, are we.

He jumped out and ran to the front of the automobile, feeling for the hood release. When he pressed it, the hood sprung open a few inches and he inserted his fingers in the gap, finding the safety latch, lifting. The lid yawned above him, the sheet metal jaws of a Detroit alligator. There was very little left under it that wasn't damaged in some way. He sighed and collapsed on the fender.

The electrical system had been torn asunder and scattered over the engine like rubber pasta. The distributor cap was gone, as was the battery. The carburetor looked as though it had been crushed in the palm of a giant. As a means of conveyance, the car had ceased to exist. It might have made a serviceable planter.

As he slumped over the fender, Rudy Vardon wept tears of frustration and bitter rage. There had been no need to so demolish the innards of the vehicle; any part of the damage would have rendered the car useless. It was a warning, a promise, and pure and simple, a show of strength. They were trapped. They were found out.

He wondered if they were helpless.

Slamming his hand once against the cold steel in disappointment, he turned and walked back toward the door to his home. His castle. He could see Eve peering out the window between the heavy drapes. She had confusion etched in her features, and worry. There were a million questions she wanted to ask, and he had answers to only a few. No answers for the biggies, though. The ones like, "What do we do now?"

In his peripheral vision he caught the cutting yellow-white blades of headlights as they sliced through the heavy darkness a few blocks up the street. First there was one set, then two, then three; the last pairs of lights backlit the first car enough for him to make out the red and blue flasher on its roof. When they passed the last cross street he knew they were coming here, for them. He knew who they were, and he ran.

He burst through the door in a rush and slammed it after him so loudly that the child, still asleep on the sofa, jerked awake and started to cry. Evelyn was more than a little frightened, he could see. Frightened of him, by him. He wanted to comfort the two of them and explain what was wrong, but there wasn't time for that any more. He threw the bolt and strode over to where Evelyn cringed by the window.

"Lock the doors and windows," he ordered sharply, but she didn't move. Instead she stared fixedly at his face, and he realized he must look like he had gone over the edge. He grabbed her, shook her. "Now, dammit."

"The car," she stammered, "is it . . ."

"They've wrecked it." He moved into the hall and picked up the phone. It was an off chance, a long shot. He expected exactly what he got—nothing. They had killed the car. They had killed the phone.

Our turn next.

He looked out the window beside the door and saw that the cars were pulling up in front of the house.

Black shapes were getting out, but at least they wer
human. For now.

"Are the monsters coming to eat us?" Margarett
asked tearfully.

"Shh," Rudy said. He picked her up and starte
toward the back of the house. "Come on, Eve. We'l
go out the back."

"And go where?" Eve asked as she hurried afte
the man and child.

They moved into the dining room. "I don't know
yet. We'll just keep moving until I think of some
thing. I wish we had a gun or something. I wish—"

A thundering pounding rolled at them from th
rear of the house. They stopped for a moment
fearful and confused, but Rudy put the six-year-ol
down quickly and, motioning his girlfriend to sta
where she was, crept toward the kitchen. Just as h
came within sight of it, the rear door seemed t
explode, bursting open with impossible force. Wha
had not shattered under the first assault did so as th
remains were catapulted into the wall on the hinges
burying the doorknob in the thick plaster. Woo
splinters and glass flew through the air like shrapnel
imbedding in the far walls. When he took his up
raised forearms from in front of his eyes, Vardon sav
man-shaped shadows filling the doorway, starting t
move into the room.

The artist turned wildly and ran back to Eve an
Margarette, who were huddled in terror in a dar
corner of the dining room. Too frightened to attemp
speech, he grabbed them both and pulled them bacl
toward the living room. There would be others ou
front, he knew, but perhaps if he could get them al

upstairs, maybe they could get out a window and escape over the roof or something. He didn't know about that, but he did know that they couldn't stay down here with those things running in the back door. It was obvious that all pretense was gone, now. The creatures had come for blood.

They had reached the middle of the room when the front window burst inward, shards of glass flying like razor blades through the air. Rudy pushed the woman and child toward the sofa, shoving them forcefully to the floor where they might avoid injury. A dagger of glass cut a deep path back along his temple, just missing his eye. Another—longer, like a sword—slid through the fabric of his jeans and imbedded in his thigh. His body twisted in pain and he went to his knees, but female screaming surged in the air like a tide, and the booming thud coming from the thick front door let him know there was no time to lick his wounds. Vardon scrambled to his feet and tried to run to the fireplace, but could only manage a jerky, spastic walk. Clouds of darkness whirlpooled in front of his eyes one minute to be replaced the next by a growing brightness that threatened to bleach his mind of consciousness. He couldn't pass out, dammit! He wouldn't!

Panting and swearing, he had just reached the fireplace when he heard the front door give way with an ominous ripping sound. Frantically he reached out and grabbed the brass poker from its cradle and then turned, issuing a low growl of his own, to fight.

"How quickly we lose our veneer of civilization, Rudy."

Joshua Gimball stood just inside the decimated

door, flanked by Alec Wall and Doc Appleby. Charlie McQuire and his two deputies walked in calmly from the kitchen, smiling.

Mack Horner spit a wad of tobacco juice against the wall, watching it roll obscenely to the floor, and cackled merrily at Vardon. "Whaddaya think, Mister Art-test? Pretty cre-ative, ain't I?"

Rudy gripped the poker in a white-knuckled hand and took an unconscious step toward his tormentor.

"Enough," Gimball hissed. It stopped them both immediately. "Horner, you're upsetting Mr. Vardon here, and we are guests in his house."

Charlie McQuire snorted.

"Do you find that statement humorous, Chief?" Joshua asked.

"Yeah, I guess I do, Professor."

"I assure you it wasn't intended to be."

McQuire averted his eyes nervously.

"Rudy. I'm so sorry to, ah . . . break in on you this way, but I feel the time has come to have a serious talk about life here in Larksboro, don't you agree?"

"What do you know about life?" Rudy asked bitingly.

"We know you ain't gonna see much more of it," Horner mumbled.

"Hah!" Gimball barked. "The man asks what I know of life. Why, Rudy, I know a great deal about life. A great deal. You might say that I've made quite a study of it. Human life and . . . other life, too."

"Other life, huh? Like you, you mean? You're a goddamned monster, Gimball. A fucking monster and I'm going to kill you if I have to follow you to

258

hell to do it." Vardon slammed the tip of the poker against the floor.

"Yes. Well, I think you'll precede me to hell by a good many years, assuming the existence of such a place. As for this accusation of monsterhood . . . Mr. Vardon, I'm truly surprised at you. Monster is such a pedestrian term. Common and ignorant." He shifted his attention to Evelyn, pointing to the crying child beside her. "My dear, if you don't soon shut that child up, I'll have one of my friends assist you. And please, get up off the floor. Sit there on the sofa, won't you? You'll catch your death down there in that draft."

Rudy took a few steps toward them, his weapon raised high. "You leave them alone, you son of a bitch. Just leave them the fuck alone, you hear me?"

"Tsk, tsk, tsk. Your language seems to be deteriorating, sir. And in front of such a small child, too. Of course, Freud did say that children were rather totally formed by four years, didn't he? Still, we can't afford to take chances on the opinions of a man like that. I think the old fraud would have even denied me reality, don't you, Rudy?"

"What are you?" Eve sobbed.

Joshua gestured expansively. "What are *we*, Eve. *We*. All of us in this room are of the same . . . er . . . persuasion, as it were. And there are even more than this, I might add. In fact, we have quite a little society here in Larksboro. Not that it isn't exclusive; we choose our members with extreme care. That's why we are what you will be soon, my dear. We are—"

"Werewolves!" Rudy yelled. "You're all were-

259

wolves!"

Horner pursed his quite human lips and howled mockingly.

"Doctor," Astin Chubb panted, limping around in tight circles. "Doctor, you promised you could help me."

Gimball shook his head. "Will you two please be quiet? Charlie, aren't you capable of controlling your men?"

McQuire pushed the pantomiming Chubb into his howling friend and said hoarsely, "Goddammit, will you two just stop it? Holy fuck!"

The two giggled but acceded.

"Very good, Charles. You must forgive the outburst," Joshua apologized to Vardon, "but there was such disgust in your tone when you said werewolves, you know. Such fear. We can smell the fear coming off of you right now in waves, Rudy. When you are a werewolf and have been for some time, you get rather used to it. You lose touch with the fact that others may find it a little frightening." The man grinned. "It's no wonder, of course. All those terrible movies. Very bad publicity, I must admit."

"We don't call ourselves werewolves, however, Rudy. The term denotes someone who has no choice in the matter—changing at the full of the moon, howling into the night, bestial of both mind and body, cursed with the curse of the wolf, suffering, in torment and agony. Well, I've been a werewolf all my life—I'm the bastard son of a priest, you see, and we're always werewolves—and I've found that all of that is rubbish. Patently untrue. Bullshit. The experience is really quite pleasant, isn't it, Alec?"

Beside him, Wall nodded. "Indubitably."

"There. And Alec wasn't always a werewolf, as I was. I've made him what he is today, as they say. In fact, none of these good people were born to a life of werewolfery; they chose it. Do you think for a minute they'd follow me so willingly if I had done something hurtful to them? They like it, Rudy. Really. But I digress.

"Over the course of the years, I have learned much about my condition—historically, medically, and otherwise. I have learned how to make the change— what I call transmogrification—a voluntary matter, as it is supposed to be. I can change at will, either way. I have even amassed the power not to change at the full moon, should I desire not to. This is how it should be.

"Shape changing was once the province of powerful shamans, sorcerers, magicians. It is a willful thing. A purposeful thing. Like all else, it was left in the hands of the incompetent and the ignorant, and so lost most of its effectivity. I have changed that situation. We are no longer at the whims of our beast nature, Rudy. Not even as much as you yourself are. We aren't werewolves, sir, we are lycanthropists."

"You're what?"

"Lycanthropists. Sorcerers who can change their shapes at will. A new species, Rudy. Of course, we'll never take over the planet or anything like that. Not only is that the stuff of fantasy and bad horror films, it would be terribly unwise. We are the ultimate predators, and your kind are our preferred prey."

"God," Eve sobbed. She grabbed Margarette and crabbed as far as she could away from the professor

261

along the sofa cushions. Rudy moved toward her instinctively.

"Not to worry," Joshua soothed her gently. "There is nothing for you to worry about."

"Right," Vardon spat angrily, putting his free hand around Eve's quivering shoulders. "Nothing to worry about. We're only your 'preferred prey.'"

"Of course we prey on humans. What else? It is in our blood. Our very nature is to stalk man, hunt him down, devour him. That is why we must keep our own population low. Otherwise, your species might get overhunted, and we would be faced with a diminished food supply. It is, after all, only good ecological sense. And I said nothing about *you* having nothing to worry about. Just Eve, Mr. Vardon. Just Eve."

"What do you mean 'just Eve'?" Rudy demanded.

"Just what I said. I have other plans for your beautiful young girlfriend."

There was a whimpering outside the door in the night. Joshua cocked his head to listen, smiled dreamily, and motioned for something to enter. When the "something" did, Evelyn collapsed, rolling bonelessly to the floor.

Margarette started to wail, "Mommymommy-mommy . . ."

Rudy could only stare at what had walked into his house.

There were two of them. They weren't wolves, at least not in the same way that Gimball had turned into a wolf earlier that evening. These were truly wolf-men. No. They were wolf-women.

One was darker than the other and seemed fiercer

262

as it nudged against Alec Wall familiarly, but both were hideous. Their heads and faces were those of wolves from hell; they were not natural, they were demonic. The covering of short hair flowed down without a break until it reached their erectly nippled breasts. There it thinned and faded into human skin, and wasn't taken back up with any fullness until it obscured the pubic area and colored the legs, feet, and buttocks. The hands were barely human, with the fingers shortened and clawed fearsomely. The feet were even more canine, complete with dewclaw, and threw their stance weight forward as if they walked on four legs instead of two. How could they run? he questioned. They would have to drop down to all fours.

Baring three-inch-long fangs and slavering repulsively, the two creatures stood beside Gimball, whimpering like puppies. As the tall blond man reached out and stroked them, they shook ecstatically.

"What do you think of my two young lovelies?" Joshua asked.

"Disgusting," Rudy managed to choke out around the bile that flooded his throat. The stench in the room was almost unbearable.

Gimball shrugged. "Ah, well. We all know where beauty lies anyway, don't we? Let me introduce you, my friend." He stroked the dark one that stood beside Wall. "This beauty is Irene Hillman, a student of mine at the college and Alec's . . . fiancé. This other," he said, indicating one of honey-brown coloration, "is the good doctor's daughter, Carol. His daughter and his mate."

"His . . . MATE?"

"Yes. Well, you must understand that we do not exist under the same set of social taboos that you do, Rudy. In our society there are no incest prohibitions. Much as there were undoubtedly none with primitive man. It is much more natural and acceptable than you might expect."

Rudy nodded, numb to his soul. "Why are they . . . I saw you when you . . . changed. You didn't look like them at all."

"Very observant. A very perceptive question. In answer, I shall tell you that it takes a rather lengthy period of time to be able to fully complete the transmogrification, as I can. As a result, you have a wide diversity of appearances within our little group. These two have not been within the fold long enough to change to any larger degree than this, although I must say that Irene is doing quite well for the short time she's been one of us."

The dark creature yelped, pleased with herself.

Alec smiled proudly and stroked her back.

"That's why you have such a wide range of belief as to what a werewolf looks like," Gimball explained. "One who is fully able to change looks like a type of wolf. Of course, his body weight and relative size remain the same. And the eyes never change, never. You can always tell who a werewolf is by looking at the eyes. Of course," he chuckled, "if you get that close, the knowledge is liable to do you very little good. The shapes in this group alone run the gamut from these very partial changes, through the Hollywood types and up to myself; I change completely, as you've seen."

Irene whimpered again, and Carol echoed her.

"God," Rudy whispered. "You're animals."

"Now there you're mistaken," Joshua said good-naturedly. "In fact, the fact that we *aren't* animals when we change is what makes us so effective—and so dangerous. You see, we have gained the keen senses and reflexes of a wolf, his form, but we have kept our ability to think and reason. The thought processes are totally unimpaired, Mr. Vardon. We do not become animals. We are a hybrid between man and wolf, combining the best of both. We are the ultimate species. The ultimate."

The two females whimpered louder. Irene barked, growled, barked again.

"Yes, you're right, Irene. I am wordy tonight. Not that it really matters. But I did promise you, I know, and we do have to be going soon. Alright. Alright."

The massive professor started to walk across the floor toward the three humans. Horner moved to accompany him, but Gimball waved him way imperiously. Rudy, who had been on his knees trying to revive Eve, shot to his feet and raised his poker defensively.

"Get away from us, Gimball. Back up, you sick bastard, or I'll crush your skull."

"Rudy, Rudy," Joshua admonished, advancing confidently. "I really don't think I can let you do that."

When he was within striking distance, Rudy brought the poker around like a baseball bat, using every ounce of strength he could summon, trying for the left-field bleachers. Joshua ducked it effortlessly, with the grace of a dancer. The big man grabbed Vardon by the front of the shirt as he straightened up and, in one fluid motion, flung him violently against the far wall without so much as a grunt. Rudy hit, the breath exploding from his lungs in a whoosh, his head denting the plaster as it rocked back on his shoulders. He slid to the floor almost in slow motion, the gash on the back of his skull leaving a trail of blood down the wall. He lay on his side, eyes glazed but seeing, unable to move, and watched what happened next.

Gimball towered over the frightened Margarette for a few seconds, grinning maliciously. Then he reached down and lifted the screaming, kicking child from where she cringed beside the still unconscious Evelyn, raising her to shoulder level and holding her straight out in front of him.

"It is time you joined your parents," he said.

Then he turned to his two females and tossed the child to them as if she were a pork chop.

The dark creature, Irene Hillman, shouldered the other out of the way and caught her in mid flight, snarling madly and chafing her jaws. Then she turned and ran through the doorway, with the lighter creature tailing along behind her into the darkness.

There was one final, trilling scream.

Then there was only the snarling and the tearing of flesh.

When the darkness came to swallow him up, Rudy welcomed it as a savior.

Doc Appleby bent over the unconscious form of Evelyn Sangellis first, examining it carefully. When he was satisfied, he looked up at Joshua and smiled, nodding. Then he walked to the battered body of

Rudy Vardon and felt the neck for a pulse, grunted, and turned him carefully on his back, kneading for broken bones or other, more subtle injuries. He examined the wound on the back of Vardon's head carefully and checked his pupils for dilation and contraction. After a few minutes he stood and straightened his clothes, looking over at Gimball once more.

"This one's going to be fine," he assured Joshua. "Oh, he'll have one bad headache and he'll be sore as hell, but there's nothing seriously wrong with him."

"Good," Gimball grinned. "Mr. Vardon figures into my plans almost as much as his ladyfriend does." He looked over Eve's still form wantingly. "The party this year should be a very festive one, indeed, my friends. Alec, will you please see that those three deliver our human guests to Moonshadow unharmed? The doctor and I will collect the females and clean up here. And Charles, take care of the Griswold cabin as soon as possible, yes? You know how I despise unfinished business."

The pain increased in intensity rapidly. It grew and grew and grew until its white-hot aches pulled him up from the depths of the dark well bottom he had been inhabiting. He didn't mind. The pain was nothing compared to the creatures—demons and devils—that chased him in the smothering blackness. A thousand years of pain would be fine if it only took him beyond the reach of their fangs, their claws. So he didn't fight it, spiraling upward into a land of agony, but also one of noise and light.

The light almost blinded him when he tried to

open his eyes. Groaning, he threw his forearm across them to block it out, concentrating instead on his other senses to determine reality. He heard faint noises; there were leaves rustling in a breeze, some birds chirping. His skin reported that no breezes touched him, and the birdsong was muffled and sounded far away. He was inside, then. He was alive. He seemed to be lying flat on his back on something soft—a bed, a cot, a couch. The pain throbbed in a tightening web around his skull.

Rudy opened his eyes slowly. First just slits. Then, when the pain levelled off and his pupils adjusted, a little more and a little more, until he was staring at a ceiling.

It was no ceiling that he could remember.

Well, now or never. He threw his legs over the edge of the cot—it was a cot—on which he was lying and sat up. The room immediately began to whiten and swirl, and he was forced to plop back across the thin mattress and take in deep draughts of air to relieve his nausea. There was a window in the wall he faced, but very little light came through it. After a few minutes he realized why: It had been solidly boarded over.

Behind him the door creaked open. He started, tried to rise and at least put his back to the wall, but his injuries betrayed him and he stumbled groggily, lacking balance. Only his desperate hold on the cot kept him from falling.

Joshua Gimball stood, observing, smiling. He bent down and patted the mattress invitingly. "Come now," he stated, "you can't feel well enough for such athletics yet. Have a seat, Rudy. I don't intend you any harm."

As if he had a choice! He sat heavily.

"You've suffered a rather nasty blow to your head, but Doc assures me that you'll be just fine if you act sensibly. Try to be calm."

"Oh, right."

"That's easy for me to say, right? How true." He leaned against the wall and crossed his ams over his chest. "Well, you must be exhausted, so I'll get right to the point of my visit. I thought perhaps I would tell you what is going to happen, and why. Would you like to know that, Rudy?"

Vardon stared at him coldly.

Gimball ignored the look and continued. "Both you and your girlfriend are going to attend my Halloween party, Rudy. You are going to die that night. She is not. Evelyn Sangellis will, on Halloween night, be admitted into our little order. After which time, she will become my mate. For life, Mr. Vardon, as is the custom with wolves."

Rudy tried once more to rise, groaning with the effort, but his wobbly legs wouldn't hold him and he fell back. "Damn you," he cursed loudly. "I'll kill you if you so much as touch her, you bastard. I'll kill you!" He tried to rise again, but Gimball kicked the cot swiftly and drove it into the injured man's knees, knocking him to the ground. In a blur of motion, the lycanthropist was standing over his victim with his feet firmly planted in the artist's throat.

"You do have spirit, Rudy. I'll give you credit for that. And you would probably make an excellent werewolf, in time, if I could cure your rebelliousness. But that would be rather embarrassing for both of us, wouldn't it? Eve would be my mate and you would, of necessity, have to constantly challenge my dominance if you should want to have her back. It seems you have doomed yourself in either case, my friend." The man removed his foot and walked back to stand by the open door.

Rudy choked harshly, rolled to his side, and vomited.

"Damn. Now look at that mess. I'll have to send for Mattie to clean it up, I suppose. Whatever. I haven't told you how you're going to die yet, have I?" A look of diabolical glee crossed his face. "This is so dramatic, I can hardly wait to tell you. After your ex-girlfriend experiences her first transmogrification, you will be her first taste of human flesh. You will be her first meal, Rudy. Isn't that poetic?"

"She won't . . ." Rudy rasped.

"Ah, but she will. The wolf blood is persuasive. she may not relish the idea, but . . . she will. It will be your last supper, but her first." He reached to go out the door, laughing at his own pun.

"Wait!" Vardon yelled after him. "Why? Why me? Why Eve?"

Joshua hesitated and looked back. "Why? Very simple, my friend. All things feel the urge to mate, to reproduce their kind. I really don't know if we can or not, but we shall try. There is no physical reason why we cannot, but . . . who knows? There are higher powers, many things I've yet to understand, I'll admit. If any of the women do conceive, I can assure you it will be an historic moment, indeed. Perhaps even a first, who can say? If we cannot reproduce, the urge is still there to be fulfilled; we must have a companion, at least. The cleaving of female to male seems to be universal, Mr. Vardon. Perhaps the Orientals were right with their yin and yang, their in and yo. Complimentarity, Rudy. Always that need to obey the biological command to complimentarity. Ah, well.

"If you behave yourself we will keep you alive for Eve. If not, you will still serve the purpose dead. Essentially the choice is yours. You may even kill yourself if you see fit. I can assure you that you will be well fed until the time arrives, however. Your needs will be seen to. Do what you must." He turned and walked out, closing the door behind him.

Rudy heard the locks, three by the sound, slip closed, and the soft tread of Gimball's footfalls as he walked away. He pulled himself back onto the cot and sat heavily, massaging his throat.

"Jesus," he swore softly. "What the fuck do I do now?"

Even as the little shafts of light that made their way around the boards across the window faded, he was no closer to an answer than he had been when they were still bright. He was, however, that much closer to Halloween.

By his reckoning, it had been two days since he awoke in this room . . . Death Row. Two days. He thanked whatever powers were to credit that his digital watch had come through all the trials in one piece. It gave him a way to tie together a pattern, to establish the rhythm of this place. It was 11:43 A.M.

They brought breakfast around eight in the morning and set it by the door. Lunch was served around noon. Dinner between six and six-thirty in the evening. Regular as clockwork, every day.

Who brought the meals was something else, seemingly determined by chance rather than any schedule. some meals it was Mattie Zimmer and the other woman. Other times it was one of the men. He had seen no regularity yet and did not have time to wait much longer.

No longer than tonight.

He had tried to pry the boards loose from the single window, but it had been nailed on so tightly that it would take a much bigger person than he had ever been to do it alone. In frustration he had turned his efforts toward the cot, trying to loosen the screws that held its metal legs to the frame. If he could work them loose, at least he would have a crude weapon when the time came. When he needed one.

He had worked long and hard. His fingers were raw and bruised, the tips resembling hamburger, and he had to stick his hands in his pockets or behind his back so they wouldn't be seen when one of them came into the room. He had cleaned up the drops of his own blood that spotted the floor with spit and the tail of his shirt. He had ripped off his fingernails and chipped his teeth. And he had finally succeeded. He had his weapon.

11:48 A.M.

Should he go tonight? No. Why not, he asked himself? Why the hell not?

They move more freely at night. They know the woods. Their eyesight is better. They have enough advantages without giving up any more to them.

So when?

Now! When they bring the lunch tray. Now!

But what if? . . .

DON'T THINK! NOW!

He heard the sound of shuffling footsteps coming up the stairs to the second floor. Where the room was. The tread seemed heavy for one of them, and he was sure it wasn't Gimball or Wall. Those two moved like ghosts, and he didn't want to tangle with either of them if he could avoid it at present.

The steps stopped at the door. Locks began to unlock.

Rudy raised the cot leg high over his head, carefully letting the cot sag toward the floor. He moved beside the door and waited, poised for the assault. There would only be one chance. God, don't let this be Mack Horner. I don't know if I can kill that psycho.

A head was thrust between the door and the jamb, looking cautiously, checking if it was safe.

Vardon closed his eyes and brought the metal post down hard. It made contact with a soggy thunk, like smashing a watermelon or a pumpkin. It wasn't at all like hitting something as hard as he thought a head should be; it gave.

Someone groaned softly, as in a dream. Something heavy slid to the floor like a sack of potatoes; a dense-sounding thud, accompanied by the stiletto rapping of knuckles and the deeper thump of the skull. The serving tray clattered and a dish broke. Then the silence settled back in and he waited for someone below to hear the commotion and come charging up the stairs. No one did.

He had yet to open his eyes.

When he did, at last, he saw that it was Mattie

Zimmer who lay at his feet, wedged half in and half out of the room. For a moment he felt the pangs of self-revulsion (My God, I've killed an old woman!) course through him; she looked so old, so grand-motherly, so human. But he had to remember that she wasn't, none of them were, so he shook it off and bent to drag her into his cell.

The rear of the woman's skull was deeply indented and welling thick blood, which streaked her hair crimson as it spilled to the floor to mingle with the trickling fluids that flowed from beneath her down-turned face. Feeling squeamish and sick, he grabbed the body under the arms and pulled it awkwardly out of the hall, shutting the door until he could get himself together again.

Suddenly the still form heaved, choked, began gurgling and coughing the blood from its throat. The liver-spotted hand flexed, broken nails scraping against the floorboards.

Mattie Zimmer tried to raise her head.

Rudy panicked. White and cold and biting pain-fully into his tongue so he wouldn't scream, he snatched the metal leg off the floor and brought it down on the old woman's twitchng body again and again and again, beating the head down, driving it like he'd drive a nail into a two-by-four, until there was little left but gore and pulp and bone fragments. Crying silently, he sprawled over the cot and vomited painfully.

"Oh Jesus," he moaned, "Oh Jesusjesusjesus."

The thought stopped his tears. Holy shit, he must have sounded like a rhythm section up here, ham-mering, hammering.

Somebody must have heard. Must have.

There was no noise from anywhere in the house. I can't be this lucky. There must be somebody home.

Picking up his weapon, he stepped over the remains of Mattie Zimmer and walked cautiously through the door and into the hall. He neither saw nor heard anyone. He crept down the stairs, staying well against the wall and centering his weight on each foot as he put it down on the riser. All those adventure shows were paying off now. By God, he could do this just as good as Clint Eastwood any old day.

By the time he had reached the first floor, his thighs ached and he was drenched with sweat, but he had still seen and heard nothing.

Cautiously, so cautiously, he snuck to the front door. My God, what if they were out there? There had to be somebody else around here. What the hell should he do now?

Look out the window first. The window.

He walked to the window, pulled the curtain away from the sill just a fraction, and looked. Nothing. Good. Then he duckwalked to the other side and did the same. And saw Astin Chubb in a chair against the far corner of the porch, hat pulled low over his eyes.

Shit!

He looked like he might be asleep: his hands sat loosely in his lap and his chest moved in and out deeply, evenly. Occasionally his foot would twitch. Maybe he could get to the deputy before he could wake up, or maybe he wasn't asleep in the first place; maybe Chubb was just faking it, trying to lure him

275

out. How the hell was he supposed to know? For Christ's sake, he'd never done anything like this before.

Cursing silently, he slowly turned the door handle and opened the front door, expecting to be ambushed at any moment. The door hinges didn't even squeak; he'd been really worried about that. He kept to the wall of the house as he crept along the porch, keeping one eye on Astin Chubb and the other peeled for anyone else who might pop out of the woodwork at the wrong moment. His hand ached from his hold on the steel cot leg; his shoulder ached from holding it so high. Only eight feet to go.

Five.

Three.

Two.

As he shifted his weight to move forward, one of the floor boards squealed like a wounded puppy.

Astin Chubb rocked forward on his chair, his hat falling into the dust. Before the front legs of his seat had hit the ground he was rising, spinning toward the sound that had awakened him, reaching for his side arm.

One.

Rudy brought the club down with a shout, but the deputy jerked his head away smartly and it smacked into the juncture of the shoulder and neck, raising havoc with the nerve center located there and pile-driving the fat man to his knees. Chubb's left arm was useless, hanging limply at his side with no more feeling or movement than a side of beef, but the deputy was right-handed. Stunned, he feebly groped for his .357, finally jerking it clear of the holster.

Vardon leaped forward and kneed Astin in the teeth, knocking him onto his back in a spray of red froth and ivory. The pistol discharged wildly, far wide of its intended target, and then the cot leg was coming down like Thor's hammer, slamming into the deputy's forehead, the angled steel imbedding itself in the ruined flesh and crushed bone. Muscle spasms jerked the trigger on the .357 once more and the shot careened into the trees, but then the grip was relaxed by the soothing touch of death, and Astin Chubb lay still.

Eve! He had to find Eve!

He ran toward the front door, drunk on his victory. They could be killed! They could be killed like anything else alive could be killed! Now he had to find his woman and get her out of here, far from here, and then he'd be back. He'd come back and kill them all because he had to; no one else would believe him, and these creatures had to be destroyed before they could murder anyone else.

The front room was as empty as he had left it, and so he ran from room to room searching, calling, and finally pleading for Eve to answer him. After an hour he stood at the foot of the steps, both physically and emotionally exhausted, wracking his brain to try to find a clue to her whereabouts. Where would that bastard put her? She could be here, anywhere in town, where else?

Damn him! Damn that son of a bitch to hell!

He heard them coming up the rutted dirt road in their truck. Not too close yet, he hoped. Not too close.

He charged out the back door and into the protect-

277

ive embrace of the surrounding trees, tears streaming down his cheeks. He had to run; he was their only chance of survival. But he'd be back. Oh yes, he'd be back for sure.

And when he crashed Joshua Gimball's Halloween party, he'd know much more about what he was fighting, and he'd be prepared.

He'd get Eve back from these demons.

And, he swore to God Almighty, he'd see everyone of them in hell.

The first time that Evelyn had awakened, she had wanted to believe it had all been nothing but a nightmare—an explicit, gruesome nightmare, oh yes, indeed, but a nightmare none the less. And so, desperately clinging to the soft textures her semiconsciousness gave both her departing dream images and the newly arriving shades of reality, she rolled to her left and reached out for her lover. First she would cuddle against him and take reassurance from his warmth and shape and texture. Then, later, after breakfast and perhaps some loving, she would read him the riot act about this paranoia of his—how it not only irritated and worried the hell out of her all day, but how it kept her from sleeping well at night.

Rudy, she thought dreamily, with your present turn of mind, there's no way I'm going to let you write the screenplay for my dreaming.

And her hand had smacked into a wall that couldn't have been there and plopped onto cold sheets—where Rudy should have been—like a dead fish. Her eyelids had launched open to show her the strange bed and the strange bedroom and she knew it had been real—no dream, no dream—it *was* real, and she found herself screaming.

Then a door behind her had opened and she had whirled, trying to rise, but had only tightened the grip of the sodden sheets she had wrapped around herself during the long, restless, haunted time of her unconsciousness. Instead of getting out of bed, she rolled jerkily to the edge and tipped onto the floor with a squeal of exasperation.

Something walked up behind her as she lay grunting and squirming on the rough wood flooring. Moaning low in her throat, she tried to crawl caterpillar-style under the bed.

The something touched her shoulder and she stopped all movement as if she had been turned off. Her skin crawled, but she barely breathed. Waiting for the first puncture of her skin, for the feel of her own blood spurting and oozing from her body.

She was lifted gently, tenderly placed back on the bed.

Still she waited.

A familiar, compelling voice said, "Eve." Simply. And she had to look.

Beyond her own control, Eve Sangellis craned her neck up and back, up and back, until she saw a luminous pair of grey-green eyes.

Then the something behind her started to speak.

The second time Eve awakened, she didn't. Perhaps she had already been awake or perhaps she wasn't even now, only dreaming wakefulness. She felt drugged, high, her consciousness scattered around the room like so many dust motes, floating lazily. She thought she remembered eating, but she wasn't sure. Had she eaten? Had she been fed?

Can't concentrate. Can't . . . what?

She sighed distractedly.

A shot? Was that a gunshot? Her heart speeded up and she could feel the tingling rush of adrenaline as it poured into her veins.

Another! It was . . . a gunshot. Why? Shooting . . . who?

And then she was in a maze, a labyrinth, following the echoes of why? and who? through corridor after dark corridor frantically until, after eons, she saw a young man she knew splattered in shadow . . . or was it blood . . . or was it shadow . . .

Rudy.

Then she was straining and sitting up heroically, ripping away the sheets tucked under the mattress that sealed her inside the bed like a letter in an envelope. And when she felt her grip on reality beginning to quickly weaken, she invoked his name, the most real thing she knew, chanting, "Rudyrudyrudyrudyrudy . . ." Falling to the floor, still chanting, shes dragged herself, dizzy and sweating, across the wood, the splinters slicing into her hands and knees, helping her to focus, to look for a door, there must be a door . . .

". . . rudyrudyrudyrudy . . ."

As her eyes locked on the doorknob—impossibly far away, tantalizingly close—it turned.

The light from the outside blinded her. All she could see was a bulking shadow, tall and wide-shouldered, but she knew who it was. She knew, and she heard him even through her sobbing.

"Ah, so he didn't look in here," it said. "But how could he, when he doesn't know this little spring-house even exists?" A chuckle, deep, melodious.

". . . rudy . . ."

"Yes, my little Eve, your Rudy has been a bad man. So rude. But we can fix that in due time, I'm sure." Joshua strode over to her and picked her up effortlessly, and she didn't resist. Tired. She was so very tired.

"But look at you," he fawned, setting her down gently on the bed and tucking her in once again. "You're all upset, and after all the effort I've directed toward your peace of mind. I tell you, Evelyn, the man has no couth. Ah, well. First I'll give you this." He held up a syringe for her to see and depressed the plunger slightly. A jewellike bubble of liquid formed at the top of the needle and flowed like a tear down its length. "And then we'll have a little chat."

"Do we go after him?" asked Alec Wall. His usually placid face was puckered with concern and sorrow.

Joshua shook his head. "No. There is no need. We will bury our dead and go on with the business of living."

Wall stood silently for a few minutes. "I want to go after him. I want to feel his flesh part between my teeth. I want to bathe in his blood."

"Alec, I understand your feelings. I grieve for our lost ones also. But don't you take this so hard, old friend. As predators, we gravely underestimated our prey; as prey, Mr. Vardon proved to be a man of great strength, courage, and resource. What has happened is sad, but it is also quite natural. You must remember that we aren't gods, Alec. Nor is Rudy Vardon a devil."

"He *is* a devil!"

"No. He is a creature enraged by the loss of other creatures of his kind, just as you are. We took from man, now man has taken from us. There is a balance to be preserved, Alec. A balance beyond our ken. You must remember he fights for his life and for his mate."

Wall huffed his displeasure. "So what do we do, Joshua? Do we sit around bantering abstract ideas like old men? Do we turn our backs to this and say that it's a shame, that's all?" He smashed his fist into the table at which they sat. It left a deep mark in the wood.

Gimball rose and walked to the far end of the room. "Don't you see, Alec; he'll come back. Before Halloween, he'll come back. He must if he wants to win back his woman, and that, I believe, is foremost in his mind right now. In his heart. He aches for her. Yes—" he turned and smiled at his companion— "he'll come to us, my friend. All we have to do is wait."

"What if he doesn't? What if he tells others, brings the authorities? What will happen to us then, Joshua?"

"Who can he tell that would believe him? Would he say there is a pack of wolf-men running around Larksboro? Do you think that he is stupid enough to do that or that anyone in authority would believe him? No.

"He could tell them we have kidnapped his

girlfriend, but she's already under my spell, you see. She'll say and do what I tell her. So let them come, and she'll deny every word of what he alleges.

"Besides, Alec, the man is enraged. We have, in effect, challenged his honor and dignity as a man. I'm sure his intention is to pick up this gauntlet on his own. He'll come back to us, and he'll come back alone."

Alec Wall grinned, displaying disturbingly long canines. "Yes, I understand now. And when he comes back, my good friend and mentor, you must let me take him. Let me bring him down, and then let your mate consume his still-living flesh. If I cannot feast on his blood and his marrow, then let me at least feast on his terror."

Joshua sat back at the table and crossed his arms over his broad chest. "We shall see," he allowed. "We shall see."

October 30. The day before Halloween.

Larksboro carried on in the normal way, not hustling and bustling, but moving gently through the autumn like a ghost through an empty house. Walter Starr stood behind the grill at the Four Starr diner every day, serving food and gossip to his customers between picking nits with Reiner, who maintained that the town just didn't feel right, not like it used to.

"Seems like the woods're closin' in on us, or somethin'," he complained. "Damned town's gone spooky all'a sudden."

"You're the one's gone spooky," Walt would shoot back with mock maliciousness. "Guess it's 'bout time we stuck you over at the Midview Rest Home so's you

283

don't fall down the stairs or such. I hear they don't have no stairs over at Midview. No spooks, either."

But though such talk was kept light, it tended to shoo everybody out into the chill air early, quietly. Others felt the same way.

With the death of Mattie Zimmer, the Larksboro Western Auto closed its doors permanently. Just as well, thought the townsfolk, because the death of both Zimmers in such a short time tended to make a body a trifle uneasy in a building that so obviously bore their mark. Nobody had really expected Mattie to last long after Fred was gone, and the heart attack hadn't come as much of a surprise to those who cared one way or the other.

Charlie McQuire bitched and moaned about being understaffed since Astin Chubb had just up and quit, leaving one night without so much as a by-your-leave. It was brought up to him on a number of occasions that, since the hiring and firing of law enforcement personnel was his responsibility, he could hardly complain about the last two weeks with only one senior deputy, but he always responded with a look so hostile that it made you shiver and walk away. Some of the junior officers said he spent a lot of time locked in his office, and it sounded like he was growling.

Aggie Cooper and her husband were just fine, thank you, and they spent a lot to time walking around the streets and talking to their constituency. Elections came up in November, and the mayor was busy with a little handshaking and baby kissing, even though everyone agreed he was a shoo-in.

The Hollywood Theater on Sycamore Street

showed a double feature—*Halloween* and *Dawn of the Dead*. Attendance was brisk, but not nearly as good as it had been for *Horror of the Wolf-beast* just the week before. Why, even that Professor Gimball from the Community College had come to see that one, accompanied by Doc Appleby and his daughter, and that Alec Wall and his young girlfriend, Irene Hillman.

With Eve Sangellis on his arm, too.

The sudden relationship between Evelyn Sangellis and Joshua Gimball, as well as the equally sudden absence Rudy Vardon, presently fired the town's minds and tongues. Being so much more dramatic than its predecessor—the taking up of that Hillman girl with Gimball's hired man—it quickly relegated that tidbit to the back of the collective mind of the good people of Larksboro. The theories ranged from Vardon's suddenly revealed homosexuality to the cunning murder of her old lover by Eve and Joshua. Generally, though, it was thought that the two made an exceptionally good-looking couple, and it was hoped that they would marry in the near future.

It was the day before All Hallows Eve, chill and crisp as an apple fresh out of the dunking tub. The sky was brilliantly blue and populated with rolling clouds of black, grey, and marshmallow white—the passions of the changing seasons. Jack-o'-lanterns grinned moronically from windows all over town, waiting patiently to be given light and life.

The children took out their masks for the hundredth time to see that they were going to be scary or pretty enough to reap the windfall profits of the season.

The dentists chuckled in anticipation.

Joshua Gimball and Alec Wall prepared Moon-shadow for the professor's annual Halloween party, a small but festive occasion for themselves and a few close friends.

And Rudy Vardon came home.

He knew better than to drive through town. There might be more of them than he thought, or other ones, and it couldn't be risked. Bad enough that he had stolen that Jeep in a little town on the Pennsylvania-New York border, but he needed fast transportation and a vehicle in which to carry his arsenal.

He had come prepared.

It hadn't taken long to locate all the things that might be needed to do the job, although the cost had drained his bank account dry. That couldn't be helped, either; there hadn't been time to haggle over prices, and even though New York was his city and he was known there, his shopping list had been bound to raise a few eyebrows as well as suspicions. Rudy had paid dearly, but he had come away with exactly what he needed.

At least that's what Tony had said. He hoped it was true.

The silver bullets had been the hardest part.

He had studied hard for a week, going to the library and rifling the shelves for volumes on lycanthropy, werewolves, demons. The number of them was surprising; six days had hardly been enough time. It seemed that almost every country in the world had tales of were-somethings, from your standard wolves to bears and eagles and leopards and even snakes. In fact, every animal that could possibly serve a man for revenge or observation, quick travel or just plain violence, seemed to be included in the list of shapes that could be assumed by a human with the right knowledge and under the right conditions.

Gimball hadn't lied to him about a thing, as far as he could tell. The things the teacher had said about the voluntary aspects of werewolfism were reputedly true. Most cultures considered the ability to shift shapes to be a mark of great magical powers such as the village shaman might possess. Witches and warlocks were reputed to have the ability, as were the sorcerers of old. In fact, it appeared that shapeshifting was primarily a learned skill, and that, when one was born with the ability—such as the bastard children of priests—it was considered no different or worse than being born with any other special and rare physical or intellectual trait.

There was very little, however, about how to become a werewolf should you so want to; there was even less about how to kill one, and he desperately needed a definite answer to that question. True, Mattie Zimmer and Astin Chubb had died easily enough, but he really had no way of knowing if they were werewolves, did he? He had never seen either of them change into wolves himself, only Gimball. So it was possible that they had just been human dupes, helpers, initiates. Whatever. Whether they were monsters or not, they had looked only too human when he had killed them, and maybe that made a difference, too.

Rudy toured the shops dealing with the occult and the arcane, which appeared with surprising frequency in the seedier areas of the city. That was a quick disappointment. Most of those he spoke to obviously had no belief whatsoever in the occult and simply preyed on what they saw as the feeblemindedness of those who did. They were shysters and con men, and as soon as they determined that the raggedlooking man before them actually believed in wolfmen, actually wanted to go out and kill someone he thought was a werewolf, they found any number of ingenious excuses to close up their shops for the day—or at least until he was safely down the street.

He was about to give up when he spotted a small store called the Druid Oak only a few blocks away, its simple sign more noticeable for the neon and glitter around it. He was greeted by a long-haired bearded man with a deep throbbing voice who introduced himself as Tony.

"So you've seen these werewolves, M? . . ." He looked a bit like a wolf himself.

Rudy sidestepped the end of the question. "Yes. One of them. I want to kill it. I want to know how."

Tony leaned back thoughtfully against the counter. "Kill it. Well, that's a pretty tall order. Now, if you jut want to drive it off, if you just want to be protected, I've got some real effective amulets in back. And some wolfbane, fresh, just came in Tuesday."

"You . . . ah . . . get a lot of requests for protection against werewolves, Tony?"

The man looked slightly affronted. "Hey, you saw one, didn't you? There's a lot more of them around than you might think!"

"Oh. I didn't realize they were so . . . common."

Tony's expression softened. "Well," he admitted, "I don't think they're all that common. You have to realize, you see a lot of crazies in this business. Psychos, paranoids, the works. I get a lot of people who think they know somebody who's a werewolf. Hell, I even got a couple who think *they're* werewolves. So I sell them the amulets and the wolfbane, you know? If they're right . . . if they're right, then they're protected. If they're just a little strange, then they think they're protected and they're only out a couple bucks. Nobody gets hurt either way, see what I mean?"

Rudy shook his head. "And you think I'm a little strange?"

"Actually. Look, not many people come in here and want to know how to kill something, know what I'm saying? They come in here for herbs and rhinoceros horn and eye of newt, right? Mister, the thing is, I ain't about to sell you something out of this shop and have you go out tonight and kill some poor son of a bitch with it because you've been watching too many late movies. You got me?"

"Look, dammit, do you believe there are such things as werewolves?"

"Sure. Really. This is an honest shop, pal. This isn't a rip-off parlor. Wicca is my personal religion, and I believe in what I sell. It's you I'm not too sure about."

Vardon laughed and put up his hands in surrender. "Okay, okay, I see your point. So, just tell me how to kill a werewolf, Tony. I'm not asking you to sell me anything. Just tell me what you know."

After considering a moment, Tony relaxed visibly

and said, "Sure, I guess I can do that." He stroked his beard and then continued, "Right. You can get them while they're still in human form; you can off them just like the next guy. A werewolf isn't immortal or anything like that, he just can't be killed with your normal stuff when he's in his wolf shape. In fact, you can injure them when they're wolves and the wound will show up on their human body, but they heal so fast that it doesn't really affect them much. But when they're human you just pull out your old .44 and Pow! No problem."

Well, that answered one question. "What about when they're not in human form?"

"When they're not . . . human . . . okay. When they're not in human form, you can draw and quarter them and bury them at a crossroads, or cut off the head and stuff the mouth full of wolfbane . . ."

"Anything simpler, Tony?" Rudy watched the sun going down. Too much time was being wasted here; he was almost unbearably impatient. "Can you stab them, shoot them, run them down with your car?"

"I doubt that running them down with your car would work, unless you managed to behead them or quarter them when you did. Maybe if you shoved them in front of a train . . ." Rudy's look told the clerk the joke wasn't appreciated. "Yeah, right. Well, I never heard of anybody stabbing them. Never. You can beat them to death with a silver-headed club— you know, like in the movies—so maybe you could stab them with a silver knife. I don't know about that. It might just work, though, if you wanted to get that close. Personally . . ."

Rudy's brain was screaming at him. Get going.

Get moving. The sun was almost down; the street shadows were lengthening and flowing toward one another. He reached across the counter and grabbed the startled man by the shoulder. "What about shooting?" he demanded. "What about bullets? Silver bullets?"

"Whoa, whoa, take it easy! I was getting to that. Sure, silver bullets. Sure. Just like in all the movies. Silver bullets will work just fine to kill a werewolf, only—"

Vardon had released his hold on the man, whirled, and almost run into the street. That was what he had wanted to hear: Silver bullets would kill them. Good. Great. He knew now what to do, where to go, and how to do it.

In a few seconds, his bedraggled customer had disappeared into the tides of people that ebbed and flowed in the street. Tony stood in the Druid Oak with his hands raised in a futile effort to call the man back. "Wait a minute, buddy. Hey buddy, I didn't tell you . . . Hey . . ." At last he gave up and resumed his place against the counter. Another weirdo. And he hadn't even been able to sell him any wolfbane! Jesus!

Yes, the silver bullets had been the hard part. Harder than the twelve-gauge riot gun, harder than the .45 semiautomatic. Harder, even, than the silver knife he had in his boot; at least he could explain that away as a gift for a collector who had everything. What had been hard was explaining why he wanted ammunition for a .45 caliber military handgun made out of silver, and why he wanted twelve-gauge shells that were loaded with silver buckshot. It had been hard to explain, so he had eventually ceased trying and resorted to flashing high-denomination greenbacks. That language was universal. There had been no shortage of whispers and puzzled glances after that, but there hadn't been any more questions.

The Jeep jounced over a rut in the dirt road, and the large ornate cross he was wearing thudded against his chest. It had been an afterthought to buy it, then have it blessed by a priest. For all he knew, it might not even be effective against these beasts. But it made him feel better, somehow, and God only knew that was enough at a time like this.

The corrugated road led him up, always up, until it dumped him finally at the front door of the Griswold's cabin.

At least, where it had been.

It seemed there had been a fire—a freak bolt of lightning, no doubt. Some careless hunter. Kids playing with matches. The sturdy structure had been reduced to a few blackened spines that stuck up from the stone foundation at all angles, making the wreckage look like the grisly remains of some giant forest dweller. Rudy could do no more than sigh in ill humor. He should have expected this. The building would have been far too hard to clean up as it was, but the fire had solved the problem quite well. Any untoward evidence had literally "gone up in smoke." Just as the whole of the Griswold family had done. He shuddered, remembering what had been done to Margarette. Not the whole family, then. Not all of them.

Their efficiency had thwarted his plans, too. He

had thought he might be able to spend the night here, undisturbed and sheltered. Not now. But there was no where else to go, really. Home, perhaps, but they were probably expecting him to come back, so they'd certainly be watching there. There wasn't anyone in town that could be trusted; hell, he wasn't even sure that Walt Starr wasn't one of those damned monsters. And he certainly didn't know these hills well enough to go out looking for a better place.

It had to be here.

He got out of the Jeep and unpacked it, dragging each bundle in turn into the ruins of the house. When he was done he drove the vehicle back into the trees to hide it away from the sight of any of those things that might happen by this way, checking. Then he walked back and crawled into the ruins himself, making himself as inconspicuous as possible. There was equipment to be checked, weapons to be loaded, a plan to be gone over. Hopefully he could get some sleep, although he couldn't see how. There was a lot of preparation to be made before daylight tomorrow. Before Halloween. Before he attended Joshua Gimball's Halloween party.

Trick or treat?

More by chance than any real planning, he found Moonshadow by midmorning. He could see no one around.

Rudy felt like a commando, or at least thought that he must look like one. He was dressed in one of the camouflaged suits that the Armed Forces had issued its ground troops in Viet Nam. On his feet were jungle boots.

The clerk at the Army-Navy store had asked what he was going hunting for. He had almost choked on the laughter.

The silver knife was sheathed and strapped around his leg. The pockets of his pants, large and accordion-pleated, were stuffed with shotgun shells and spare clips of ammunition for the pistol, which was slung on a web belt around his waist. He carried the riot gun.

A black ski mask, pulled over his face, completed the outfit.

His hands were sweating, and the mask made him feel as if he were suffocating. There was no movement from the house, the barn, or the yards. There were no sounds. Nothing. His legs cramped and his head ached from staring, and still he waited.

This was lunacy. How was he supposed to fight and kill a pack of werewolves? Who the hell did he think he was, anyway? Eve was probably dead by now, or one of them, and now he was going to burst in and get himself killed, too!

Shit!

But Gimball had said he wouldn't do anything to her until the party tonight, and Rudy would bet that he hadn't changed his mind. He would stick to his plans, unafraid, unworried that Rudy had managed to escape. The man was arrogant, confident, and capable.

His opponent, on the other hand, is scared shitless, Rudy grimaced. Jesus, I wish I were John Wayne. I wish I were Clint Eastwood. I wish I were Bruce Lee.

I wish I were absent.

A cramp shot through his right thigh, and he stifled a moan as he shifted his weight. He had been here for an hour, and still he had seen nothing. To wait any longer was crazy. If Eve were here, she could be in any of these buildings, and he wasn't going to find her hunkered out here looking at them.

One more quick look around the area revealed nothing threatening, so he rose stiffly and ran toward the house, finding the front door unlocked when he reached it. Pausing for a moment before entering, he tried to control his rapid breathing and concentrate on picking up whatever sounds might indicate the presence of a person, or a thing, inside. It seemed as quiet as a grave, although he immediately cursed himself for drawing such a comparison.

Feeling slightly foolish, like a thirty-year-old man playing army, he raised his shotgun across his chest and swivelled into the room, pushing the door open rapidly and moving out of the back light to press himself against the wall.

The room was empty.

Gaining confidence with each empty room he discovered, he moved over the whole downstairs, finding nothing at all.

The upstairs rooms told the same story as those below as, room by room, he came up blank. Even the room in which he'd been held prisoner had been thoroughly cleaned, the cot removed, and the boards taken off the windows. All that happened to him might well have been a nightmare, for all the evidence this place gave. It was disconcerting.

But then, these people were past masters at hiding evidence and cleaning up messes, weren't they?

He walked down the stairs and out of the house, closing the door after him. All that was left to do was wait. They could be anywhere. Eve could be anywhere. He would have to let them come to him. They would be here later on for the party, and they would have to bring Eve. After all, she was the guest of honor, wasn't she?

Yes, and you're supposed to be the hors d'oeuvre.

Rudy Vardon settled back against a tree, cradling his gun in his lap. He checked to see that it was loaded, hoping that they'd come back to Moonshadow one or two at a time. It would be so much easier that way, because he had a little treat he wanted to give to each of them. A little something to make this Halloween night one that they'd never forget. A present, for teaching Rudy Vardon how to hate.

Somehow, he had fallen asleep. Maybe it was from having to sleep curled up and shivering amidst the ruins of the Griswold cabin the night before, and maybe it was to escape the horrors that he knew awaited him this night. It might have been his mind's attempt to take refuge from the memories of what had happened—what he had seen and what he had felt. For whatever reason, sleep had come upon him while the sun was still fairly high in the sky, although it was already westering. It had been a good, deep, sound sleep without dreams.

The sounds of the party woke him after dark.

Rudy's eyes opened suddenly, as if the rubber band that had been holding them shut had snapped. There was no trace of what the doctors call the hypnogogic state—that space between sleeping and waking when you drift slowly up through ever more distinct layers of consciousness, aware but not really awake. Instead, Vardon's waking was one closely akin to soldiers long in combat. One moment he was sound asleep, and the next it was as if he had never felt the need for sleep in his life. When his eyes opened, all systems were go.

It looked as if every light in every room of the main house was on. Laughter and muffled conversation drifted out into the night on the currents of yellowish light that flowed through the windows, forming incandescent lakes on the ground below the sills. Gimball's baritone was easy to separate from the rest as it rumbled from behind the thin drapes that hampered Rudy's view of the living room. Focusing his attention, the artist thought he could make out about a half-dozen shapes moving behind the diaphanous material. There was one that towered over the rest easily, and this he assumed was Gimball. A second was quite lithe and also rather tall; this one was probably Joshua's ever-present companion Mr. Wall. The portly figure was probably the chief of police. Then there seemed to be three or four others that were much smaller and thinner. Perhaps women or old Appleby. Maybe the mayor. Silently, he cursed himself for falling asleep. They might all be here by now adding to his disadvantage.

All he had now, he reasoned, was surprise.

After checking to see that all his weaponry was in order, he separated himself from the trees and ran quickly across the yard to the corner of the house. When he reached it, he flattened himself against the wall, trying to make himself part of the paint. His breaths came strained and rasping, the respiration of an old man, and trying to forcibly control it made him cough. Damn! He was in no condition for this even without the weight of all his equipment. His trousers alone, stuffed with shells, seemed to weigh a hundred pounds, and he was sure they had made the shotgun of lead.

He started to peek around the corner on to the front porch. If that was clear, he could sneak up to the window and see just who was in the living room waiting for him. Then he could burst through the front door shooting. Or maybe it would be better to create some kind of diversion and pick them off as they came outside.

As he eased his head around the corner, a red eye winked at him from the distance. He jerked back so quickly he almost fell, and did bang his head sharply against the wall.

"Oh m'God," he breathed. "I'm dead."

He could hear it coming now, walking his way across the wooden porch. If it had seen him, it wasn't hurrying. No, it was just walking casually in his direction, booted feet clomping against the planking.

Rudy closed his eyes and forced himself to think about what had just happened. Had he been seen? He had poked his head around the corner, and the red eye had winked . . .

A cigarette! There had been a man on the far end of the porch, just coming on to the planking, and he had been smoking a cigarette. It had to be a guard, maybe one of the town deputies. Chubb was very certainly dead, Rudy was sure of that, so that left

Mack Horner or else somebody he didn't know about.

The steps walked closer now. Very close. Nearly at the corner.

Whether he'd been seen or not was irrelevant. Whoever it was, was almost on top of him. Vardon took a deep breath and held it as he raised the riot gun stock first. He had to get this bastard quick. Quiet.

He never even considered running. He was too scared to move.

Horner took a puff of his cigarette and stopped at the corner of the porch, looking at the clear night sky. It was beautiful up in these mountains at night, and he wasn't at all sorry not to be inside with the rest of the pack. It was better out here, and he was quite content to play sentry until the time came to induct that Sangellis girl into the group.

The deputy sighed as he thought of her and brought the cigarette up to his lips. Stepping off the porch to continue his circuit of the property, he allowed himself to fantasize about what he'd do with that fox. Personally, he didn't give one good shit what the professor said about the fidelity of wolves to their mates. If he could ever see his way clear to a piece of that fine stuff, well, he'd sure as hell rip one off.

As Horner turned the corner, he heard the scuffle of feet on gravel and saw a black shape dart toward him along the edge of the house. His cigarette made a red trail in the night as he raised his arms to ward off the blow he sensed was coming, but something like a semi smashed into his face, smearing his nose as if it were clay and punching through his front teeth. He fell like he'd been clotheslined, his groans reduced to gurgles by the blood that flowed down his throat from his mouth and nose. A tooth caught halfway down his gullet and he started to choke and vomit. A piledriver smashed into his temple, mercifully knocking him out of his wrecked body and sending him spinning off into a comforting darkness blacker than the night.

Was he dead? Oh shit, it's Horner, the evil bastard. Was he dead? No, probably not. Not Horner. Probably not. So Rudy pulled out his knife and stabbed him six times in the chest, just to be safe. Question: How many times do you have to stab a werewolf with a silver knife to kill him?

Blood-spattered and shaking, Rudy pulled the corpse along the wall to the back of the house and then returned to his corner. There was a black-cold ball in his stomach that was just lying there, and it tried to rush up into his throat when he saw the dark blood on his hands. Moaning, he wiped them on his pants.

Okay, alright, try again. Get around to the porch and see who's in there.

Shit, there's so many of them! How the hell can you expect to kill all of them? Dynamite! You should have brought dynamite and blown them all to hell and back.

What if you can't kill them like that? That guy didn't say anything about dynamite, for Christ's sake!

Then Rudy was yanked off the ground and slammed into the side of the building so hard the breath caught in his throat, and a voice hissed evilly, "Your ass is mine."

Charlie McQuire had decided to go out for a breath of good air and to check on Horner. It wasn't that Horner was unreliable or anything like that, but he did tend to take life a little too easily sometimes. Tonight shouldn't be one of those times, not if what the professor said were true. If what he said were true, they just might have a little extra entertainment tonight in the form of that artist fella. Not that the man hadn't been invited, nothing like that, but his spirits might just be a little high tonight. He might tend to get a little rowdylike, and Joshua didn't want anything to upset the . . . the . . . ambience of the evening. That was it.

What the fuck was ambience, anyhow?

He had walked down the porch, seeing no sign of his guard, and circled around the back trying to find him. When he had turned the rear corner, he thought he had found him. There was the dark silhouette of a man at the front corner, crouched low to the ground, and the chief almost asked what the hell the idiot thought he was doing until he realized that it just didn't feel like Mack Horner over there. You couldn't really judge the size with the guy crouched down like that, but Horner wouldn't have any use for sneaking around toward the front of the building. Whoever this was, it looked more like he was hiding than guarding.

So Charlie McQuire began his stalk, and the closer he got to his quarry, the bigger the smile was that spread across his face. By the time he was at arm's length, he was barely restraining the triumphant growl that perked in his chest. It was Vardon! The professor was right. Vardon had come back, and now the bastard was his. McQuire reached down, grabbed Vardon with both hands, and smashed him into the side of the building like a man beating a rug. His prey looked just like a deer before it was pulled down—eyes wide and staring, mouth open, shocked.

It wasn't that Rudy knew what to do—he didn't. And it certainly wasn't the lightning reflexes brought on by years of encounters in combat situations. Vardon had only been in three fights in his entire life and had lost all of them, with the exception of the one his father had broken up when he was eleven, and he had been on the shit end of that one, too.

What it was, was an attempt to push his attacker away in the throes of white panic, combined with the fact that he still had the fanglike silver knife enfolded in his sweating hand. He struck out with his hands at the face and chest—the only things he could reach of Charlie McQuire. The fat man leaned his head back and away, and the glinting blade passed under the wattles that quivered below his chin, slipping smoothly up the hilt and into his neck.

The fat hands opened, fingers splayed wide, releasing him involuntarily to slide painfully down the rough wood to the ground. McQuire towered above him, teetering unsteadily, for just an instant before he crashed to his knees. As Rudy watched, the fat man pulled the dagger from his throat and dropped it into the dirt. Each breath wheezed through the gaping hole with a spray of blood. A sausage-fingered hand attempted to pinch the wound shut while the other

302

reached out for Vardon, the fingers wiggling like grubs.

Whether Charlie reached out to him for salvation or revenge, Rudy didn't know.

Then the man toppled forward like a felled tree, and Rudy had to roll quickly aside to avoid being crushed. There was the hollow-sounding rap of a skull against wood, the squishing pop of gristle and bone separating, and last a mournful sigh. Then, silence.

The river of blood became a trickle, an ooze, then stopped completely. Rudy reached to find a pulse beneath the jawbone and found none. Charlie's head sat, squat and round, on top of Charlie's broad back. The body lay on its stomach

Something about the head, ill-supported by the broken neck, reminded Vardon of a Halloween pumpkin. A Jack-o-lantern.

Trick or treat.

He realized he couldn't retrieve his knife; he couldn't pull it out from under the dead, cold flesh of Charlie.

Without hesitating and without looking back, he picked up his shotgun and slipped noiselessly around to the front porch, where he dropped to all fours and crawled its length to the front window.

The party was in full swing.

Eve was the first thing he saw. She sat passively in an overstuffed chair by the fireplace, her eyes glazed and unfocused. She looked as if she'd been drugged, maybe hypnotized.

How do people look when they're hypnotized? He didn't know.

From some deep part of his mind another word surfaced—enchanted.

Joshua Gimball stood proudly by her side, the massive hands that he rested on her shoulder saying all that needed to be said about propriety. There could be no doubt that he considered the woman his.

Alec Wall and Doc Appleby were standing in front of him, involving him in an animated conversation, while the doctor's daughter, Carol, and another, darker, woman nodded and talked a short distance away.

Rudy could see no one else, and he started to worry. There were more than this, he was sure. Horner and Chubb were dead, and so was McQuire. so were Mattie Zimmer and her husband, Fred. That was five, and it was just possible that Walt Starr and the others were just normal people, as normal as they appeared to be. But still, he would have bet money that there were others, especially the mayor and his good wife, Agatha. He scanned the room again. No one had entered or left. Gimball was looking quite amused by what Wall was trying to seriously point out. Appleby looked on with interest. Carol seemed to be showing off a piece of jewelry to her dark friend.

Rudy was struck by the mundaneness of the scene. If he painted it, he could arrange for it to be reproduced ad nauseam and sold for $4.99 at every Woolworth's across the country. It was a study in mediocrity, and Rudy was chilled when he wondered how many other blasé, ho-hum facades hide such hideous realities.

There was a humming behind him, low and insistent, which he first dismissed as the song of the night insects. But it kept getting louder, little by little, and he had just started to turn to get a fix on what it might be, feeling the beginnings of fear, when it resolved itself into words.

It became, "Aggie, who's that by the window?"

Rudy turned, tripping over his own feet in his haste and falling against the wall, which propped him up. There were two shadows running toward him, one slightly in front of the other. The one in front was larger, broader, and ran with a much longer stride than the thin form behind it. Martin and Aggie Cooper.

The shadow that was Martin Cooper shimmered like a heat mirage in the starlight. It growled angrily.

Rudy raised the shotgun to his shoulder and fired. The recoil rammed his shoulder backward painfully into the building, deafening him. He pulled it more tightly into his shoulder and, as the figure running toward him staggered out of the shadows in front of him, fired once again, point-blank.

Martin Cooper was thrown backward into the shadows and driven to the ground. He never moved.

Agatha Cooper saw her husband, his chest pulped and oozing blood like pus. She sensed there was no life in his still form, even as her teeth lengthened into fangs and her nails into claws. This was a thing she didn't understand. Joshua had said they couldn't be killed. But the man on the porch, that Rudy Vardon, was swinging the barrel of his weapon toward her now, and she suddenly didn't feel so strong, so brave, so omnipotent. Her grotesque feet scrabbled against the earth as she tried to turn and run back into the

305

safety of the trees.

There was a roar and a flash like lightning, and she was spun off her feet like a top and slammed to the ground. Something wet was running down the left side of her body, down her arm, but she couldn't raise it to her face to see. Instead, she held out the arm she could use in a gesture of supplication and tried to ask for mercy from this fiend that had killed her mate. And was trying to kill her, as well.

"Please," she begged, "No. No. Please . . ."

As he pumped another round into the chamber, Rudy saw the thing's arm extended toward him, and he paused. This wasn't Agatha Cooper anymore. It was a THING, a thing that looked part Aggie and part dog. Part wolf. But still, Aggie Cooper was there, and maybe she could be saved, somehow. Maybe . . .

The Aggie-thing's mouth worked, chafed, and finally emitted a sound. It was low, guttural, bass. It was the most disgusting, vile sound that Rudy Vardon had ever heard, or ever hoped to hear. It sickened him.

Drool crawled thickly over the thing's jaw, leaving silvery snail's tracks on the tufted hair. Bubbles of it formed at the corners of the thing's black lips.

Crying with disgust, Rudy fired again, and the Aggie-beast's stomach disintegrated in a puff of gore.

From within the house he heard the sound of strident voices raised in alarm. A woman shrieked in fear. There was a scrambling and the sound of furniture being turned over. A lamp shattered.

Something growled.

Time had run out. Vardon spun and kicked at the

front door. The jamb splintered, but the door remained closed. He levelled the shotgun and fired. As the door was blown ajar he shouldered his way by it into the living room, raising his weapon and spreading his legs for balance.

Snarling and changing, Irene Hillman had tried to reach the attacker before he could get inside, but she hadn't reacted fast enough. As she saw him raise the shotgun to his shoulder and take aim at her, she tried to changed direction quickly and run out through the kitchen and escape. The full load of silver buckshot caught her between the shoulder blades as she turned.

Something was surging through Rudy that he had never felt before—a madness, a power, a thrust of vitality that shrivelled his fears in its white-hot glare. It consumed him like a fever.

There was a smile on his face as he swung the barrel of the twelve-gauge to the next available target—Carol Appleby. As he worked the pump, ejecting the spent cartridge and shoving a fresh one in front of the firing pin, the doctor saw the danger to his daughter and mate and, in a very human reaction, jumped in front of her to shield her from danger.

The sound of the discharge shattered the air, and the buckshot chopped and blended pieces of the two of them together as the force of the blast piled them in a bloody heap in the corner.

Rudy spun around to find his next target and saw a thing that had once looked like Alec Wall flying through the smoke-filled air toward him. He ducked instinctively and raised his weapon to protect his face

307

and head, but the leaping bulk caught him on the shoulder and knocked him to the floor, the riot gun flung away uselessly through the window.

The .45 was in Rudy's hand before he had finished rolling, the massive flow of adrenaline adding speed and precision to his movements. As Wall swerved to pounce on him, he fired twice, the silver bullets catching the dancer dead center in the chest and pitching him face first to the floor. Yet, even as Vardon jumped to his feet and inched away, Alec continued to change, digging his claws into the wood floor and dragging himself toward his adversary.

Rudy fired once more, point-blank, into the werewolf's back, and it lay still.

When he turned to face Gimball, the man was smiling. He removed his massive hand from Eve's shoulder and started to move sideways around the perimeter of the room.

"I see you've done your homework," Joshua said appreciatively.

"Yes, you bastard. Yes, I have."

"Silver bullets in the pistol?"

Vardon nodded.

"And silver buckshot in the shotshells, I suppose. Very ingenious, Rudy. I commend you."

"I'm going to kill you, Gimball," Rudy swore in a monotone. "I'm going to send you to hell where you belong."

"Assuming there is a hell, Rudy," Joshua corrected. "If there is, I'm sure you're quite right. I guess you wouldn't consider letting me go, would you?"

Vardon's laughter was bitter, vile. "Have you hurt

her, Gimball? Have you . . . changed her?"

A twinkle lit in Gimball's eye for just an instant, then it winked out. "I really shouldn't tell you, should I? I'm sure you would kill me anyway, but I should make you suffer for it. But I won't. No, Rudy, Eve has neither been hurt nor . . . altered. That was to happen tonight but, well, I'm afraid that's pretty impossible now, don't you think?" His eye twinkled again unnervingly. "I believe that I have, however, managed to change her mind on a few things while you've been away."

Vardon pointed his gun menacingly at his opponent, tightening his two-handed grip on it until his knuckles were blanched white. "Stand still, you bastard," he spat. "I mean it . . . just stand fucking still."

Gimball smiled ruefully, shrugged, and complied.

"Now what do you mean that you've 'managed to change her mind on a few things'?"

Joshua cocked his head and grinned in a particularly disturbing, doglike gesture. "Shall I show you? Of course. If you'll just direct your attention to the lovely lady . . ." His voice lowered and became harsher, more commanding. "Eve, show our friend Rudy your knife."

Still seated in the overstuffed chair and staring sightlessly ahead, Eve raised her right arm slowly and precisely, puppetlike, until her hand appeared from under the folds of her full skirt like a small white dove from a hat. Clutched in her thin fingers was a black cylindrical object that filled her palm. Her arm raised until it was fully parallel to the floor. Then it stopped, holding that position unwaveringly.

309

"Now open it please, my dear."

With the slightest twitch of her finger there was a soft click, and an eight-inch blade snicked smoothly out and locked into place, a single steel fang.

Rudy tore his gaze violently away from the sparkling metal and stared at Gimball incredulously, eyes wide and questioning. There seemed to be something cold, slimy, and multi-legged crawling around in his guts. "What have you done to her?" he managed to gasp out.

Gimball stuck his hands in his pockets casually. "Most people would call it hypnotism," he mused, "and they would be . . . close. But you, Rudy, you are a bit more open-minded than most; perhaps you would call it enchantment."

Suddenly Rudy was shivering as if the temperature had plunged twenty degrees, but sweat cascaded down his rib cage and sogged his palms. He redoubled his grip on the pistol.

"Ah, I see you like the word," Joshua continued smugly. I have studied clinical hypnotism, actually, but that is to this what a firecracker is to an atomic bomb." He pulled his hands from his pockets and stroked his chin, flashing a toothy grin, and the teeth seemed somehow longer, sharper. "I underestimated you before, Rudolph, and I do apologize for the slight. That oversight cost me two dear friends." His complexion darkened, and his baritone voice grew even deeper. The smile disappeared and was replaced by a sneer. "But then," he made a sweeping gesture of the carnage around him, "you *are* full of surprises, aren't you? Yet so am I."

As he turned his massive head toward Eve, still

310

eated, still holding the knife straight out in front of
er, Rudy saw that Gimball's snout was lengthening,
is ears pointing . . ."

"Evelyn, my love," came the rasping command.
"Please rise now, and stab this young gentleman to
death."

And as her lover watched in disbelief, she rose—
slowly, ever so slowly—from her chair and began her
deadly clockwork march toward him.

Vardon's mouth went dust-dry. Oh shit oh shit oh
shit, he thought, and actually whispered it out loud.

The werewolf's laughter came to him as if from a
million miles away, but distinctly. "Yes," he chuckled. " 'Oh shit.' A quite concise summation, actually.
You see your quandary, then?" The voice was deepening steadily, rasping and gravelly now. "Either she
will kill you, or I will. Even if you kill me, she will be
. . . shall we say, adamant? And if you kill her . . .
but Rudy, *can* you kill her?"

But it didn't come out "her"; it came out "hur-
rrr". . . .

It was enough. Rudy tore his gaze away from the
dull plastic orbs that were Eve's eyes, knowing that
Gimball had misdirected his attention away from the
most immediate danger. He led with the pistol barrel,
swinging to the point where he had last seen the
lycanthropist standing and past, past, until the front
sight began to eclipse a head and face barely recognizable as Joshua Gimball on a body barely standing
erect . . .

. . . and he fired.

There was a loud yelp. The grotesque form lifted
off the ground and spun backward into the wall, but

311

the sound of impact was covered by a hideous banshee wail from Rudy's flank.

Again he swung, arms locked and leading with the front sight, and again he was in time. But the face bisected by that forward sliver of metal didn't belong to a wolf or a dog or some hybrid monstrosity; it belonged to Evelyn Sangellis, his lover and friend, and in a single heartbeat he answered Gimball's last question . . .

(But, Rudy, *can* you kill her?)

. . .and that answer was no.

She came at him screaming, knife raised, Norman's mother in *Psycho*, and the sight of it sapped all the strength from his limbs. His arms dropped until the .45 hung loosely from one hand at his side. He watched her sweep forward as implacable as the tide, and he knew he was waiting to die by her hand.

But then, what would happen to *her*?

Vardon's mind gave him one quick glimpse of Eve changing, transmogrifying, coarse hair tufting her beautiful face and drool stringing down from those soft, full lips . . .

At the last second he twisted away from the descending blade and grabbed his attacker at the same time, but not before she had succeeded in burying half its length in the meaty part of his chest. Then his arms encircled her and her forward momentum carried them backward and down, twisting so that Evelyn landed underneath, her head thunking violently against the floor as Rudy's weight toppled on top of her, punching the air from her lungs.

For a second there was silence. Stillness punctuated only by Rudy's staccato breathing. Eve lay beneath him like a grotesque rug, slack, breathing shallowly, eyes open but unseeing. Drops of blood dripped from his chest wound and pattered on her cheek.

Vardon let himself relax fractionally, thinking, "Oh God, let it be over. Please."

Moaning, he kneeled, then stood, and with one unthinking tug pulled the knife from his chest. Blood spurted for a second in a freshet, then slowed to a steady ooze. Gorge tried to climb up his throat in a hot pillar, but he swallowed hard to force it down.

He glanced back toward Gimball's body, lying still along the wall, blood smeared bright red and wet where he—it—had slid down the plaster.

Dead.

It must be dead.

The thought almost made him smile.

Then he reached down as best he could and tried to haul his lover to her feet, wondering if he could manage a fireman's carry.

She came alive with a vengeance.

There was no warning—no moaning, no crying, no eye-rolling. One second she was limp as a beanbag in his grip, and the next she leapt at him, a cat, a buzz saw, tearing long strips of skin from his cheeks as she tried to put out his eyes.

Rudy could take no more. Once again he bellowed in rage; something senseless, primal. Then he drew back his fist and began to beat his attacker with no feeling but frustration, anger, and the will to survive.

The first blow seemed to weaken her; she staggered.

The second and she began to sag.

313

He pulled his fist back to strike again . . .

. . . and heard an abomination growl, "You DARE strike my mate," as he was yanked toward the ceiling.

Below him, Evelyn fell unconscious to the floor.

His head snapped around ands he was looking at a vision from hell.

It was the face of Joshua Gimball: a long, hairless snout with a leathery black nose; black and pink mottled rubbery gums drawn back over six-inch-long tusklike yellow fangs. Fetid drool ribboned from coarse bristle covering the lower jaw and, running from the corner of one tearing grey-green eye to the bleeding hole where an ear had once been, ran the ragged furrow plowed by Rudy's last shot, leaking thick blood and fluids.

"Youuuu darrrre . . ." Gimball rasped.

And, without plan or knowledge, Rudy Vardon screamed, "JESUS CHRIST!"

There was a deafening howl of pain, and suddenly he was flying through the air, through a window, feeling slivers and blades of glass imbed themselves in the muscles of his back and buttocks. He landed jarringly on the porch, slid its width, and tumbled into the moist grass, something hard and cold jabbing him painfully in the lower back.

Broke my back, he thought, but he could wiggle his fingers, could wiggle his toes . . .

A roar of hate rumbled from the innards of the house, causing the remaining glass to fall from the window frame. Then there was a shadow, dark in the empty frame, bulking as it grew nearer. More human, for some reason he couldn't understand, but still horrible.

Shaking his head to clear his thinking, Rudy rolled to his stomach and tried to push himself up, grabbing for whatever might be beneath him at the same time because he had dropped the pistol inside. He had no weapon, and what he was lying on was . . .

. . . the shotgun.

He heard the thumping of padded feet behind him and a grunt; he tried to stand, work the pump, and turn at the same time but it was too much, too late, and he ended up sitting with his legs stiff out in front of him with the pump worked but the gun only halfway raised—too late to aim . .

Suddenly, he was calm. Calm, even though he heard himself screaming as a black shadow flew through the air at him in slow motion, jaws open incredibly wide, canines gleaming wet, saliva streaming like crepe.

It seemed to fall over him, and when it did he thought he heard himself scream even louder and thought that weird; he didn't think he had it in him. Then, before he could fully realize that it wasn't him screaming after all—it was IT screaming—there was an explosion and something rammed into his solar plexus so hard that it launched him into darkness.

Rudy floated back to consciousness to the tune of the night insects. Floating, floating . . . something warm and soft and heavy covering him . . .

Remembering.

His eyes snapped open only fractions of an inch away from grey-green ones, wide and staring. Something cold and hard lay against his cheek. His hands, trapped between his body and this other, lay in something wet and sticky.

Gasping, he threw the weight from atop him and scrabbled away, stopping only because he was too weak to crawl further.

He looked back at the remains of Joshua Gimball, lying limp and broken in the frame of light cast from the cabin. And he did nothing but look until he was sure that, this time, he was dead.

Perhaps there is a God, Rudy mused. A Good Power. Because it was obvious that no skill had saved him at the last. No, what had pulled his chestnuts from the fire could only fall into one of two categories—luck or intervention.

Was there a difference?

Gimball's final leap had carried him true—through the window and onto his prey. Unfortunately the impact had been severe enough to impale him on the shortened gun barrel as well as to cause Rudy's finger to jerk the trigger in reflex.

Besides being impaled, Joshua Gimball had been nearly gutted.

Rudy rose and circled the corpse warily. I have to get Eve, he thought, and I should take the shotgun, just in case. But, after minutes of silent debate he found he simply couldn't bring himself to get that close to the lycanthropist, even if he was dead.

No. No way.

Weak-legged, he looked back into the living room to where his lover lay unconscious. She hadn't moved. She hadn't cried out. She hadn't so much as blinked since he'd struck her, as far as he knew. As he entered the house and walked across the room,

Rudy wondered what Joshua had done to her, how long it would last, and if it would ever end at all. He himself was a mass murderer now, as far as the world would believe. Nine people were dead by his hand. He would have to run, change his identity, hide.

He found the pistol gleaming dully where he had dropped it, picked it up, and ejected the old clip, inserting a fresh one before allowing himself to think about the future, wondering if either he or Eve even had one. Then, suddenly, he was falling forward, crashing toward the floor.

His hands went out to break the fall, and they did cushion it somewhat, but his right hand refused to give up its grip on the pistol and he bounced off his left, feeling rather than hearing the wrist snap. Pain bolted up his arm and shoulder and neck to clog his skull, but the snarling cut through it somehow, and he twisted to look toward his feet.

He saw Alec Wall, an Alec Wall-thing, clutching his boot desperately with one clawed hand, the nylon and leather parting easily under the grip. Blood throbbed from its mouth and nose in time with the beating of its heart; more trickled out the pointed, tufted ears. It snapped its jaws, fanglike teeth clicking, and tried to pull him closer.

He screamed.

He rammed the muzzle of the .45 into the face of the creature and yanked the trigger over and over until he realized that the fresh clip was empty, that the firing pin was hitting an empty chamber, that the hirsute form clinging to him even in death no longer had a head.

That he was still screaming.

That he was crying.

That, somewhere far behind him, far away, Eve was saying, very weakly, "Wha . . . wha . . . what's . . . Rudy? What's . . ."

On his way out, with Eve dazedly tucked under his arm to keep her from falling, Rudy set fire to Moonshadow. He stayed there long enough, in the dark, to be sure that it had caught.

Reading wasn't the same as Larksboro.

But then, neither Eve nor Rudy were the same, either.

He thought this for the millionth time as he rose from in front of the TV to answer the jangling phone. The coffee sloshed from his cup as he set it on the arm of the chair, and he thought, Waste of good scotch.

He had spilled it already when the phone had first started to ring. The old nerves just weren't what they used to be.

It was bad to answer the phone. What if it was the police or the FBI or somebody, looking for the murderer of those people over in Larksboro? Whenever he answered the phone—he usually let Eve do it—and they asked for him, even under his new name, he hung up.

He picked up the receiver like it was ready to bite him. No, not bite. Don't think about that. "Hello?"

"Honey?" It was Eve, calling from the library. She was researching a new book. Eve wrote gothics now. It seems her fairy tales had gotten a little too heavyanded. Macabre.

"I was afraid you wouldn't answer the phone." There was an edge to her voice. Something wrong.

"What is it? What's the matter?"

"Oh, it's probably nothing, hon. It's just something I read and I . . . it's just a myth, you know. Probably not even true, but—"

"Dammit, Eve! Will you tell me what the fuck's wrong?" he snapped viciously, reaching for his coffee.

"Well," she was obviously hurt. "I was reading about—about THEM, you know? And I found a book that says . . . it says—"

Vardon gulped his coffee, but it didn't help. Suddenly it had gotten cold. So cold.

"It says that, to really kill them, you have to cut them into pieces or burn them into ashes, Rudy. It says, if you don't do that, they . . . they—" Her voice broke, "Oh my God, Rudy! It says they don't stay dead! It says they come back!"

"Come back?" Rudy tried to shout, but there was something large and cold and slimy in his throat, and he had to talk around it. He croaked, "Come back as what?" but he was already thinking back, trying to remember how many of the bodies hadn't been in the house. How many hadn't burned.

Eve's voice was a whisper. It sounded like a bad connection, static over the line. "As vampires."

In Reading, a coffee cup dropped from a quaking hand and fell to a carpeted floor with a muzzy thud, spilling its contents into the nap in a darkening stain.

In Larksboro, in the cemetery, a different container entirely spilled its contents out onto a carpet of leaves with a splintering creak. But what came out of it was dark also, as dark in its way as the night that surrounded it, as dark as evil and hate and the unholy lust for revenge.

Among other, equally unholy, lusts.

And what came out of this container sat up and brushed the dirt from its chest and hair and smiled broadly.

For it was not alone.

And it was not without purpose.

Strangely gleaming grey-green eyes shone like twin moons in the shadows as it rose to lay claim to its new world.